LEGALLY WED

Rick R. Reed

A NineStar Press Publication

Published by NineStar Press
P.O. Box 91792,
Albuquerque, New Mexico, 87199 USA.
www.ninestarpress.com

Legally Wed

Copyright © 2020 by Rick R. Reed
Cover Art by Natasha Snow Copyright © 2020

Printed in the USA
NineStar Press Edition
April, 2020

Print ISBN: 978-1-951880-97-2

Also available in eBook, ISBN: 978-1-951880-59-0

Love comes along when you least expect it.

That's what Duncan Taylor's sister, Scout, tells him. Scout has everything Duncan wants—a happy life with a wonderful husband. Now that Seattle has made gay marriage legal, Duncan knows he can have the same thing. But when he proposes to his boyfriend Tucker, he doesn't get the answer he hoped for. Tucker's refusal is another misstep in a long line of failed romances. Despairing, Duncan thinks of all the loving unions in his life—and how every one of them is straight. Maybe he could be happy, if not sexually compatible, with a woman. When zany, gay-man-loving Marilyn Samples waltzes into his life, he thinks he may have found his answer.

Determined to settle, Duncan forgets his sister's wisdom about love and begins planning a wedding with Marilyn. But life throws Duncan a curveball. When he meets wedding planner Peter Dalrymple, unexpected sparks ignite. Neither man knows how long he can resist his powerful attraction to the other. For sure, there's a wedding in the future. But whose?

For my husband and my son and his husband.
Mazel tov and all that.

Sometimes love comes along when you least expect it.

Chapter One

Same-sex marriage had just become legal in Washington State, and Duncan Taylor didn't plan on wasting any time. He had been dating Tucker McBride for more than three years, and ever since the possibility of marriage had become more than just a pipe dream, it was all Duncan could think of. He thought of it as he gazed out the windows of his houseboat on Lake Union on days both sunny and gray (since it was late autumn, there were a lot more of the latter); he thought of it as he stood before his classroom of fourth graders at Cascade Elementary School. He thought of it when he woke up in the morning and before he fell asleep at night.

For Duncan, marriage was the peak, the happy ending, the icing on the cake, the culmination of one's heart's desire, a commitment of a lifetime, the joining of two souls. For Duncan, it was landing among the stars.

And for Duncan, who would turn thirty-eight on his next birthday, it was also something he had never dared dream would be possible for him.

Now, too excited to sleep, he was thinking about it—hard—once again. It was just past midnight on December 6, 2012, and the local TV news had preempted its regular programming to take viewers live to Seattle City Hall, where couples were forming a serpentine line to be among the first in the state to be issued their marriage licenses—couples who had also for far too long believed this right would be one they would never be afforded. Many clung close together to ward off the chill, but Duncan knew their reasons for canoodling went far deeper than that.

The mood, in spite of the darkness pressing in all around, was festive. There was a group serenading the couples in line, singing "Going to the Chapel." Champagne corks popped in the background. Laughter.

Duncan couldn't keep the smile off his face as he watched all the male-male and female-female couples in the line, their moods of jubilation, of love, of triumph, traveling through to him even here on his houseboat only a couple of miles north of downtown. Duncan wiped tears from his eyes as he saw not only the couples but also all the supporters, city workers, and volunteers who had crowded together outside city hall to wish the new couples well, to share in the happiness of the historic moment.

And then Duncan couldn't help it; he fell into all-out blubbering as the first couple to get their license emerged from city hall. Eighty-five-year-old Pete-e Petersen and her partner and soon-to-be-wife, Jane Abbott Lighty, were all smiles when a reporter asked them how they felt.

"We waited a long time. We've been together thirty-five years never thinking we'd get a legal marriage. Now I feel so joyous I can't hardly stand it," Pete-e said.

It was such a special moment, and it was all Duncan could do not to pick up the phone and call Tucker and casually say something like, "Hey honey, you want to get married?"

But he knew he had to wait even if patience was a virtue Duncan had in short supply. On Sunday, when the first marriages would take place, he planned on bringing Tucker to their favorite restaurant, an unpretentious little joint on Capitol Hill called Olympia Pizza. There, amid the darkened and—for them—romantic interior with the smells of garlic, basil, and tomato sauce surrounding them, Duncan would propose, saying something clever like:

"I'm thinking about changing my Facebook relationship status to 'engaged.' Would you mind?"

In his mind, Tucker would chuckle and then rub at the tuft of blond hair that grew from his chin, regarding Duncan with his dark-blue eyes. Duncan could see the flicker of the candle lighting up his man's features as he held the silence for a few moments, building the suspense. Then he would say something like, "I think I'll change mine too."

That would be one way it could play out—very twenty-first century.

Duncan would then imagine all his friends and family congratulating the newly minted fiancés with "Likes" and words of encouragement and shared happiness. Maybe he could get their waiter to take a picture of them, holding hands over a sausage and mushroom pie, right after the moment when they went from two guys dating to two guys anticipating...marriage.

Duncan found himself wiping yet another tear from his eye. Sunday was going to be perfect.

*

Because Tucker spent Saturday night on Duncan's houseboat, they rode over to the Hill together and parked on Fifteenth, just a few steps away from the pizza restaurant where they had been regulars ever since their first date here three years before.

Even though it was only 5:30 or so in the afternoon, the day had grown dark, and there was a damp chill in the air.

Duncan locked his Ford Escort and hurried down the street, eager to get inside, eager to set in motion, well, the rest of his life. His heart beat a little faster, and his breath came a bit more quickly. Inside, he felt filled with brilliant light.

Tucker called from behind him, laughing. "What's gotten into you tonight?"

Duncan slowed to turn and cast a glance back at Tucker, who looked very fetching in a pair of worn Levi's 501s, a form-fitting black T-shirt, and a black leather jacket that contrasted wonderfully with his almost white-blond hair.

"What do you mean?" Duncan asked.

"Well, there's a real *spring* to your step is the only way I know how to put it. This is different from the usual swish in it." He laughed and caught up to Duncan, squeezing his bicep to show he was only kidding with that last remark.

"Just hungry," Duncan replied. But hunger was actually the last thing on his mind at the moment as his hand worried the velvet box in the pocket of his cargo pants. He hadn't planned it, but on Saturday he was downtown, and he couldn't resist wandering into Ben Bridge just to see what they had in the way of wedding bands.

He saw it right away. He knew that the fact his eye fell upon it first thing was fate talking to him. Before he had even spoken to a salesperson or glanced at another item, he saw the simple white-gold, diamond-studded band in the display case. "That's for Tucker," he whispered to himself. He hadn't planned to buy an engagement ring, and he certainly couldn't afford its exorbitant price tag, but the thought of the light that would come into Tucker's eyes when he opened the box was so thrilling and romantic, he couldn't resist.

The clerk, a young woman whose dark hair, olive skin, and green eyes mirrored Duncan's own, came up to him. "Can I show you something?"

Duncan recalled being at a loss for words. This little side trip into the jewelry store had really been intended as only a fantasy; a sort of appetizer for the better things to come.

"I just love that simple band with the diamonds right there." Duncan had pointed down to the ring.

"Oh, it's a beauty. Would you like to try it on?" She was already stooping down to take the ring out of the display case.

"Oh, it's not for me." And suddenly, Duncan stopped. He was so filled with love for Tucker, he was unable to speak. He gnawed for a moment at his lower lip, looking away from the smiling and expectant face of the clerk and drawing in a deep breath to compose himself. What did he have to lose, anyway? He smiled and looked down to see his hands trembling. "It's for my, my..." His voice had trailed off. What to call Tucker? He was his boyfriend, he supposed, yet he seemed like so much more. But partner was so presumptuous because they didn't live together for one and had never registered as domestic partners in the state for another. "It's for the guy I hope will be my fiancé," he had finally blurted out, hoping the clerk didn't notice the tear he could feel standing in the corner of one eye.

He wondered what she would do. Would she regard him with disdain? Would her attitude change? Would she laugh?

But her face had immediately brightened, and her smile was as wide as his own. "That's fabulous!" she exclaimed. "I'm so happy for you." She had pushed the ring across the counter. "He's a lucky guy. And I'm not just saying that because he'd be getting this gorgeous ring, but mostly because he'd be getting you." She winked. "You're a catch."

Duncan had picked up the ring with one hand and reached for his wallet with the other.

Now, in the restaurant, he was just about to burst with what he wanted to ask Tucker. With anticipation. With excitement. With the promise of a seismic shift in his and his boyfriend's lives.

Wait. Wait, he told himself, over and over, as they followed the hostess to a table near the back. *Wait*, he told himself again as they perused the menu, both ordering a Stella Artois.

When the pizza arrived, so would Duncan's proposal.

Duncan forced himself to make small talk as they sipped beer. He let his gaze wander over to the table next to them where an older couple sat, indicating with his eyes that Tucker should look as well. Tucker looked at the man and woman, who both appeared to be in their seventies, with gray hair and clothes that kind of matched, baggy jeans, cardigan sweaters. She wore a brightly colored scarf around her neck, and his glasses were square, blocky and, whether he knew it or not, kind of cool in a retro sort of way.

"How long do you think they've been together?" Duncan asked, leaning forward and placing a hand atop Tucker's.

Tucker leaned back, putting his own hands in his lap and screwing up his gaze in what Duncan would surmise was deep thought. "Gee. It's hard to say. Probably a long time. I'd guess Gramps and Granny there are in their seventies, and I bet they're each other's first, so maybe fifty years or more."

"That's what I was thinking too. Notice how quiet they are together?" Duncan admired the way they stared into each other's eyes and how the woman held her fork aloft with a piece of fried calamari on it for her husband to try.

Tucker snorted. "They're probably all talked out. After half a century, they probably can't think of a single new thing to say to the other." He laughed. "He's probably thinking he can't wait to get home so he can plop down in front of the TV and crack open a beer, and she probably just wants to bury her nose in a Harlequin romance, so she can get a glimpse of what she doesn't have anymore."

Duncan felt the statement cut through him and tried to convince himself that Tucker was merely going for the obvious interpretation, the one most people would make. "Oh, don't be such a cynic!" he cried. "I think they've just been together so long they're really contented around each other. They probably don't feel the need to fill the silence up with idle chatter." *As you're doing right now*, Duncan chided himself.

"Maybe." Tucker scanned the restaurant. "I hope that pizza gets here soon. I'm starving."

"Me too." Duncan rubbed the dark stubble on his chin. "I'm sure it'll be worth waiting for." Making sure Tucker wasn't looking, he moved the boxed ring from his pocket next to him on the booth bench, so it would be ready when the moment arrived.

The waiter, and the moment of truth, showed up just then. The waiter was a lanky kid with a neck tattoo and a shock of auburn hair that fell over one eye. "Here you go, guys. Careful, that pan is hot."

"And so are you," Tucker quipped.

The waiter grinned, his gaze cutting to Duncan, who did not grin back. Duncan swallowed, suddenly feeling a distinct lack of spit in his mouth. His heart beat just a little harder.

The waiter wandered away.

"God, that smells terrific."

The aroma of the pizza wafted up, embedded in the steam rising off the hot, cheesy pie. Even though the smell of tomatoes, garlic, Italian sausage, and basil were the sweetest perfumes to him, Duncan didn't feel hungry.

His proposal was now front and center in his mind, and he swore he could not entertain the thought of taking a bite until he got his special moment underway. Later, the dinner could turn into a real celebration. Hell, the whole night could.

Tucker was about to reach for the spatula to lift a slice onto his plate when Duncan grabbed his wrist. "Wait. Before we get started, I have something I want to ask."

Duncan reached down, feeling for the box at his side. His nervous reach hit the box and knocked it to the floor. "Shit," Duncan whispered. When he quickly ducked to grab for the box among the shadows and grit beneath the table, he whacked his forehead on the edge. He saw stars.

"What the fuck?" Tucker was laughing.

Duncan groped around in the dark, feeling for the box. *This isn't the way things are supposed to go at all. Where is that damn thing, anyway?* Finally, his hand lit on the velvet box. In the fall, it had opened. He reached inside and found, to his horror, that the ring itself had rolled away. He groped around on the floor some more until he felt the metal of the ring under his fingertips. He breathed a sigh of relief and grasped both box and ring, righting himself and being careful not to hit the back of his head as he reemerged from beneath the table.

What could he do but laugh? So he did, putting the ring and the box on the table in front of him. "Hey, it'll be a good story to tell our grandchildren, right?" Duncan continued to laugh, rubbing at the knot already forming on his forehead. He thrust the ring toward Tucker. "This is for you." He managed to make himself stop laughing even though there was something giddy going on inside that he didn't quite understand.

Was it joy or the beginning of a heart attack?

Tucker picked up the ring, examining it. He looked with a questioning smile across the table at Duncan.

"It's legal now," Duncan gasped, the carefully chosen words he had imagined and planned on saying deserting him.

"What? Pot?"

"Don't be stupid." Duncan stared across the table, feeling as he once had when he was a teenager on Thanksgiving weekend driving on a slippery highway. It had rained earlier and the temperature had dropped. The roads were slick, but not frozen—until he tried to make it across the overpass. The car did a figure eight, and all he could do was wait for the impact, whether it was with a guardrail or another car. He knew the only thing that would stop the desperately fishtailing vehicle was a collision. He could still feel the impact all these years later.

He felt that way now, helpless to do anything but push onward.

His mouth was utterly dry. He took a gulp of beer and licked lips that felt chapped. "Marriage. We can get married now."

Tucker's laugh was high-pitched and nervous.

"You and me?"

Duncan laughed again, but there was no mirth in it. Reality couldn't have been more different from his fantasy. "That. Was. The. Hope." He managed to get out between breaths that verged on panting. He looked desperately into Tucker's blue and now, he could see, uncommitted eyes. He tried to swallow again but was unsuccessful and finally said, "That's an engagement ring."

The words he had planned on saying, clichés all, now came back to him, and even though he knew he was in a car headed for a collision, he forced himself to say them. "Tucker McBride, would you make me the happiest man in the world and agree to be my husband?"

Just then, the one-eyed waiter waltzed up to them. "Get you guys a couple more brewskis?"

"Get out," Duncan hissed, out of character but fearing he would scream.

The waiter hurried away.

Tucker didn't meet his gaze. Instead, he stared down at the ring, turning it around and around with his fingertips as if endlessly fascinated by the shiny object.

Finally, Duncan asked, hope barely there, his voice just above a whisper, "Would you marry me, honey?"

And, at last, Tucker looked up at him, tears standing in his eyes. He put the ring back on the table and then shoved it toward Duncan.

"No," he said.

Duncan stared hard at this man across the table, this man with whom he had spent the last three years, through good times and bad, through hot summer nights and hot winter ones, too, through dinners, movies, bar crawls, and quiet evenings at home and suddenly felt as though Tucker was a stranger. Duncan blinked back tears. He put a hand to his stomach, which was churning with what felt like acid. Not a single coherent thought formed in his head, so he certainly couldn't think of what to say in response to Tucker's eloquent refusal.

He picked up the ring and stared at it and almost wondered how it had made its way into his hand.

He slid the ring onto the third finger of his right hand and grinned at Tucker. "Guess I bought myself some bling this weekend then." He held his hand out in front of him as though to admire the ring, but all he was really feeling was the fear that the smell of the pizza and beer were going to make him throw up.

The two men sat for a while in silence.

Finally, Duncan recovered sufficiently enough to ask, "No?"

Tucker gave him a sad smile, one that Duncan was horrified to see was fashioned mostly from pity and concern. Tucker shook his head and removed his gaze from Duncan's to scan the restaurant. Duncan watched as he made what must have been eye contact with the waiter, and he pointed to their beers and held up two fingers.

"I'm sorry, babe. I thought what we had was kind of an easy thing, you know? No strings? That's why I liked having my place and you having yours." He went silent as their waiter brought two more beers, setting them down before them silently and then hurrying away. Duncan stared at the sweating bottle before him as though it were a pile of something a dog left behind, a St. Bernard, maybe.

He didn't touch it.

"You're talking in the past tense."

"Huh?"

"You're talking in the past tense—what we had, what you *liked*."

Tucker smiled sheepishly. "I guess I am, huh?" He scratched at his neck. "I didn't realize it, but maybe my mind is getting ahead of me."

Duncan toyed with a paper napkin on the table. He didn't look at Tucker when he asked, "So, you're not only saying no to my proposal, you're breaking up with me as well. Right?" He stared down at the diamond ring on his own finger. How could he have been so stupid?

"I didn't intend to, honey."

"Oh stop with the terms of endearment already." Duncan felt like he was about to cry, and that was the last thing he wanted Tucker, or anyone else in the restaurant, to see.

"Okay, I didn't intend to." He reached across the table to grab one of Duncan's hands, and Duncan snatched his hand away. Tucker grabbed it again and held it.

"I don't know if I can stand your kindness," Duncan whispered. He was pretty sure Tucker hadn't even heard him.

Tucker licked his lips and went on. "I had no intention of breaking up, but now that I see how far apart we are in terms of what we want, maybe we should." He squeezed Duncan's hand.

"That's it? You don't even want to try? I thought you loved me."

"I do. I do. I love being with you. I love having sex with you." Tucker gnawed on his lower lip for a moment and then said the line that had stung lovers' hearts worldwide since the beginning of time: "But I don't think I'm *in* love with you. That spark just isn't there."

Duncan looked up to see Tucker staring sadly, hungrily at him as though he was looking for something. What? Forgiveness? Absolution? For him to say Tucker was excused?

"You don't need to go on," Duncan said. It was odd. Moments ago, he felt near tears, edging on hysteria, and now he felt nothing. A curious numbness, almost like shock, had crept in, leaving him feeling dead inside.

"But I want you to understand how much you meant to me, what good times I had with you—"

Duncan cut him off with a bitter laugh. "There you go again with the past tense."

"Sorry."

"Why don't you just go?"

Tucker stared at him as though Duncan had reached across the table and slapped him. Finally he said, "Without eating?"

Duncan stood. "Enjoy it." He reached into his back pocket and pulled out his wallet, then threw a couple of twenties on the table.

"No, Duncan, don't. Sit down."

But Duncan was already moving rapidly away from the table and out of the restaurant.

Outside, rain had begun to fall. Not the typical Seattle winter rain, which was more like a mist, a fine drizzle that left one feeling damp instead of drenched. This one was a downpour, splattering hard off the sidewalk and cars, blinding. Lightning lit up the sky and thunder rumbled, also rare for Seattle.

But did Duncan hurry through the sheets of water pouring down from an angry sky?

No.

He wandered, almost leisurely, back to his car, letting the rain soak through his clothes, run in icy rivulets off his head, down his neck, to trickle down his spine, chilling him to his very core.

He didn't care.

The rain matched his mood.

Once he got to his car, he sat with his head on the steering wheel, shivering. He thought about how city hall today was an assembly line of weddings. How, all over the city, gay couples were celebrating being, for the first time in his state's history, legally wed. He pictured the scores of couples right now at the Paramount Theatre downtown, where the city was throwing "A Wedding Reception for All." He thought of the smiling faces, the linked hands, the hugging, the kissing, the shared dreams and hopes for the future, the joy of the witnesses, the popping of champagne corks, and the slicing of wedding cakes topped with two brides or two grooms.

He had never felt more alone.

Drawing a big breath, he wiped the tears and rain away from his face, turned the key in the ignition, threw on the windshield wipers, and pulled out of his parking space to start home.

He turned on the radio and tuned to the "adult contemporary" station he preferred to listen to while driving.

Karen Carpenter's plaintive voice emerged from the radio speakers. "We've only just begun," she sang.

"Oh shut up, Karen. Have a hamburger." Duncan snapped the radio off.

Chapter Two

When Duncan woke up the next morning, it was to dull gray light seeping through his sole bedroom window and a little man with an ice pick behind his eyes, hammering away. The gentle rocking rhythm of his houseboat, usually a comfort that lulled him to sleep or made him feel secure, now only made him nauseous.

Rain tapped insistently against the window.

He had spent the night alone with an old trick—one named Jack—Jack Daniel's. Duncan, who often embarrassingly or proudly admitted, depending on the situation, that two drinks were his limit, had downed half the bottle, drinking shot after shot of the amber liquid until he passed out on his couch in front of a television that continued to broadcast images of happy, just-wed, same-sex couples.

He sought oblivion and got it. He didn't even remember crawling into bed, but here he was with his clothes in a heap on the floor beside the bed, to boot. He lifted his head to glance down at his pale-blue sheets and mattress-ticking-striped comforter and was relieved to see neither had spatterings of puke.

He sat up, wincing as the pain in his head intensified. Why he thought drowning his grief in alcohol had been a good idea was beyond him. Now he simply felt alone, rejected, and sick.

He scooted down on the bed a bit to look outside at a pale tangerine line on the eastern horizon above the Eastlake neighborhood across the water. The houses, apartment buildings, marinas, and houseboats rising up from the steel-gray water were blurred as the raindrops made contact with his window and trailed down, leaving distorting smears in their wake. A red-and-white striped tugboat made its way purposefully across the water, pulling its load of what looked to Duncan like nothing more than rock.

He lay back down hard, flinging an arm over his forehead, thinking again of the Carpenters. It was not only Monday, it was a rainy day.

Duncan's first thought, ever responsible, was that he needed to make a phone call. No, make that two phone calls. The first would be to the school where he taught, letting them know he was sick (Did heartsick count? Did being hungover?) and that they should try to find a substitute. Duncan never missed school, but he figured he owed himself a mental health day. Hell, after last night's fiasco, he owed himself a mental health month.

Would he ever heal?

He snatched his iPhone from the little ledge jutting out from the side of his bed, brought up Cascade Elementary, and punched the screen to call his employer. He felt bad that he was putting them in the position of finding a sub this late in the morning. He didn't want to talk to his principal, Bruce Harrington, because he didn't think he could bear the kindness and sympathy in the other man's voice. Bruce was the kind of guy almost all the teachers went to at one time or another for a shoulder to cry on, for a sympathetic ear, for a hug.

He was too sick for any of that this morning.

And he was in luck—he got the school's voice mail. "Hey, it's Duncan Taylor. Sorry to call so late, but I'm feeling really sick this morning, and I'm not going to be able to make it in today." He thought of adding something about a possible bug, or food poisoning, or even a touch of cancer, but was too exhausted already to embellish his excuse.

Besides, he *was* sick.

Heartsick.

Hungover.

The second call he needed to make would be to his sister, Scout (his mom had been a big fan of *To Kill a Mockingbird*—the movie—not the book) back in Summitville, PA, Duncan's old hometown on the Ohio River just west of Pittsburgh.

But for a talk with Scout he would need coffee, and he would need a shower. He would need to feel less like one of the living dead. Right now the only noise he felt capable of making was that distinctive *erp* sound that preceded vomiting.

He forced himself from his bed, surprised to see that he was naked, and rooted around in the heap of clothes on the floor for his boxers and T-shirt. He donned those and headed to the kitchen on the opposite wall. He went through the ritual of making coffee, adding a couple extra teaspoons for good measure. "I like my coffee like I like my men: strong and black," he whispered to himself, in hopes of eliciting a laugh. Duncan realized he was not in the mood. Grimly, he started up the coffee maker. He then groped around in one of the kitchen cabinets for the ibuprofen and downed three of those with a big glass of water. He belched after finishing the tumbler of water, refilled the glass, and gulped its contents down as well.

Why did drinking make one so thirsty? A question for a science lesson for his fourth graders, maybe? Scratch that.

Food. The very idea of it made his stomach pitch and then do cartwheels. But Duncan knew having something in his gut would most likely result in him feeling marginally better. He opened the small refrigerator to his left and rooted around. The crisper held a few apples, a head of cauliflower, and a bag of baby carrots. The shelves above were crowded with spelt bread, eggs, jam, shrink-wrapped chicken breasts and tilapia, an assortment of condiments, a container of takeaway Thai, and what his stomach told him, most unwisely, he really wanted—a half-eaten cheeseburger, wrapped in foil from Saturday night's dinner with Tucker at Blue Moon Burgers in Fremont.

He pulled out the bleu cheese and bacon burger, sniffed it, and downed it in three or four bites. Miraculously, rather than coming back up, it managed to settle the churning in his stomach, and Duncan was glad he didn't regret the decision.

He poured himself a cup of coffee and walked with it to the houseboat's front door. He slid into the pair of deck shoes he kept by the door, slipped outside, and stood just over the threshold. A small awning kept him dry, but not warm. It was a bit of an endurance contest to be out here in December, but the cold, damp air and the smell of Lake Union actually invigorated him. He sipped his coffee and watched as two shells filled with early morning rowers glided by, heedless of the rain and chill. Their coxswain called out directions, her voice carrying dimly to Duncan across the water.

There was serenity here, and Duncan had never regretted buying the little houseboat, which had always seemed to him like a romantic place, small and cramped as it was. He liked that he could step out his door in warm weather and practically be *in* the water. He loved the activity on the lake: the sailboats, the touristy land-water vehicles—the "Ducks," the seaplanes landing and taking off. But most of all, he loved the feeling it gave him of being removed, his own little warren right here in the heart of the big city. Even though all he had to do was look south to see the skyline of downtown Seattle, the houseboat gave him the feeling that he was set apart, a pioneer of sorts.

Maybe, he wondered, Tucker had never liked the houseboat. Maybe that was why he hadn't wanted to get more involved with Duncan, because Duncan was forever singing its praises and waxing rhapsodic about it with statements like "I don't know if I ever want to leave this place." And he didn't know. The houseboat was secure. Cozy. Home. That, plus being on the water appealed to his Cancerian sensibilities.

And besides, who knew what Tucker wanted? Duncan leaned forward to look to his right, so he could bring the northern edge of Seattle's Capitol Hill neighborhood into view. He peered up at the lovely dome of St. Mark's Cathedral at the top of the hill and thought that, nearby, Tucker probably slumbered in his apartment on Boston.

He wondered if he was alone.

He shook his head. He would need to stop thinking about Tucker. He shivered and gulped down the remainder of his coffee, which had quickly gone cold in the forty-degree weather. He ducked back inside and closed the door firmly behind him.

The houseboat's warmth erased the chill. Duncan grabbed a flannel robe from the back of his bathroom door and shrugged into it, poured himself another cup of coffee, and made himself comfortable on his bed, fluffing the pillows behind his back.

It was time to call Scout, his big sis. She was his port in a storm, the woman he turned to whenever he had good news or bad. She always cared, making him feel as though what was happening in his life was the most important thing in the world. And she did this despite the fact she had her own adored husband, Bud, and twins, a boy and a girl who had just started their first year of high school.

He brought her up in the contacts in his phone and stared down at her photo for a moment. It was one he had taken on a visit home last fall, in Scout's backyard. Behind her, a maple tree had burst into scarlet life against a backdrop of deep-blue sky. She looked a lot like him. Oh sure, she had much bigger boobs and a much smaller nose, but the Italian/British ancestry was there in plain view. Scout had the same muddy-green eyes that turned emerald in sunlight; she had the same coarse dark-brown, almost-black hair that turned to ringlets when there was any humidity in the air at all. And she had the same Cupid's-bow lips as Duncan, a mouth that spoke both of warmth and sexiness at the same time.

Duncan snorted; he wished his mouth had the same pull as his sister's. She was one of the most happily married people he knew. So was everyone in his family. His younger sister, Jemima—they called her Jem and Duncan knew, though his mom denied it, this was another *To Kill a Mockingbird* reference—adored her cop husband, Vince. Their union had produced one child, a little girl called Debbie, who was the biggest tomboy

Duncan had ever seen, always getting into scrapes with other kids, always coming home with a fresh new sports injury, despite the fact she was only six. Yet, in spite of their rambunctious charge, Jem and Vince seemed like newlyweds, mooning at each other at family gatherings as though they had just met, still in the bloom of early love though they had been together for more than a decade. Even his mom and dad, now retired and living in St. Petersburg, FL, were one of those insufferable couples who rarely did anything without the other.

"All I ever wanted," Duncan said to the knotty pine walls, "was to be like them. To know the simple happiness of having a soul mate. Is that too much to ask?"

Duncan pondered the question, the phone held down at his side for a moment, and surmised that it was. Here he was, pushing forty, with a string of broken relationships behind him and nothing to show for it but heartache and tears.

His life was a country western song.

The thought of that did cause him to chuckle, in spite of himself, and spurred him to action. He pressed the button that would connect him to Scout. Since it was three hours later in Summitville, he had no worries about waking her.

Scout's deep, raspy voice came across the miles to him, immediately lowering his blood pressure and making him feel surrounded by an embrace. God, he loved his big sister. "What are you doing?" she asked, her standard opening line, for years, to their every phone call.

"Just sitting here, staring out at the rain."

"Why aren't you at work? Isn't it, like, eight thirty out there?" Duncan listened as, presumably, she looked around for a clock or a watch.

"I called in sick."

"Oh, poor baby. Calling in sick on a Monday usually means you had a good weekend." She laughed.

When Duncan didn't join her, she stopped. "Okay. What's wrong?"

Duncan thought there would be small talk before they got to the heart of the matter. He thought they might discuss the weather, Bud's job at the fabricating plant where he worked as a welder, one of Duncan's more cantankerous and humorous classroom charges, the twins' teenage angst, or anything other than getting right down to the real purpose of his call.

But that was Scout for you. Direct. And somehow, even though they had only this tenuous connection across thousands of miles, she was always quickly able to discern when things were out of whack.

"You said you were sick. Everything okay with your health? Your job going okay? Tucker?"

Her last word sent a frisson of heat though him, making him feel, absurdly, ashamed and embarrassed. Scout was obviously not going to let his reluctance to talk keep her from getting at the heart of things. It was her way. It was why he both adored and sometimes hated his sister.

"It's Tucker," he said, his voice coming out just above a whisper. His gaze moved to the window, and he noticed the rain had stopped and there was even a patch of blue in the sky. He guessed the universe, and the sun, had not gotten wind of his heartbreak.

"You guys okay? He seemed so nice when you were back here last fall."

Duncan didn't say anything.

"You broke up, didn't you?" Scout asked, sympathetically. Duncan could feel the sorrow in her voice, almost as though they were psychically connected, which, in fact, maybe they were. "Oh honey, why does it seem like it never works out for you?"

"Gee, thanks, sis."

"No. No, I mean you're such a great guy. You shouldn't be alone. You're kind and sweet and funny. Handsome as all get-out—how could you not be? You look like me. Great with kids. You make a mean red gravy with meatballs." She laughed.

"Now you sound like Mom. I can do no wrong."

Scout said, "So what happened? Why did this fool let a catch like you slip through his fingers?"

"Well, we did break up. But it was more than that."

"Oh?"

"You heard about the elections in Washington, right? I told you about same-sex marriage being legal now?"

"Oh yeah." Scout sucked in a breath. She was so intuitive. Right away, Duncan knew she knew. "Don't tell me you proposed?" She didn't give him a chance to answer. Her next utterance was tinged with outrage. "And he said no? To you? I can't believe it." She was quiet for a moment and then said, "I never liked that guy anyway."

Duncan couldn't help it. He laughed. "You just said a minute ago how nice he was."

"Oh, everybody says shit like that. It doesn't mean anything. None of us liked him."

"Really, sis?" Duncan was touched by her allegiance, by how she was always on his side. "Really?"

She didn't say anything again for a moment, and he assumed she was considering whether she should tell him the truth. "No, not really. We did like him, but it was only for a long weekend, and I'm sure he was on his best behavior. Who can tell what anyone's really like from *that*?"

"You're so sweet. You don't have to suddenly hate him because he rejected me."

"But why?"

Duncan told her all about his week—the hope that had filled his heart on Wednesday when he watched the first couples line up at city hall for marriage licenses, buying the engagement ring, the disastrous pizza dinner, and how all he had left from that fiasco was a lump on his forehead and a shredded ego. He didn't even get any pizza.

"Poor baby. And this is why you stayed home today?"

"Of course. Wouldn't you? I couldn't go in there and face a class of boisterous fourth graders. I don't know how I'll face anyone again." He said this last bit so softly he wasn't sure Scout had even heard him.

"Honey, take the day, take a couple days. Eat chocolate. Watch bad TV. Drink. Cry yourself to sleep." Scout paused for a moment. "And then get back out there. You're a hottie and charming, and you'll find someone else."

"Sis, do you know how many men I've gone through in the last eighteen years?"

"Are you bragging or complaining? Because to this girl, who's been dining on the same diet since she was sixteen, I'm not so sure I want to hear about all the men you've had."

They both chuckled. Duncan said, "No, really."

"I wasn't keeping count."

Duncan stood and paced around the small confines of his houseboat, glancing outside as a seaplane took off from the water. The noise of the engine would have drowned out any conversation, so it gave him time to do a quick tally, one he was certain was conservative.

"More than a dozen," he finally said. "And that's not even counting the disasters—the one-time-only dates with lunatics, egomaniacs, and Mama's boys." He plopped back down on the bed. "A dozen guys and every one of them dumped me, for one reason or another." He snorted. "Remember Tyler?"

"Oh, he was a sweetheart!" Scout exclaimed.

"Yeah, the guy he was seeing on the side, the one who was all of twenty years old thought so too."

"Sorry." Scout asked, "But what about that lawyer? What was his name? You guys went out for almost a year."

"Hunter. Yeah. He was smart, looked like he stepped out of *GQ*."

"Why didn't that go anywhere?" Scout wondered.

"Well, after that year, Hunter told me he wanted to open up our relationship. Told me he wanted to try three-ways and more-ways." Duncan shook his head, remembering. "I'm a one-man kind of guy. I want the husband, the dog, the white picket fence, maybe even a baby someday. I couldn't stomach the thought of sharing, of bringing tricks back home with us. Of watching while he—"

"I get the picture!" Scout interrupted. "I would never have guessed he was like that."

"Oh sweetie, you don't really know gay men, do you?" Duncan sighed. "I have known so many gay couples for whom arrangements like that are standard operating procedure. That or they have their own 'don't-ask-don't-tell' arrangement where they look the other way while their other half sluts around." Duncan didn't say anything for a long moment. He certainly didn't tell Scout he *had* tried a three-way with Hunter, just to make him happy. Scout would never understand. The experience had been a disaster, leaving Duncan feeling very much the odd man out. Things certainly hadn't gotten off to a good start when the guy asked if Duncan wouldn't mind leaving the bedroom. And even now it hurt to think about it, watching the passion on Hunter's face as the bearded guy they brought home from the Cuff that Saturday night fucked him. The thought of it was like a knife twisting in his gut.

Was he the only gay man who could settle for just one? Sometimes it seemed like it.

"Well, you never know," Scout said. "I've heard that just when you least expect it, love comes creeping around."

Duncan shook his head sadly. "Not for me." He opened the door again, letting the cold breeze wash over him. "Maybe I'll get a cat."

"Oh Duncan—shut up. Get a cat, by all means. We have two and they're hellions and we have the shredded couch to prove it, but they make good company. But don't give up on finding that special someone. He's out there. I know it."

Duncan shivered in the chill coming through the door, yet made no move to close it. He was touched by his sister's pronouncement of hope and her confidence in him, but after you take so many wrong turns, never ending up where you want to go, it begins to feel like you're permanently lost.

"How do you know?" Duncan asked, not really thinking Scout had an answer. "I'm not getting any younger and the possibility just seems to dwindle, getting smaller and smaller, with each year that passes with me alone."

"Look, you're entitled to feel sorry for yourself *today* and maybe tomorrow, too, so I'll put up graciously with your whining."

"Gee thanks."

"Seriously, little brother. Remember how you told me about watching all those couples get their marriage licenses on TV?"

"Yeah."

"Well, doesn't it occur to you that *lots* of people have found someone they can share their lives with? I did it. Mom and Dad did it. Jem did it, although she had to trap her fella by getting herself knocked up," Scout snickered. "My point is us and all those people you watched, those *long* lines of people as you said, all found someone. So I think the odds are in your favor."

Duncan closed the door and checked to see if there was still coffee in the pot. He knew his sister was trying to make him feel better, to force him to see that there were plenty of fish in the sea, yet what she said didn't make him feel more hopeful, it only made him feel more alone.

He wouldn't say this to her, but the fact that all these people found their soul mates, their spouses, their families, no longer gave him hope. It just made it seem as though he were the only schmuck not invited to the party, the poor, pathetic soul doomed to always be on the outside looking in, his nose pressed to the glass.

"Thanks, Sis," he said finally. He poured himself another cup of coffee, set it on the nightstand, and crawled back into bed. He yanked the covers over himself, thinking that maybe he would just sleep out the day. At least if he were asleep, he could have a little oblivion, if not peace and contentment. "I'm gonna do what you said—wallow in self-pity for the day."

"Sounds like a wonderful plan." Scout sucked in a breath. "Honey, I hate that we're so far apart. Why don't you move back here? I so want to just give you a big hug, make you a big bowl of *pasta fagioli*, and get you to help me wrap Christmas presents. You always did do a better job of it than I ever could."

"It's a gay thing," Duncan mumbled. "You wouldn't understand."

Scout chuckled. "You want me to look into flights? I could come out for a few days. It's been forever since I've seen you."

"You don't have to do that." Duncan knew his sister didn't have much money, not when her whole family lived on her husband's welding wages. A plane ticket, especially one bought at the last minute, would probably be what she'd spend on groceries for a month or two. "I'll be okay."

"Are you sure?"

"Yeah, like you said, I just need to take a little time to get over the disappointment."

"And then hop back up on the horse," Scout snickered. "Or a guy hung like one." She snorted. "Did I just say that?"

It was nice; she made him laugh. "And on that note, I'm gonna go."

"I'll call you in a day or two, see how you're doing."

"Thanks. I love you."

"Love you too."

They said their buh-byes and hung up.

Still in bed, Duncan turned away from the window to stare at the wall. Yes, he was miserable, and it wasn't even so much about Tucker. Maybe, in his heart, he had known Tucker wasn't the "one," but he simply had cast him in the role because he wanted so badly for it to be true.

No, what made him feel like pulling the covers over his head was that this latest breakup, this latest rejection, had about it an air of finality. Options closing. Doors slamming shut.

He didn't know if he could bear dating again, playing the game, the awkwardness of the hunt, the embarrassing dinner conversations that felt more like job interviews. Yet dating, *real* dating, where you made plans and went out to dinner or a movie, was the only way Duncan wanted to connect with a man.

He had seen the hookup sites. He had been to the bars, and had even taken a couple of trips, both disasters, to one of the local bathhouses.

Sex was easy.

Love was hard.

And marriage? It was never gonna happen. Not for him. Maybe he should just accept that, concentrate on building a tight-knit circle of friends upon whom he could rely, go back to Pennsylvania more often, get to know his nieces and nephews better. Get that cat. What was that breed he liked again? The Maine coon cat. He had heard they were like dogs.

That would be fun, wouldn't it? A kitten?

Duncan pulled the pillow over his head and moaned, wondering what was to become of him.

Chapter Three

Duncan slept for eight hours. When he woke, the light was fading as dusk encroached. The rain had returned and drummed on the roof of the houseboat.

Duncan rolled over to peer out at the grayish light, doing a quick mental check to gauge how he was doing after his slumber, which had felt, initially, deep and dreamless. In fact, he was surprised to see it was only about five in the afternoon. He had imagined that it would be morning.

He sat up with a little cry of surprise. His sleep had *not* been dreamless. Images rushed back to him as he realized he had had one of the strangest dreams he'd ever experienced.

"Oh God, what's wrong with me?" Part of him wanted to flush the dream images from his mind and the other part took a strange comfort from them.

He had been in a beautiful garden, the grass beneath his feet almost supernaturally green and vibrant, so bright and verdant it didn't seem real. Same with the sky, which the poets would label azure, stretching in its infinite blueness above his head without the interruption of a single cloud.

A warm breeze blew, carrying the scent of hibiscus. Duncan found himself standing, facing an assemblage of people, all seated as an audience before him. There were his parents, his sisters, and their husbands and kids. His grandma, dead now for five years, pressed a hankie to her nose, peering at him intently through her horn-rims. There were work colleagues, friends from high school and college, even old boyfriends. With the exception of Grandma, it was like an event organized by Facebook.

He turned to his left and confronted Father Frank Safara, his priest from the Catholic church he had attended as a boy. Duncan had never known what had become of the man, but he hadn't aged at all and looked rather royal in his white, cobalt, and gold vestments. The priest smiled.

A string quartet began to play Pachelbel's Canon in D. Duncan recalled thinking it was a clichéd choice, but he wasn't the one getting married.

Or was he?

The priest nudged him and whispered, "Stand up straight, young man; she approaches."

Wait a minute. *She*?

Even in the dream, Duncan had wanted to burst into giddy, uncomfortable laughter. He turned to Father Safara and said, "But I'm a gold-star fag."

"Shhh, we don't have time for that," the priest admonished. "She approacheth."

Duncan looked at the man of the cloth oddly. Seriously? *Approacheth*?

Gently, the priest turned Duncan's shoulders so he was facing the crowd again. From behind a trellis laden with blooming, climbing hydrangea, *she* emerged. A woman. Clad in a satin wedding gown adorned with lace and seed pearls, its long trail sweeping the ground behind her, she carried a bouquet of calla lilies. A veil obscured her face. She moved toward him and Duncan wanted to say to the priest, "This is wrong, father! You got the wrong guy." And again, reiterating that he was a gold-star fag, which meant, in gay parlance, that he had never had sexual contact with a woman.

But he couldn't open his mouth. For one thing, the guests were rising, smiling and dabbing at their eyes, as wedding guests are wont to do. The music, now morphed to the Wedding March, increased in volume.

Behind his bride, Duncan spied the flower girl and ring bearer, two Boston terriers on their hind legs, one brindle and white and one black and white, carrying their respective tokens—a pillow with rings and a flower basket—on their forepaws.

That was when Duncan woke up. Although he initially hadn't recalled the dream in his waking moments, he thought it was the images of a bride *for him* and the two dogs as wedding attendants that had yanked him rudely out of his coma-like slumber.

Weird. Duncan got up and went into the small bathroom to pee, brush his teeth, and shower, all the while trying to piece together some interpretation of the dream that would make sense. He wasn't able to come up with much of anything other than the fact that he was certain it was *not* his subconscious trying to inform him that he was, in reality, straight.

That idea was as laughable as it was absurd. Duncan thought he could trace back to when he knew he was gay and that was at the ripe old age of six, when he went for a boys' swimming class at the Summitville YMCA. Their instructor was a young blond man named Jan who wore board shorts, sported a tan and, even to Duncan's boyish eyes, the most amazing hairless pecs he had ever seen on a man.

Duncan had been in love. He became the best swimmer in the class, not because he was like a fish in water, but because he wanted to please Jan. He dreamed about Jan and, when the class was over, he gave Jan a bouquet of dandelions picked from a patch of weeds outside the Y. Duncan still remembered the grace with which Jan had accepted the offering.

Duncan never, ever questioned his sexuality from his very first sexual experience in sixth grade, when he got naked with the African-American boy next door in his bedroom. All they did was rub their erections together, but Duncan had never felt shameful or strange or guilty, but natural and, well, good.

He loved women, Lord knew he did, but dining at the vaginal buffet had never been an option that had crossed his mind. *Ever.* Honestly, though, he felt more comfortable in the company of women, preferred talking to them, found their (mostly) nurturing natures and senses of humor (mostly) less hard-edged than men's, even the gay ones. In fact, he thought there was a weird conundrum at work. Straight men, the ones who were supposed to be all about the ladies, actually seemed to prefer the company of men, except in the bedroom. Look at how they stuck together even when there were women around. Growing up, Duncan recalled many a Sunday or holiday when all the men gathered in the living room, watching some incomprehensible sport on television, while the women stayed together in the kitchen, with Duncan sitting unobtrusively in the room, listening with pleasure to their talk and the music of their laughter.

And now, he wondered, drying himself, had his subconscious been trying to tell him something with his odd dream?

But what? He knew he wanted to get married, wanted to find that special someone. But a woman? Really? He laughed out loud. And then stopped, abruptly.

He threw on a pair of flannel sleep pants, a T-shirt with the Elephant Car Wash logo emblazoned across its front and sat at his kitchen table to ring up Pagliacci Pizza. He ordered a pepperoni with black olives, large, as a big "fuck you" to Tucker.

Tucker could break his heart, but Duncan would be damned if he would deny him his pizza.

As he waited for the pizza, he rummaged around in his refrigerator and was delighted to find a six-pack of Mac and Jack, a local ale out of Redmond. Tucker had probably left it in his fridge at some point, since Duncan himself was more of a martini or wine drinker.

But now the beer sounded good. Drinking it all would be yet another "fuck you" to his ex. It would be great with the pizza.

And it promised even more oblivion.

By the time the pizza arrived, Duncan was browsing the Seattle-Tacoma Craigslist and had already worked his way through half the six-pack.

It wasn't until his fifth beer that a combination of the dream, post-traumatic stress, garlic and tomatoes, and perusing, curiously, the men for women (m4w) ads on Craigslist, inspired in him an idea. One that, even in his drunken heart of hearts, he knew would be better left alone.

But who among us, three sheets to the wind and nursing a broken heart, has ever listened to a sensible inner voice?

Duncan went to the upper right-hand corner of the main m4w page and, laughing, hit the Post link.

He slurred, "What could it hurt?" and began uncertainly typing out an ad.

GAY MAN SEEKS STRAIGHT WOMAN FOR MARRIAGE

So, you're probably sitting there looking at that headline of mine and thinking, "WTF?" Why, you might very reasonably ask, would a gay man seek a straight woman for marriage? Yes, it has been done, but usually by confused people who did not intentionally set out to join their lives in sexual incompatibility.

First off, sister, get the word sexual out of your mind. This ain't about sex, nor will it ever be. Nosireebob, or nosireejane, or whatever. This is about a marriage of the minds. A marriage, if you will, of the hearts.

Except for in the bedroom, everybody knows that gay men and women get on better than just about any other combo. And if you don't agree, move along, there's nothing for you to see here.

So, now that she's gone, we can talk. Why do I, an avowed homosexual, want to marry a straight woman? Especially when gay marriage is now legal here in Washington?

Number one. Kids. I want 'em. You want 'em. And it's just easier when you make an omelet with an egg and sperm. Yum! Of course, the mixing would be done in a lab and not in the natural way, which for me, and I do apologize, is out of the question. I haven't taken the drive up Vaginal Way and I don't intend to point my Chrysler in that direction anytime soon.

But I think a gay dad and a straight mom could be a kid's dream parents.

The other reason I want to marry a straight woman is because I love you ladies. I have two sisters; I have a mom; my best friends have always been girlfriends, and not in a campy slang way either. I confide easier in women. I enjoy being with them—I tend to be more relaxed, more myself.

Why does a marriage have to be about sex, anyway? Don't those fireworks fade after a while? What do the good, long-term marriages have in common? It isn't the old in-and-out.

No, it's companionship. Respect. Making a family. Wanting to grow old together.

I have just come to the rather stunning conclusion, at the ripe old age of 38, that a marriage, for me, would be better with a woman.

As Mary Magdalene sang in *Jesus Christ Superstar*: I've had so many men before, in very many ways... Well, me too. And not a one of them has worked out. Maybe you've had similar experiences.

So, maybe you and me, we could be a match? I'd look good on your arm, I'm Italian and some other stuff, but the Italian wins out in my coloring (dark), hair (dark), eyes (green), nose (big), and smile (totally warm). If it matters, I'm about 5'11" in pretty good shape, currently tipping the scales at 175. I keep my hair cut short and usually sport a little goatee. I've been told I'm cute by many gay guys.

But not cute enough to marry, I guess.

Maybe you'll feel differently.

Should we meet up for coffee and find out if this crazy thing just might work?

Duncan looked down at what he had written. It was too long. It was too lucid. It was too crazy. He realized, with horror, he wrote better when he was drunk. His finger hovered over the Delete key, but he eventually moved it away and cracked open the last of the six beers.

He stared at the ad for a long time. *What the fuck are you doing?* a little voice in his head chided, sounding much like his sister, Scout. *Are you crazy? You are not really thinking of actually posting this, are you? This can only lead to heartache, not to mention who knows what kind of crazies might respond. Delete that fucker. Delete it right now.*

But Duncan knew, drunk or not, giggling over what he had written, that he didn't want to delete the ad. In spite of having to retype every other word several times as he composed the ad and in spite of those same words being ever so slightly out of focus, Duncan realized there was truth there.

And what would be the harm in simply seeing what might happen?

He was sober enough to realize he would feel differently in the morning and would delete the ad. He was sober enough to know this was nothing more than the drunken ravings of a brokenhearted homo, desperate for love.

But what the hell? He was posting it.

He paused only to upload a picture of himself, one taken last spring, at the school's field trip to Volunteer Park and the Asian Art Museum. The other fourth grade teacher, Tee Soldano, had snapped the picture of him as he stood outside, looking up toward the sun, a smile on his face. He looked happy in his khakis and short-sleeved plaid shirt. There was something unguarded and...well...hopeful, about the pose.

It was perfect.

He hit Post and waited to get the email that would complete the posting process. When he got that, he finished up and ensured that his post would go live.

Straight women of Seattle, watch out. Duncan Taylor is coming for you! He laughed until he put his head down, hard, on the surface of the kitchen table and fell asleep, snoring.

Chapter Four

Duncan didn't check his email until two days after he posted the ad. Tuesday he returned to school, hung over and feeling weak and depressed, but happy to be getting back to his routine. He realized there was nothing like a classroom of boisterous fourth graders to take one's mind off one's troubles. The day passed in a blur, and he told no one about his posting on Craigslist, although he had confided in Tee Soldano in the break room about his disappointing, if not heartbreaking, weekend. She was suitably sympathetic but, like Scout, confident he would find someone even better. "A man like you? Come on! Word just hasn't gotten out," Tee had said with a smile. "Once it does, trust me, they'll be lining up."

Duncan wished he had an ounce of his older friend's confidence.

Anyway, Tuesday was a day of catching up, exhausting especially when Duncan's energy reserves were at their lowest point at the start of the day. While he hadn't forgotten his ad—who could?—he simply couldn't bear to face his email when he got home, fearing that he would either have no responses, or that his email box would be full of replies, each one stamped with its own special brand of crazy.

So, Duncan forced himself to get off the houseboat, make the short walk over to Fremont, and buy himself one of his favorite comfort dinners at Sinbad, just behind the huge statue of Lenin that stood in the heart of the funky and eclectic neighborhood. The chicken shawarma and fries, spicy, hot, and delicious, were like a little balm on his heart.

When he got home, he fell asleep in front of a DVRed episode of *Chopped* on the Food Network, dreaming of a man who was just as adept in the bedroom as he was in the kitchen. Duncan awakened to scattered images of eating pad Thai off the small of a muscular and tanned back.

It wasn't until Wednesday afternoon that Duncan had the courage and the energy to face his email.

There were a lot of replies from Craigslist, so many in fact Duncan laughed nervously and contemplated checking every one and hitting delete.

Instead, he counted. There were nearly twenty replies, twenty if you included the confirmation email from Craig. Who was Craig, anyway, and how did his list become such a part of the fabric of twenty-first-century life?

Never mind. He began opening emails. The first touched his heart, but he knew immediately, it was too much for him to take on. As much as he wanted to help the woman, he knew this was far out of his league. Kelly had written:

> I'm a single mom. As luck or fate would have it, I have been blessed or cursed six times with kids, all with different daddies, all deadbeats. I struggle to survive, since six kids is a handful and adding a special needs kid—Down's—into the mix makes it even more difficult. I work downtown at a call center and have worked my way up to senior

customer service representative, which means I make the astounding sum of $15 per hour. Please don't get any ideas about marrying me for my money! I get by on what I make, living in a section 8 two-bedroom where I do not feel safe and constantly worry about my kids, and government assistance.

Like you, I have been disappointed in men. Over and over, as I suspect you have. My brother, out in Pocatello, Idaho, is gay and he's the only man I can think of that I can rely on. He's great with the kids and even sends me money when he can, but he's a car mechanic with his own boyfriend, so he doesn't have much to spare.

Look, I am not looking for money. But I will be up-front—having someone help share the financial burden would be a blessing.

But, like you, I am looking for someone I can share this fucked-up life with, someone to watch TV with at night after the kids have FINALLY gone to sleep. Someone to sit down at the table with over a plate of macaroni and cheese and talk about our days. Someone who maybe would like to take a trip on the ferry some summer day over to Vashon Island for a picnic.

I don't know if that's you. If it is, get back at me. I don't care what you look like. All I require is a kind heart.

By the time Duncan finished reading that particular message, he had tears in his eyes and wasn't sure he could go on if this were the kind of thing he would find in the other messages. He had an almost irresistible urge to send this woman his next paycheck and, perhaps, his life savings.

He shook his head and moved on, relieved to find none of the other messages were quite as dire as the first.

Some of the women were angry, which he hadn't expected. The general tone of those messages was that Duncan had overstepped some imaginary boundary, and he was weirdly competing with them for the available guys in the world. He had to chuckle at the lack of logic there. The men he wanted would never have been interested in those women anyway. Right?

Other messages wanted to know why he was doing such a thing and said that he could never end up happy. Sure, they said, he might find someone with whom there was a comfortable meeting of the mind and the heart, someone with whom he even shared common goals, but his ambition was doomed to failure because a spark always ignited real love. One woman had written, "And in the real world, honey, that spark is sex."

They urged him to abandon this course and keep looking for the right guy. He wondered if Scout had gotten wind of his latest "project" and was flooding his inbox with sensible advice.

He deleted all such well-meaning responses.

Then there were replies from women who were too old (he loved his mom dearly and with devotion, but he did not want to marry her), too man hating, too desperate, too lonely, too crazy. One wanted to marry him so she could watch him "get it on" with a "variety of hot studs." She offered to suck the cum out of his ass. Lovely.

That one made him stop reading and reconsider what he had done.

*

Marilyn Samples had called in sick that Wednesday from her job as senior client services representative at the Aloha Dog and Cat Clinic in the city's Capitol Hill neighborhood. The title was just a fancy way of saying she was the chief front desk receptionist and, as such, did more than her share of answering phones, greeting clients, taking care of payments, filing, and making a fuss over every Pomeranian and Siamese that waltzed in the door.

It was an okay job, she thought, as she idly stroked her orange Tabby, Mike. Mike was going on ten years old and, once a boisterous young man who enjoyed nothing more than scratching the *hell* out of the arms of her favorite chairs and training for competition in the drapery-climbing Olympics, had now settled into a calmer and more dignified middle age, much as Marilyn herself had.

Today, she was holed up in her little one-bedroom warren on 17th, within walking distance of her employer, nursing the remains of a cold that had reached its peak, as Murphy's Law would have it, on her days off: Sunday and Monday. She thought she could manage going back in tomorrow, but resting today was her insurance that she could make it through Thursday, Friday, and the very busy Saturday.

But all these days off had induced in Marilyn a terrible *ennui*. Now that she was feeling more herself, the normally busy and somewhat hyper Marilyn didn't know what to do. She had watched everything she had saved up on her DVR—*Project Runway, RuPaul's Drag Race*, a gaggle of Lifetime original movies, mostly about women in peril, *Philadelphia* on the Retro channel (Marilyn, weakened by her cold, had wept buckets over that one), and several episodes of *Modern Family*. Marilyn had read through four of the novels on her Kindle—*Promises* by Marie Sexton, *Still* by Mary Calmes, *Racing for the Sun* by Amy Lane, and an older one she had, for some reason, never gotten around to—*Nocturne* by Z.A. Maxfield.

She had tried calling and texting her best friend, Christian, but he had never responded. No surprise there. What had drawn the pair together was their shared interest in gay men and, as long as Christian had played the field, which was mostly over the course of their friendship, he was a wonderful companion and confidante. Marilyn couldn't deny, when she was alone with only herself and Mike to talk to, that Christian's no-holds (or holes, in his case) barred descriptions of his sexual escapades, taking place everywhere from tricks' apartments, to the trails of the Washington Park arboretum, to the seedy confines of adult bookstores, titillated her. She supposed that's why she kept him around. His adventures added a little color to her life, and she could live vicariously through the many, many men Christian hooked up with, sometimes imagining herself in his place, although not when he came crying to her with his latest sexually transmitted infection.

Christian seemed an ironic name for such a slut, Marilyn thought for the thousandth time, and snorted. Idly, she picked up the phone and texted him again, asking where he was, what he was doing, who he was with, the fact that she was sick.

No response.

Christian was the kind of man who loved having Marilyn as an audience, which worked fine as long as he was performing.

But recently Christian had met someone, a man who owned a little wine shop in Wallingford, and the two had fallen truly, madly, deeply in love. Marilyn had been happy for the pair until she realized their union left her shut out in the cold.

Once Christian and Paul were established as a couple, Marilyn was no longer needed, and Christian, quite callously, left his "Grace" to fend for herself. It was an old story.

Ah well. She'd known what she was getting herself into when she befriended Christian. Christian had always been about Christian. The man had probably asked her three questions about herself during the course of their friendship, and two of them had concerned her opinions on how *he* looked.

Marilyn knew this latest fling would burn brightly and passionately for a month or two and then would fizzle out under the weight of Christian's need for variety. Then Christian would call, acting as though he hadn't ignored her for months, and ask if she wanted to go see what was on sale at the Nordstrom Rack downtown and if she was interested in Bloody Marys afterward on the Hill.

Marilyn set the phone back down and realized she didn't think she would welcome Christian back with open arms. Not again...

Of course, she could try her other BFF, Hannah, but Hannah was deep into plans for her wedding in June, and she, like Christian, had let her fervor over a man cloud what had once been a very deep and abiding friendship.

"Fuck 'em all, Mike," Marilyn whispered in the cat's ear, which flicked at the feel of her breath. Mike jumped from her lap.

Marilyn had her fill of TV, her fill of gay romance novels, her fill of lounging around all day, drinking Bloody Marys and eating Doritos, olives, and frozen pizza. She almost wished she had gone into work today.

She picked up her iPad and thought she would play a game of Hearts, but the purple icon for the Craigslist app called to her. She snorted. "Let's see what the boys are up to today," she called across to Mike, who seemed uninterested. He had settled himself into a corner of the couch, and his eyelids were at half-mast. The only thing that would rouse him now, Marilyn supposed, were his favorite words: Fancy Feast.

But when she opened the Craigslist app, she paused before going into the men for men area, her finger hovering over the screen. Did she really want to read about the scores of men out there hankerin' for a blow job, or a big dick up the old whazoo? She shrugged and tapped something she rarely tapped, the men for women section.

It opened for her and Marilyn scanned the ads, most of which were younger guys looking for girls who wanted to party, sprinkled with those men looking for more serious relationships. Marilyn chuckled and whispered to the screen, "Good luck with *that*."

Did anyone *ever* find a serious relationship on Craigslist?

And then she saw an ad that caught her eye and made her, for just a second, hold her breath. She swore, in that same second, her heart stopped beating.

The ad's headline read, "Gay Man Seeks Straight Woman for Marriage." "You gotta be fucking with me," Marilyn said aloud, causing Mike to look up. But she was intrigued and began reading.

*

Duncan didn't get to bed until almost eleven that night. He had stayed up late to watch a string of *Golden Girls* episodes on the Hallmark Channel. The old show was TV comfort food for him, and the final string of episodes he watched, the story arc that ended the show for good, was all about Dorothy at last finding her true love, her soul mate, and getting married.

It happened when she least expected it. It happened to the last character on the show viewers expected to see married. Duncan had, to his chagrin, shed a few tears as the girls said their final goodbyes.

He forced himself to switch off the flat screen and hoisted himself off the couch to brush his teeth in preparation for bed.

Just as he was pulling back the covers and leaving jeans and T-shirt on the floor in a heap, he eyed the desktop Mac on the table across the room. Maybe he would check to see if he had any new messages from Craigslist, just real quick.

And maybe, a sensible inner voice told him, now would be a good time to delete that silly ad.

He sat down in his boxers at the computer and logged in to his email.

The messages from Craigslist had slowed to a trickle. This was not surprising, considering the constant deluge of messages pouring into the forum. The good and bad of that fact was that messages were quickly buried.

He deleted one email with the oh-so-clever subject line "Me So Horny" without reading it, but the subject line of the other message caught his eye.

It read, "You're an Ass."

For some reason, Duncan laughed at that. Although certainly offensive, there was something refreshing about the line.

He opened the message.

> You're a fool. What they call in the South, an idjit. You've either got your head buried in the sand or up your ass. Take your pick.
>
> That ad you posted? Homo Looking for Hag for Love, Marriage and Children? Were you serious about that? Really? I mean, come on!
>
> I have known many, many gay men and all of them worship dick too much to even consider what you propose (pun intended) to do. And I can certainly understand that point of view myself.
>
> So what? You got your little heart busted one too many times? And you think a big soft bosom would be the perfect place to rest your weepy head? Poor baby!
>
> It will never work. But you know what? You tickle me. And I will meet you just because I want to see what kind of freak would post an ad like yours.
>
> So, if in spite of all I've said, you still want to meet, how's about we meet for coffee this coming Sunday afternoon. Say 4? I don't know where you are in the city, but I do know where I am, and I don't have a car, so I suggest meeting at Going to Ground, a little indie coffeehouse on Olive Way.
>
> Be there or be square, sucker. Oh, and that makes me wonder: you still going to suck once we get

hitched? How's that gonna work? Never mind. You can tell me on Sunday—the Lord's Day.

Duncan shook his head. Something about this one was unglued, but so bracingly honest and funny that he *did* want to meet her.

Before he gave his common sense a chance to take over, he quickly hit reply and wrote: "See you Sunday! You'll recognize me by the puppy-dog eyes, hangdog expression, and the wedding ring on my *right* hand."

Again, before he gave himself a chance to think about it, he hit "Send."

He could always cancel later. But somehow, he knew he wouldn't.

In spite of the fact he felt like he had just been royally reamed out, he went to bed for the first time since Sunday with a little grin on his face and relaxed enough to fall immediately asleep.

Chapter Five

Duncan knew the woman wouldn't show up. Of course, her message was not the message of a woman with a sense of humor, but the missive of a nasty bitch who hated not only gay men, but men in general. The email he had read, thinking back on it now, had fairly screamed hostility.

So why was he sitting here at Going to Ground, looking up every time the door opened, searching for a woman whose name he didn't even know. Worse, he had no idea what she even looked like. She could be one of the group of teenage girls sitting opposite him, giggling as they texted into their phones. He thought the one with the blonde ponytail and neck tattoo had been casting surreptitious glances at him.

Perhaps he *had* been punked. It wouldn't surprise him. After all, his posting that ad on Craigslist had left him wide open for ridicule, not to mention things even worse and more dangerous, if he cared to stop to think about them, which he didn't.

Duncan was fairly certain he knew how this little adventure would play out. He would sit here for an hour or so, nursing his skinny soy vanilla latte and then would reluctantly leave, knowing that either the woman hadn't shown up and hadn't, in fact, ever had any intention of doing so, or she had been there the whole time, watching him and laughing on the inside.

Hell, she might not even be a woman. "She" could be that character in one of the comfy chairs near the window, sporting a handlebar moustache and bolo tie and reading a beat-up paperback of *Giovanni's Room*. She could also be the harried mother of twins, making herself more harried by her jumbo cup of coffee as she pushed her double stroller back and forth on the weathered wooden floors, her babies whimpering inside.

He should just get up and leave now, he told himself. Cut his losses. The day was still young.

But just as he was tipping his chipped cobalt blue mug back to get to the dregs of his caffeinated beverage, she came in.

And Duncan knew it was the woman who had written. Not only was the searching way she looked around the coffee shop a giveaway, but Duncan simply felt this woman matched the words he had read.

He slouched down in his chair, holding his oversized mug up to his mouth, because he wanted to give himself a few seconds to observe her before she approached.

As he looked at her, the term *zaftig* sprang to mind.

She was, perhaps, a bit older than he had expected, but not *that* old. Duncan would put her in her early forties, which was only slightly older than he was. She had wide hips and a big bust, but the effect was kind of attractive in an earth mother sort of way. Her bulk looked good on her; it suited her. She wore a pair of black tights and a loose-fitting black tunic top that exposed one shoulder, upon which was a tattoo that Duncan was amused to see was of the Cheshire cat. She wore clunky sterling silver jewelry—big teardrop earrings that almost brushed her shoulders and a necklace that could have doubled as a breastplate. But the look worked. Her hair was too black to be naturally that color, but it had been cut in a short asymmetrical bob, and Duncan had to admit he liked the swatch of burgundy that ran through the left side of it. Very Seattle. She wore quite a bit of mascara and her full lips were not, as he would have expected, a bright crimson gash, but a softer color, one that would have undoubtedly been called something like Cinnamon Toast.

She looked like a thinner Dawn French BBC television character, and since *The Vicar of Dibley* was another of Duncan's comfort TV shows, he was charmed, rather than put off by her assertive and somewhat eccentric appearance.

He sat his coffee cup down, caught her gaze, and smiled. Shyly, he raised his hand to wave.

*

Marilyn spied him as soon as she entered Going to Ground, although she didn't want to give herself away, so she pretended to be looking over the assorted crowd hanging out.

God, he was cute! Cuter even than his photo, which hardly had done him justice.

She hadn't expected this Italian American hunk, who looked as though he should be sitting at some café near the Spanish Steps in Rome. He was handsome in a classic Mediterranean sense, with nearly poreless olive skin, piercing green eyes, and the kind of dark, dark five o'clock shadow that made Marilyn want to purr...or growl.

He sat casually in his chair, legs crossed, wearing a pair of simple black cotton pants, not jeans, a soft butter-colored chamois shirt, open to reveal a distressed-looking gray V-neck T-shirt. Marilyn loved the fact that he wore a pair of suede wingtips sans socks. With the way the light was hitting him, that weary, milky winter sunlight, why, he would fit perfectly on the cover of *GQ*. And, Marilyn was relieved to note, he was not dressed in gay clone fashion—tight T-shirt, rolled jeans, laceless Converses.

Why in the hell would a hottie like this, she wondered, be posting on Craigslist looking for a gal? This guy could have his pick of Seattle's finest men.

Marilyn paused, freezing when she saw he had spotted her and was giving her a shy little wave that was simply fucking adorable. She pretended she hadn't seen and hurried, breathless, to the counter.

"Give me a drip, black," she barked to the kid behind the counter, who looked to be all of twelve. He looked confused for a moment, and Marilyn wondered if she was the only one still around who simply ordered a plain cup of joe anymore.

"Coming right up." He turned to get her coffee.

Out of the corner of her eye, Marilyn regarded her date once more. Christ, the guy even had dimples. If he were straight, he'd be completely out of her league. The last date she'd had had been two years ago, courtesy of Match.com, and the guy looked like Wallace Shawn. He worked as an actuary in Everett.

They had had absolutely nothing in common.

But the sex had been phenomenal.

The guy caught her looking and waved again. She could no longer pretend she hadn't seen him, so she held up a finger, which was meant to say, "Hang on there, pardner, while I get my java here."

He seemed to understand and went on regarding her with a smirk.

And then she got it; the smirk gave him away. This was someone's weird idea of a joke. This hunk of burning love was out to amuse himself at her expense. With a shaking hand, she handed the guy behind the counter three singles and took her coffee from him. She took a sip and wanted to spit it back out because it was so damn hot, but how would *that* look? Another funny aspect of the story Mr. Gorgeous here would tell his buddies later when he met up with them at the Cuff, the Lobby, or Purr. Marilyn didn't know why someone would want to see what kind of pathetic female would answer such an ad and surely could not comprehend what would be amusing or at least interesting about it. That was part of the reason she had answered with open hostility, although what she had written *had* made her chuckle. But the hostility, fake or not, had been an early attempt at self-defense, should this be some sort of prank.

And now, looking at this guy, in all his toothsome glory, she was sure it was.

She sauntered over to his table at last, wondering if she ought to sit. She remained standing.

"I don't think you gave me your name."

The guy shook his head and opened his mouth to speak.

Marilyn held up her hand to stop him. "No. Let me guess. You're going to tell me your name is something like Cole, or Travis, or maybe," Marilyn added, thinking of one of her pal Christian's favorite adult film stars, "Dawson."

A hint of crimson rose to the guy's cheeks, making him even more handsome. The dimples deepened as he grinned with just a hint of sheepishness. "Duncan."

"Right! Duncan," Marilyn sneered, thinking that the guy's real name was probably Pete, or Dan, or Mike, but Duncan fit the profile of trendy gay guy better.

Duncan laughed. "What? You sound like you don't believe me."

Marilyn smirked at him. "What's going on here?" Even though she hated to admit it, even to herself, Marilyn was feeling a little weak in the knees, so she sat.

"What do you mean? Aren't you the woman who answered my ad on Craigslist?"

Marilyn thought she could cut this whole thing, with its potential for humiliation, short right here by simply responding, "No. I don't know what you're talking about." But she knew, right away, that the fact she had sat down with him had already closed the door to that particular exit.

She would see this through. She would not let "Duncan" here make a fool of her. "Yes, I'm the woman." She gestured to her Rubenesque figure with a downward flourish of her hands and raised her eyebrows. "You like? You want to, maybe, marry?" Marilyn threw back her head and laughed loud enough to cause the chatter at the next table—a coven of teenage girls—to cease abruptly.

What was wrong with her? *You're nervous, hon, that's all. You should never have done this. You should have stayed home with Mike. He may hiss at you occasionally, but he never laughs.*

"Well, I don't know if we should get to the marriage part just yet," Duncan said, and Marilyn could see that he looked nervous as well, which eased her own nerves a bit. But still, she wanted to get this over with. It was more than obvious to her that she was being set up and, even if it wasn't outright, she was being laughed at.

She was sure of it. "Look," she said at last, leveling her gaze on Duncan. "Let's put our cards on the table, shall we? I didn't fall off the turnip truck yesterday. It was actually a week ago," she let out a nervous snort of laughter. Duncan smiled. "I know when I'm being made a fool of. My bad for even answering and being lured into whatever little setup you've got going on here, but now I'm pretty positive I'm just here for comic relief, right?" Marilyn could feel a little twinge of hurt inside, but she was determined not to let it show. For some reason, this moment brought her right back to when she was a sixth grader and was much more overweight than she was now and the kids thought it was the height of hilarity to call her "Large Marge." "Large Marge, Large Marge," they would sing. "She's as big as an ocean barge!"

"So you can admit it and let's just go our separate ways. This is *so* not funny." Marilyn stared down into her black coffee, feeling its depth and hue matched her mood.

"You've got me all wrong," Duncan said softly.

"Oh I do, do I?"

"Why? I mean, we haven't even exchanged more than few words yet. I don't even know *your* name. Why would you think I'm here to make fun of you?"

Marilyn rolled her eyes. "Come on, Duncan, if that *is* your real name, look at yourself. Look at me."

"Yeah?"

Marilyn let out a puff of exasperated air. "Why? Why? Why?"

"Why did I place the ad? The answer was right there in the ad."

"Really? *Seriously*? A guy that looks like you—a hunk, a hottie, a stud, a ten, by any yardstick—and gay to boot, is looking for a woman to marry? Why?" Marilyn looked him up and down and, in spite of her discomfort, she couldn't help it: she was pleased by the way his pants clung to his long legs, revealing the bulge in his crotch, and inducing in her a desire to *touch*. "You could have anyone. They must line up around the corner for you."

Duncan snorted. "I wish!"

"Oh don't go all Mary Modesty on me, fella! You've looked in a mirror."

Duncan stared down at the table, tracing the initials someone had carved in its scarred wooden surface. Marilyn thought she could see some embarrassment, maybe even sadness, stamped on those gorgeous features.

"I've got your number, don't I?"

*

Duncan shook his head, and then looked up to eye the woman across the table. He saw only wariness on her features, features that, in another situation, might be perceived as warm and open, if not a bit mischievous. "Well, this is embarrassing. If by having my number, you mean I have, as you so gracefully put it in your response to my ad, made an ass of myself, then, yes, I suppose you do.

"See, I came here fully expecting to be made a fool of. In fact, before you got here, I was under the paranoid delusion that any number of people in this very café were watching me and laughing into their coffee cups at the deluded homo."

The woman cocked her head. "That's not what I—" she began to say, but Duncan interrupted her.

"I don't know why you showed up. You certainly don't look like someone who'd consider what I am proposing, but maybe you're angry at me for poaching on grounds reserved for straight men, or maybe, as you said, this whole idea tickles you and you wanted to see the tickler so you could have a good laugh."

Duncan sat back in his chair, balancing it on the two legs. This woman, with all her charm, her bigger-than-life appearance, her confidence, her take-no-prisoners attitude, probably had more than her share of admirers, so he was certain she was not there to meet him regarding the possibility he had put forth. Sure, she was not the conventional idea of beauty these days—some starved, twenty-something waifish girl with surgically enhanced boobs and lips—but there was something about this woman, an authenticity, that Duncan could see would have its appeal on his more grounded and forward-thinking straight brethren. She was think-outside-the-box pretty, striking in a way that you might not at first notice, but would later realize you hadn't forgotten.

And right now, the words he had spoken seemed to have knocked the wind from her sails, because she looked like she didn't know what to say. Had he caught her? Did he have her number? Was she doing this on a lark? As a way to brighten up an otherwise boring weekend?

Duncan was determined to find out before they went their separate ways.

She said, so softly Duncan wasn't sure he heard her, "I think you've got me all wrong." She smiled, "And much as I am loath to admit it, I think I may have gotten you all wrong." Her warm brown eyes drank him in.

"What's your name?"

"You mean my real name? Or shall I make up something trendy like Blakely or Connor?"

"My name really is Duncan, by the way. Let's get that clear. My mom named me after an old Paul Simon song. You can Google it. It came out a few years before I was born."

"Yeah, were you born in the boredom and the chowder?"

Duncan smiled. "You know the song. It brings tears to my eyes every time I hear it, not just because of my personal connection to it but because the lyrics are so sad and he brings out such emotion when he sings."

Marilyn smiled back at him and he could see something turn, very slightly, in her expression. Some of the wariness vanished, some of her guard went down. Maybe she was beginning to like him. "Really?"

"Yes, really. I know the name is trendy-sounding, but it's mine." He extended his hand across the table, "Duncan Taylor, at your service."

She stared at his hand for a moment, and he was wondering if she expected something magically to appear in it, a mouse perhaps, or a coin. Then she grasped his hand with a surprisingly firm grip and shook it. "I'm Marilyn. Marilyn Samples."

Duncan regarded her across the table for several moments without saying anything more. Finally, he blew out a breath and said, "My coffee is gone and I wonder if your curiosity has been sated enough. Should we go our separate ways?" He didn't know if his naïve and hopeful dream of finding someone like the women in his own family would ever come true, especially when reality slapped him in the face as it just had. Perhaps it was time to cut his losses and go home, type in on Craigslist "Maine Coon Cats" instead of "Bride for Gay Dude."

"As opposed to what?" Marilyn took a sip of her coffee.

Duncan had been pretty sure the woman would be relieved to let this awkward encounter die a quick death, so he hadn't really considered an alternative. He shrugged. "I don't know. I guess as opposed to having another cup of coffee."

"I'd love another cup." He watched as she finished her coffee. She held out the mug to him. "I take it black. Just plain old coffee. No double shots; no foam; and certainly no soy."

Duncan took the mug from her and again found he liked her for her brazenness. He supposed that quality might put some people off, but to him it was a breath of fresh air. He stood to get them refills.

As he was moving away from their table, she called, "Duncan?" He turned. "I was eyeing those cupcakes in the display case. Do you think I could get one of the chocolate ones with the salted caramel frosting?"

Duncan laughed. "Sure, let's both have one. I'll get the same."

When he returned to the table, laden down with two mugs of coffee and the cupcakes, he noticed Marilyn eyeing the sweet with a rapture he would have put in the realm of the sexual. "Oh, you're a girl after my own heart."

"What?" she wondered.

"You like your sweets."

Once again, she gestured at her generous figure. "Hey, it takes a lot of calories to maintain this." She laughed and bit into the cupcake. She chewed and then said, "I require a husband who has the ability to keep me in cupcakes, doughnuts, pies, and cookies until death do us part. Are you up for that?"

"Since I require the same," Duncan said. "I think that will pose no problem."

"Good," Marilyn said. "I require the same stipulation regarding alcohol. In addition to coffee, girlfriend likes her margaritas, salt on the rim, and on the rocks."

Duncan nodded. "I'm glad you're not a beer drinker, like my last guy."

"Forget him. If he let a morsel like you slip through his fingers, he had to be some kind of moron."

"You have a good head on your shoulders, Marilyn."

Out of nowhere, she asked, "You like cats?"

Duncan laughed. "I guess this conversation isn't following any linear path, but yes, as a matter of fact, I do. I don't have one currently, but I was thinking of getting one, a Maine Coon maybe."

Marilyn nodded, looking as though she was considering his response. "That's good. And, just for my own reassurance, the Maine Coon, that is the only pussy you're interested in?"

"Oh, Marilyn, I think we're going to get along just fine."

Duncan passed a very pleasant afternoon with Marilyn Samples. He didn't know if he would marry her, but he did like her wit, her directness, and the fact that they had a lot in common: a love for animals, a passion for reality TV, a dislike of overly polite Seattle drivers, an appreciation for days when the mountain, otherwise known as Mt. Rainier, was out.

"It's magical," Marilyn said, referring to the mountain, which often did appear as if it had been conjured, its snow-capped magnificence often looking as though it floated atop a bank of clouds.

Neither of them were fans of Broadway musicals (although they both agreed they liked the "dark ones" or, as Marilyn put it, "ones where someone dies" like *Cabaret, West Side Story*, or *Rent*).

Their differences were surprising. Marilyn loved to go out to the gay bars, a pub-crawl on a weekend night was a little slice of heaven to her mind. Duncan? Not so much. "I love being around all those gay men in their natural habitat!" Marilyn had squealed. "I can be content with a few drinks and just observing all night." She had leaned close to Duncan and said, "Do you realize you guys have perfected the flirt into an art form? I mean, gay men can say more with their eyes than most women can say with a carefully crafted essay of five hundred words or more."

Duncan explained he had never considered that, but conceded that gay men did know how to say much with a simple glance; he had borne witness to that enough times to know she was right. Yet, he told Marilyn, he was the kind of guy who enjoyed a quiet evening at home much more, with a nice dinner, a good bottle of wine, and maybe an old movie to watch.

"Ah, you're an old man! Once we get hitched, I'll get you off your damn couch. Mark my words!"

And Duncan looked forward to that day.

Chapter Six

As winter gave way to spring, Duncan found his friendship with Marilyn had deepened more rapidly than he would have imagined possible. Over the course of the past three months, he spent more and more time with her, either on his houseboat, which she loved, or in her little apartment on Capitol Hill. Duncan swore that Marilyn's cat, Mike, was about as gay as they came because the feline seemed to go nuts for Duncan every time he walked in the door and settled on his lap for most of his visit, purring like he was in some kind of kitty seventh heaven.

Duncan wouldn't have had it any other way. And, Marilyn, a lover of gay men from as far back as she could remember, was pleased that her cat had those inclinations, which she had always suspected, but never seen confirmed until Duncan came into her life.

And Mike's.

True to her word, Marilyn had gotten Duncan off his couch and out of his houseboat. The pair now had a Friday night ritual—happy hour at C.C. Attles, followed by dinner at a nearby restaurant on the Hill (Duncan preferred Dinette, while Marilyn favored the Honey Hole), followed by a pub crawl around the neighborhood. Duncan had gained ten pounds since meeting Marilyn and was certain most of that had come from calories imbibed. He would have to check out those Skinny Girl cocktails he had heard tell of.

But, in spite of being a bit less chipper on Saturday mornings and his Levi's a wee bit tighter around the waist, Duncan appreciated the time he spent with Marilyn, who introduced him to clubs even he wasn't aware of, such as the bear bar, Diesel. "If I could grow a beard, I would," Marilyn confided. "Just so I could be one of the guys at Diesel."

And he enjoyed their conversations, lubricated by alcohol and salted liberally with Marilyn's off-kilter worldview. Duncan shared with her how he had become "the gay man who loved women" as she now dubbed him. "Probably because—" he said one late night in a dimly lit bar "—I grew up around women. Two sisters. A mom I adored." He laughed. "Growing up around so much estrogen, you either learn to love the ladies or you run away from them as fast as you can. I learned to love them, only not in *that* way."

"Always preferred sausage over pie, did you?"

Duncan told her he was a gold-star fag, through and through. "When it comes to pussy, I'm like 7 Up and caffeine."

"Huh?"

"Never had it. Never will."

The two leaned their heads close together and snorted with laughter. Marilyn placed a hand on Duncan's thigh and whispered, "More's the pity."

They spent weekends together, indulging in movie (horror or old weepers like *Imitation of Life*) and TV (*Survivor, RuPaul's Drag Race, Top Chef*) marathons. Duncan taught Marilyn how to make his family's spaghetti sauce (which they called red gravy), instilling in her the importance of slow, all-day cooking, and the addition of some kind of pork to add a layer of flavor that simply could not be had without it. Marilyn taught Duncan how to mix a proper margarita. "Never, never, never use any of those dreadful sugary mixes. All you need are some good limes, some good tequila, preferably Patrón Añejo, and a little splash of triple sec. Oh, and a salted rim." She had grinned at him. "The rimming is very important."

"Oh, I do like to rim!" Duncan shouted, clutching his heart.

"I know you do! But you be careful," Marilyn admonished.

In spite of the fact that Marilyn was actually preventing Duncan from having much of an opportunity to rim, or do any other sexual activity with one of his own kind, he was content.

They never spoke about the ad that had brought them together, and Duncan always assumed it was because the whole idea had been so preposterous. Yet, sometimes, as he lay on Marilyn's couch after a late night, Mike curled up between his legs and warming his balls, he would listen to the silence, interrupted only by an occasional snort or giggle from Marilyn, slumbering in her bedroom, and feel that they could make a go of it as a married couple.

But his dick would remind him in those quiet, middle-of-the-night hours just how unsatisfying *it* would find such an arrangement. His dick would raise its head, sniff the patchouli in the air, and perhaps give its version of a frown. His uncut, south-of-the-border buddy would remind him how starved he had been for affection these past few months and that he hoped Duncan might at least make a little more effort to end the drought he himself had created.

"Your hand, lubed as nicely as it is, just doesn't cut it after a while," his dick might inform him. "I need to rub myself up against something hard, warm, and furry. Even better, something tight and slick that grips me like a glove."

"Down boy," Duncan would whisper, promising Mr. Penis—and himself—that the following week, he would get out there and make a bit more of an effort to get laid.

Yet it never happened.

Marilyn always had plans.

*

It was on one of their Saturday night outings, this one in March, that the pair ran into a man from Duncan's past. They were dining at Duncan's favorite restaurant in Seattle, Dinette, on Olive Way. He adored the casual atmosphere and the chicken liver pate on toast was to die for, making believers out of die-hard liver-haters like Marilyn.

Duncan had had a long week and wasn't sure he was up for the pub crawl that usually followed dinner. And then he saw *him*, and his mood lightened.

Blond hair. Stocky frame. Wide blue eyes that one could simply melt into.

At first, Duncan thought, with a sick lurch to his gut, that it was Tucker who was sitting across the restaurant. Tucker, who had dumped him back in December and who had begun the whole twisted chain of events that had led him to Marilyn and this very table, this drizzly night in early March. Tucker, the man he loved with all his heart and who refused his very generous offer of marriage, crushing Duncan's heart under his heel as casually as he might step in a pile of dog turds.

But the freeze that seized his heart in that moment immediately thawed when he saw it was not Tucker at all, but his brother, Ben. Most people assumed they were twins, but there was, in fact, a full year and a half between them, and their big difference was that Ben preferred women over men, or as Marilyn might have put it, "pie over sausage."

We both love women, Duncan mused, *except he likes them most in the way I like them least.* Still, Ben was a super nice guy, kind-hearted (he even worked as a fundraiser for the Seattle Animal House, a not-for-profit, no-kill shelter for dogs and cats), with a warmth and honesty his younger brother never seemed able to emulate.

Why couldn't Duncan have ended up with Ben? Why were sweethearts like Ben always, or at least in Duncan's experience, straight?

"What the fuck are you staring at?" Marilyn strained to turn around in her seat, to try to follow the line of Duncan's gaze. Marilyn never wanted to miss out if Duncan spotted a hot guy. Looking out for one another was one of the many ways they cemented their friendship. That, and the way they rated men, using a food system:

Dee. Lish. Us. was the top of the heap: the guys who could stop traffic, open doors, inducing in the viewer heart palpitations. These were men who either were models or could have been, with little effort. The DLU guys were so gorgeous that both Marilyn and Duncan realized—and accepted—they moved on a different plane from mere mortals. Thus, they could never be approached, for to talk to them would risk one being blinded by their magnificence. They saw very few men who actually warranted the DLU label, but when they did, oh boy, did they love to look, in spite of the intimidation their beauty inspired.

Yummy. These guys were the good-looking ones that were still hot but fell into the realm of the approachable. They could be young or old, tall or short, stocky or thin, hairy or hairless—they could be anything, as long as something about them caught the eye of either Marilyn or Duncan, who had very similar taste in men. If there was a commonality to these men, it was that they were most often regular guys who, more than their good looks, exuded a sense of confidence and masculinity that was immediately apparent and, often, immediately magnetic. Duncan's sole sexual experience these past several months had been with a yummy man: a shaved head, bearded guy who worked on one of the commuter ferries in town. Duncan thought he had hit pay dirt until he had gone home with the guy and seen his Barbie collection. Oh well, they had spent a pretty amazing night together, one for which Duncan had been long overdue, but he declined when Abbott, as his name was, called to see if Duncan wanted to go along with him to a meeting of his favorite social group, Gays and Dolls, a group of doll-collecting gay men. As lovely as it sounded, Duncan didn't think the group was for him and probably Abbott wasn't either.

Edible. Truth was, most guys fell into this category. These were not the men you stopped on the street to admire. These were the run-of-the-mill guys that most people did not notice. But Marilyn and Duncan had found, if you took the time to really look, you could always find something quirky or wonderful about these men to admire. It might be something as simple as a pair of cool retro glasses that shielded a pair of amazing brown eyes, or a brilliant tattoo-sleeve of dragons or birds running down one manly arm, or perhaps something not easily identified, such as kindness, a genuine warmth that came across in a smile.

Not quite appetizing. While Marilyn used this appellation more often than Duncan, he had to concede she was always spot-on in her estimations. The NQAs were guys who just didn't appeal. They may not be terribly unattractive in any obvious way, but there was simply something about them that made them disagreeable. For example, a very good-looking man, one who might be a DLU, could become an NQA if he gave off too much of a self-absorbed vibe. Duncan had seen one such situation in a men's room at a bar once, where a man they had both admired (and Duncan followed into the bathroom, even though he didn't have to go—hey, he *was* gay, after all) had disappeared. And there, Duncan had witnessed a full-fledged love affair the guy had—with the mirror. Duncan would later swear to Marilyn he hadn't even seen Duncan or any of the other men entering the restroom as he adjusted his black hair just so, gazing rapturously at himself, and even, at one point, treating himself to a smile and a wink. Not all NQAs were of this variety, but they all did not appeal for one reason or another.

Tofu. These were the bottom of the barrel, the flavorless guys, the ones who, sadly, just failed to register at all on their attraction meter. For Duncan, these men were as rare as the DLUs, because he could usually find something worthwhile about a man, be it a strong nose, or a good haircut, or even the way he carried himself across a crowded dance floor. Marilyn was less kind but even she too would admit that very few guys were actually tofu and those that were, well, they probably never noticed them anyway.

"Do you see a DLU?" Marilyn turned back to Duncan, eyes bright with anticipation.

"Well, kind of, in my eyes, anyway."

"Where?" Marilyn did an almost Linda Blair-like swivel of her head.

"Over there," and Duncan tried to nod subtly in Ben's direction.

"That blond?"

"Yeah."

"He is a sweetheart but not a DLU."

"DLUs—and anything else—are always in the eyes of the beholder, hon. You know that." Duncan cleared his plate of the last of his merguez meatballs, which in the culinary world, ranked high on his DLU list. "But no, Ben is probably more yummy than DLU."

Marilyn stared until Duncan kicked her under the table. "Ow!" she cried, rubbing her calf.

"It's rude to stare. And I don't know if I want to talk to him."

"Former trick?"

"No. He's straight."

"He is?" And Marilyn whipped her head around again and got another kick under the table.

"Control yourself, woman. He's the brother of Tucker."

Marilyn thought for a moment. Then she pointed to the simple, diamond-encrusted band on the third finger of Duncan's right hand. "The one you bought *that* for?"

"The very one."

"Tucker looked like that?"

Fortunately or unfortunately for the pair, they had yet to run into Tucker on one of their outings.

"Almost exactly."

Marilyn patted his hand sympathetically. "You really did lose out."

"Thanks, Marilyn."

"He's cute."

"Yes, he is. And so was Tucker. The big difference between them, aside from sexual orientation, was that Ben was sweet where Tucker was sour. If Ben were the gay one, maybe I wouldn't be sitting here with you."

"Well!" Marilyn puffed herself up with outrage.

"Calm down, girl. I just meant that Tucker's rejection of me led me to place that silly ad on Craigslist, which led me to you." He squeezed her hand, treating her to both a wink *and* a smile. "For which I thank my lucky stars every day."

"Flatterer."

"I mean it."

Marilyn's feathers gradually unruffled. She settled back into the chicken thighs she had ordered, cutting a bite off and placing it in her mouth. "So, is he, like, homophobic? This Ben?"

"No. Not at all. Why would you ask that?"

"A lot of straight guys are. You know that. You act like it surprises you."

"Well, Ben always welcomed me with open arms—"

"If not open legs."

Duncan paused for a moment and then went on. "He was sweet. I would say that he treated me more like one of the family than even Tucker did. This one time, when Tucker and I were still together, I got really sick with some stomach bug. Wanted to die, I tell you! Tucker called to check in over the course of the three days I was down with this thing, but it was Ben who came over when he heard, with bags from Safeway. He brought me three big things of Gatorade, chicken soup, and pudding cups. It was sweet. That's the kind of guy Ben was. Is."

"You gonna talk to him tonight? Because I'd sure like to meet him."

"Oh, I don't know. I'd probably have to hear all about Tucker and how he's found a new boyfriend, a rich and handsome one, and I don't know if I'm ready for that." He eyed Marilyn. "Why are you so eager to meet him anyway? You said he wasn't a DLU."

"DLUs bore me. I like the yummy ones and Ben over there is certainly that. I stopped staring at him because if I kept it up, I was going to need to use my napkin for something other than my mouth."

Duncan paused for a moment, considering. "Oh God, you're disgusting. You know that?"

Marilyn smiled. "Just one of my many charms. Aren't you glad I attended that finishing school in Paris?"

Duncan shook his head and rolled his eyes. "Well, don't get yourself all moist for nothing. That boy has a live-in girlfriend that he's crazy about. Marta. She looks like that model? What's her name? The one who can't pronounce L'Oréal?"

Marilyn snorted. "Heidi Klum?"

"That's the one."

"If he has a girlfriend who looks like Heidi Klum, I would never stand a chance, if that's his type. Put me next to Ms. Klum and you've got Dorothy and Toto and I am *not* the one wearing the blue-and-white checked dress."

Duncan patted Marilyn's hand and said, completely serious, "You're beautiful."

Marilyn looked at him out of the corner of one eye. "Get out. You have to say that because you're my BFF and maybe—" She winked. "My future husband."

Duncan thought Marilyn had forgotten all about that. But before he had a chance to think about it, he sat up straighter and whispered, "Here he comes."

He smiled as he met eyes with Ben, who was crossing the room. He stood up and extended a hand to Ben. "Well, what a surprise!"

Ben knocked Duncan's outstretched hand out of the way and grabbed him in a bear hug, squeezing him so tightly Duncan would swear he heard something crack. Still, he couldn't deny the all-encompassing and enthusiastic hug felt great.

Ben whispered in his ear, "Man, it's so great to see you. I've missed you." He pushed Duncan back and looked him up and down. "You look great. That brother of mine is an idiot."

Duncan felt a ball begin to form in his throat at this sudden kindness and quickly attempted to swallow it down.

"How come you haven't called me, man? Just because Tucker's too dumb to know a good thing when it bites him on the ass doesn't mean I still didn't want to see you."

Duncan could have been argumentative and said that phone lines and email and Facebook were all two-way streets, but that would have been mean. Besides, he was feeling all bright and shiny inside from Ben's effusive happiness at running into him. "I don't know, I just thought that Tucker got his own brother in the divorce."

"Oh, that's just stupid. Well, I'm glad I ran into you. You still have my details?"

Duncan nodded.

"Let's get together then. Have a few beers."

Duncan couldn't help it. "How's Tucker?"

Ben rolled his eyes. "Who knows, man? He left town shortly after you two split up. He said he was going to get a fresh start." Ben shrugged. "He's out in Boise of all places, working as a clerk at Walmart. Some fresh start, but that's my bro for you. I got all the brains." Ben chuckled.

And all the heart.

"There's probably some guy involved."

Duncan nodded, struck dumb, feeling a twinge of jealousy stab at his gut. He wondered if he would ever get over Tucker, even though logically he knew the guy was a fool, immature, and not even worthy of him. *The mind knows what it knows and the heart knows what it knows and, sometimes, the twain never shall meet.*

Ben grinned. "So let's have a beer or two sometime. You still on the houseboat?"

"Still there."

"Man, I loved that place. It was so cool!" He looked down at Marilyn. "You seen it?"

It was like someone switched a light on underneath Marilyn's skin. She practically glowed when Ben shifted his focus to her. "Who, me? I didn't think you guys even noticed little old me sitting over here." She smiled and Duncan fully expected her to bat her eyelashes next.

"The shy wallflower," Duncan said, his voice loaded with sarcasm. "This is my friend, Marilyn Samples."

Marilyn stayed seated, but held out her hand, smiling. "Charmed."

"Oh, and this is Ben McBride."

Ben took Marilyn's hand and Duncan watched as Ben first peered soulfully into her eyes, then kissed her hand gently. From anyone else, the gesture would have seemed craven, but from Ben it was genuine and almost unbearably sweet.

"Oh my!" Marilyn said. Duncan had never heard her voice hit such a high note. He wanted to snicker.

Ben eyed Marilyn a moment longer, then said, out of the corner of his mouth to Duncan, "You doing ladies, now?"

Marilyn heard and tittered. Yes, actually tittered.

Duncan smiled. "Well, this one here, she's making me think about it."

Ben dropped Marilyn's hand and turned to stare at Duncan, mouth open. "Seriously, dude?"

"No, not at all. But if that were even possible, which it is not, Marilyn would be the first woman I'd run to."

Ben turned back to her and smiled, "I can't say I blame you for that."

Duncan watched as a line of crimson rose from Marilyn's rather prodigious cleavage up to envelop her face. For once, the woman was speechless.

"She's a sweetheart, but I should warn you, she's not declawed."

"Duncan!" Marilyn whined.

Ben looked at both of them, and Duncan wasn't sure what must be running through the straight man's mind. "Well, I gotta run. I'm meeting Marta at her place when she gets off from work at Swedish." Swedish was one of the larger hospitals in Seattle, where Marta was a nurse in the pediatric ward. He grabbed Duncan's hand again and squeezed it. "I'm so glad I ran into you, man." He hugged him quickly again and Duncan couldn't help the tightness he felt in his jeans. *Down boy, that bone's not for you.* "Let's get together soon. I mean it. This was fate, right?"

"Right." Duncan grinned.

"You, too, Marilyn. We'll all get together. Duncan here can have us all over to the houseboat, especially now that the rumors are starting that spring is in the air."

"I'd love that," Marilyn said, "When?"

Duncan glared at her.

"Next week? Friday?"

Duncan, feeling as if he had no say in the matter, nodded, "Sure."

"I'll text you," Ben said and hurried away. "We'll get it set up."

Duncan resumed his place at the table.

"What a nice boy!" Marilyn cried. "Not only cute, but the sweetness practically oozes out of his pores. I hope that Marta knows what a prize she has."

"Right?" Duncan took a sip of his wine, an excellent pinot grigio. "I always liked Ben. He's—" Duncan paused as he grasped for just the right words. "He's everything Tucker isn't: thoughtful, kind, considerate. When you talk to him, he makes you feel like you're the most important person on the planet; you know? Like he just can't wait to hear what you'll say next. And he's all touchy-feely, not in a disingenuous way, but sincere. I always feel connected to him." Duncan shook his head. "Tucker is like him only in the looks department and I guess, speaking objectively, he's the better-looking of the pair, but Ben, to be honest, is more of the catch. Sweet trumps hot any day, at least in my book. Sweet lasts; hot fades."

"And sweet guys are seldom caught up in their own sweetness, if ever," Marilyn added. "Hot guys usually can't walk by a mirror without at least taking a peek."

Duncan nodded. The two fell silent for a while, each eating the remainder of their dinner. When Duncan finished the last of his meatballs and was resisting the urge to lick his plate, he looked at Marilyn. She had a faraway gaze and held her wineglass as though she had forgotten it was there. Her eyes were shiny and Duncan thought, with alarm, she looked like she was about to cry. Marilyn never cried. She was all vinegar and salt; he was the human marshmallow when it came to emotions.

Duncan put his hand over Marilyn's. "What is it, hon?" he asked. "You okay?"

Marilyn looked as though his words almost startled her, as though they had roused her from sleep, or a trance. She took a long swallow of wine and set her glass down. "I'm fine. I'm just looking back. Looking forward."

"And?"

"And I can't see a man like Ben anywhere in my past." She cocked her head, and her lips drew down in a frown. "Or in my future, for that matter. I just gain weight and accumulate wrinkles, knickknacks, and cat hair." She looked away from him and wiped under one eye. "I'm never going to meet a Ben."

"This isn't like you, Marilyn."

"Hey, even an old broad like me gets to feel sorry for herself once in a blue moon."

"Now, stop it, you're not old or wrinkled. I told you, you're beautiful."

"I noticed you left out fat."

"What?"

"You left out fat when you said what I was *not.*" She snickered.

Duncan rolled his eyes. "But you aren't fat! I *like* your proportions. You're curvy and you have big boobies. Men love that."

"Yeah. Where are they?"

Duncan squeezed her hand and said softly, "Right here."

Marilyn looked into Duncan's eyes and he felt, for a moment, as though she were looking into his soul. There was a connection in their gazes, a moment that blocked out the restaurant, the voices around them, the soft jazz music, and the clatter of cutlery and wineglasses. "Are you thinking what I'm thinking?" Marilyn asked.

Duncan honestly didn't know. At that very moment, he wasn't thinking anything in particular, only feeling. He felt close to Marilyn, as close as he was to his sisters, to his beloved mother. Very rapidly, she had become one of the most important people in his life, and there was an enormous sense of contentment as he sat with her, belly full, holding her hand and completely satisfied. Whatever the evening held in store, he was glad it would be spent with Marilyn. "I don't know what you're thinking. Tell me."

"I think we should do it."

"Do it? Like, the horizontal mambo? I told you: homey don't play that."

Marilyn rolled her eyes. "I am trying to be serious here."

"Oh please!"

"Come on, Duncan. I am trying to propose, I guess." Marilyn barked out a short laugh. "You want me to get down on one knee? I will." And she did, sliding from her chair to kneel on one knee at his feet. Duncan grinned, looking nervously around him. Several of the other diners had stopped eating to stare.

Someone giggled.

"Duncan Taylor, will you make me the happiest woman on earth and marry me?"

Duncan was overwhelmed. He knew he had packed the snowball that had started this emotional avalanche, yet he hadn't seen it coming. He had really forgotten all about his one-time wish to be like everyone else and marry a straight woman. There was a lump in his throat. He wanted to yank Marilyn back into her seat. He wanted to hug her. He wanted to tell her he loved her. Yet, it was hard to get his brain and tongue to connect enough to form words.

But what he did manage to say was, "Yes."

Marilyn smiled and turned to the other restaurant patrons, who had grown silent. "He said yes!" she announced. She curtsied and sat back down with Duncan, grabbing his hand and squeezing.

And the whole restaurant broke into applause.

Their waitress, who had obviously been watching from the bar, rushed over with a bottle of champagne. When she popped the cork, it set off another round of applause among Dinette's patrons. The atmosphere in the little restaurant had ramped up to celebratory; somehow Duncan and Marilyn had unified the place into one joined in merriment.

Marilyn awkwardly settled back into her seat, and Duncan observed a line of sweat at her forehead. She was breathing faster. He felt, if he were being completely honest, a bit in shock, as he remembered the sensation from his car accident many years ago. Yes, this was a completely different kind of thing; but there was that same sense of unreality, as though he wasn't sure what had just happened.

Had he said yes simply because everyone in the restaurant had been listening? Or had he said yes because he really wanted to be with Marilyn, regardless of the difference in their orientations? Could that work?

She *did* make him happy.

She *was* a woman, straight, who presumably needed the recommended daily allowance of dick just as much as he did.

Was this all a big mistake?

But a big *wonderful* mistake—one that would allow them to write their own life rules and chart their own course to a unique kind of happiness. Who said they couldn't? Sure, not every state in the country had got on board with gay marriage, but none had the wherewithal to say a gay man couldn't get married—to a woman, which was really kind of absurd, when you thought about it.

With a hand he was trying to prevent from shaking, he lifted his champagne flute to Marilyn and smiled. "To us," he said.

She clinked his glass. For once, Marilyn was speechless.

They sat in silence for a long time, listening as the conversation level rose once again in the restaurant. Their moment of brief fame had already been observed and people were moving on. They had no idea, Duncan mused, what they had just witnessed.

He had either accepted the potential for happiness into his life, or he had just made a huge mistake.

He smiled at Marilyn, who had yet to let go of his hand. He squeezed her hand tightly and said, "I love you."

"And you, my man, my fiancé, are the cat's pajamas." Marilyn sipped her champagne and eyed him over the rim of the glass.

Chapter Seven

"Oh Lord, what have I done?" Marilyn rolled over in her bed at just past four a.m. "Huh, Mike?" Her tabby, who stared at her from atop the bed's padded headboard, offered no response, even though he did appear to be carefully considering her question.

"Yeah, right," Marilyn whispered, rolling over hard and snatching the bedclothes up to her ears. "Keep your own counsel. That's probably wise." She turned back to Mike. "And the coward's way out!" she shouted at the cat.

Mike leaped from his perch and stalked out of the bedroom, tail upraised in indignation, Marilyn guessed.

"Fuck you, Mike!" Marilyn yelled and then burst into laughter.

Marilyn was more than a little drunk. After she and Duncan had gotten engaged—and just the thought of this sent Marilyn into renewed fits of giggles, marveling at the unreality of it—they had moved from Dinette to Neighbors, Purr, and finally, the Lobby Bar, where they celebrated their upcoming nuptials with beer, vodka, tequila shots, and no end of laughter that bordered on hysteria. They shared their news with everyone with whom they came in contact, which got them varying reactions, from high fives, to "Are you guys nuts?", to the one man who simply walked away from them, as though what they had might be catching.

This only made Duncan and Marilyn laugh all the harder.

They had packed things in for the evening when the Lobby closed its doors at two. Duncan accompanied Marilyn on her rather unsteady and never-in-a-straight line walk to her front door. After the hilarity and all the drinking in the bars, the pair was oddly silent on their late-night trek.

"You sure you don't want me to stay? It *is* the night of our engagement, after all," Duncan had asked.

"It's not our wedding night," Marilyn had responded. "Don't get any funny ideas. You haven't bought the cow yet." She kissed the tip of his nose (she had been aiming for his cheek). "No. You go home and get some shut-eye, pardner. I'll see you for Bloodys in the morning."

"I don't know about that!" Duncan had called after her. He then grabbed a cab to take him to his houseboat.

Inside her apartment, she had fallen asleep almost immediately, stopping only long enough to throw her clothes on the floor as she moved from living room to bedroom and to give Mike a quick hug and a wet kiss, which the cat very much resented.

After a couple hours of drunken, comatose sleep, Marilyn woke suddenly, as though someone had gripped her eyelids and yanked them up. She didn't feel nearly as drunk as she had when her head hit the pillow. Now all she felt was foggy-headed and thirsty.

She got up to pee and get herself a big glass of water and stumbled back to her bed, where she began her conversation with Mike.

Now she was alone—her usual state. And neither beer, wine, tequila, nor even vodka was enough to obliterate the sudden onrush of thoughts she was having.

Second thoughts.

And yet, as easy as she knew it would be to pick up her phone and call Duncan, whom she suspected would also be awake, and just tell him the whole night had been a wicked flight of fancy, a thing that should never have happened, something prevented her from doing so.

Other second thoughts. In the opposite direction.

Marilyn settled back among the pillows and tried to take a few deep breaths. First, she thought that in the morning this whole crazy night would seem like a dream. She and Duncan would get together for a late brunch, maybe at the Dish in Ballard, which was over near him, and they would laugh over what had transpired while downing their omelets. Of course, Duncan had rapidly become her best friend and the guy was a sweetheart, one of the most decent men Marilyn had ever met, but marriage?

Come on! The guy was a dyed-in-the-wool homosexual. His blood flowed in rainbow hues. What would she get out of a marriage to a man who absolutely could not abide what she had between her legs?

And an inner voice, the one that loved nothing more than holing up once upon a time on a weekend with two or three gay romance novels, rushed in to inform her she would get a lot out of such a marriage, perhaps even more than many of her sisters got from their straight husbands.

Putting sex aside for just a moment (Really, Marilyn? The saucy, horny part of her asked, and she quickly told it to "hush!"), Marilyn considered all the advantages to a union with a man like Duncan.

He was gorgeous. And the very best part was he didn't even know it. Regardless of what went on in their bedroom, he would look damn good on her arm at the vet clinic's annual Christmas party. And when she went back home with him to Idaho, all her female relatives would be green with envy, as would Thoth, her gay cousin.

But Marilyn was not a superficial gal, never had been, and even though she started her list with appearance, there were other more significant reasons to go ahead and marry Duncan. The homo.

He was kind. Come on, the guy taught in elementary school. Not only taught, but was passionate about it. He loved kids and had an infinite supply of patience, even though he was always joking that he had none. Marilyn, on the other hand, could learn a lot from him, especially in the patience department. But Duncan was the kind of man who always stopped to give the homeless his spare change, who worried for hours after seeing a dog someone had leashed to a post outside one of the stores at the University Village mall. He cried easily. While Marilyn snorted with laughter at the antics of the staff on *Grey's Anatomy*, for example, she'd look over and see Duncan trying to hold his emotions in, the tears running down his cheeks.

He was thoughtful. He brought her things, little presents, for no reason—truffles from Fran's, a new book she had wanted, an action figure of Cher.

He listened to her. So many of the straight men she had dated pretended to listen, but she lost count of the number of men she caught staring at her rather prodigious chest while she talked. Once she had called one of them on it, asking sweetly and innocently, "Do I have something on my décolletage?"

The straight man had looked confused and reddened.

Duncan knew what a décolletage was.

Duncan liked the same things she did when it came to dining out, movies, books, and television. They never argued over what they would do or how they would spend time together because they always were passionate about doing the same thing.

Duncan didn't like sports. She never had to hear about the Seahawks or the Mariners, whatever *they* were.

Duncan loved her.

And wasn't that enough? Wasn't that, in the end, what we all search for?

Marilyn, though, in spite of her passion for romance novels, was a realist and knew that those books she read with their happily-ever-after endings were fantasies. And she knew, deep inside, such a union in spite of all their commonalities and shared interests had little chance for survival.

Even though most marriages became less about sex as the years wore on and more about companionship—and Marilyn knew this from her observations of long-married friends and relatives, even gay ones—they had a spark, usually, to begin with. And that spark was sex.

Could she doom herself to a life without it? Even with all she would be getting as consolation prizes?

She shook her head, tossing in her bed to try to get more comfortable, to try to quell the headache beginning behind her eyes.

Even the memory of sex, she thought, was a sustaining thing for couples, especially the "lifers" as she had once jokingly called them.

Common sense and her heart were at war.

Marilyn was too tired to battle. As dawn crept stealthily into the room, Marilyn fell back asleep just as she heard Mike pounce upon the bed.

Chapter Eight

Duncan was up early, in spite of the night of revelry that had just passed. Surprisingly, and perhaps because of the large glass of water he had drunk and the aspirins he had taken before retiring, he was also feeling not too bad, all things considered.

At least he could say he was feeling fairly energetic, fairly *alive* in the physical department.

The emotional, mental, psychological department—whatever you wanted to call it—well, that was a whole 'nother story.

He made some coffee and took it out to the deck of his houseboat, wearing his flannel sleep pants, T-shirt, and a heavy terry-cloth bathrobe. As he sipped, he watched the sun rise over the Cascade Mountains across the water, somewhat obscured by blue-gray, early morning clouds. The sun painted them in fiery hues of yellow and tangerine. A breeze ruffled the waters.

He imagined sharing a quiet moment like this with Marilyn and thought it was doable, ignoring the fact that the houseboat had only one bedroom and the question as to where they would both sleep had yet to be answered. Twin beds, maybe?

He took in a deep breath, smiling, and sipped his coffee. Slowly, he shook his head. Was that what he really wanted? Twin beds? A sexless union that was full of companionship but no fire? Two good friends supporting each other through holidays, vacations, celebrations, and heartaches through the slow passage of time to old age?

Would he be happy? Truly?

In many ways, he would. Marilyn did something that few other people could, as much as he enjoyed their company: she made him laugh. And though that might seem like a small thing on a score sheet of plusses and minuses, it was a big advantage to Duncan's way of thinking. Was it the *Reader's Digest* that had once said "Laughter is the best medicine"? Laughter, Duncan realized, could make up for a lot. A home filled with laughter was a happy home.

Yet, sex niggled at him, as it always did, even before Marilyn. Duncan, God help him, liked sex. He liked the feel of a hard, possibly hairy, body pressed close against his. He adored looking down and seeing how excited a man was at the thought of further sexual contact with him. His mind drifted as he thought of that same cock and all the things it could do for him and he with it.

A nice cock, like laughter, was kind of an integral part of his happiness, wasn't it? A nice, purple-helmeted warrior, dripping precum and just aching to be touched, to be sucked, to have him whirl his tongue in slow strokes around the head of it, beneath the corona, squeezing with his throat muscles along the shaft... Duncan's mind drifted.

Stop it! You're trying to have a reasonable dialogue with yourself here and your dick is urging you to go inside and whack off, perhaps to one of those videos you could so easily find online.

Was that what his future as a married man would be relegated to? Whacking off to porn, his fantasies of a man, letting loose with all manner of positions and topping and bottoming?

Or would their marriage be one of convenience, and they would come to an understanding? Would he have his night or nights out with the boys as part of their marital arrangement? Would Marilyn do the same? And when would one of those boys, for him or for her, want more?

What would happen to their comfy marriage then?

Duncan sighed deeply. These were serious questions for an early morning, especially one in which he felt slightly depleted by a night of drinking and the very unrealistic memory that last night he had become engaged.

To a woman.

He laughed out loud, his laughter sounding a bit insane as it drifted across the water.

He drained the last of his coffee and decided his stomach was still enough to endure a little breakfast, with the end result that he would feel even better and more clear-headed. A poached egg or two, perhaps, soft, on hot buttered wheat toast sounded like just the ticket.

And then he would air this argument he was having with himself with the one person he knew wouldn't roll on the floor laughing when he told her what he had done, the one person who always listened, and who always gave the most level-headed advice—Scout.

He got up and went inside.

Scout picked up on the first ring. "Hey, little brother, I was just thinking about you."

"I hope it was good."

"Is it ever? I was remembering the time you said you wanted to hypnotize me. 'Look deep into my eyes. Deeper.' And then you slapped me across the face. Not funny, Duncan."

"Oh, will you never let go of things? I was a little boy."

"A rotten little Dennis the Menace."

"Are you going to make me regret calling you?"

"Of course not. What's up?"

"I got engaged last night." Duncan let the words tumble out without preamble because he feared, if he thought at all about what he and Marilyn had agreed to, he would never get around to telling Scout, for fear she would call out the men in their little white coats.

"What? Really? You never even told me there was a new guy! I thought you were still mooning over that Tucker. That fucker." Scout laughed.

"I didn't get engaged to a guy."

"Oh, don't tell me. A dog? A nice Labrador retriever? The fundies predicted this would happen when we started allowing the gays to get married." Scout snorted with mirth.

"You think I'm kidding?"

The line went silent for a long time.

Finally, Scout spoke. "Seriously? A woman? Brother, I put away those dreams when you told me about the crush you had on Mike Blair, that quarterback with the muscles, back in high school. What are you doing, Duncan? Having a little fun at my expense?"

"No, really. Her name is Marilyn. And she's really great." Duncan suddenly found himself not sure how to continue.

There was another long silence on the other end of the line as his sister presumably absorbed the information. Finally, she said, "Tell me about her."

"Um, she works for a vet. She's cute in a voluptuous, sort of post-Goth way. She has a cat. She makes me laugh. We like all the same things—drinking, movies, food, men. She loves to read gay romance novels. She likes going out to the gay bars and knows them even better than I do; she's introduced *me* to a few." He scratched his head and said, again, "She makes me laugh. She's sarcastic and witty."

"Well, those all sound like great qualities, for a best friend. Why marriage? I mean, we know people like Uncle Carl who married Aunt Eleanor because he was in the closet, and they stayed together for years. But they met back in a time when gay men feared for their lives sometimes, when they were open to ridicule that was socially acceptable. Uncle Carl probably was doing just what society told him was right. But you? You live in a state that just made marriage legal. I know you still struggle sometimes with homophobia, but things are a lot better, you have to admit, than they were back in the '50s, when Uncle Carl married Aunt Eleanor."

Scout had a point. But he thought then of his aunt and uncle and how they were still together, living in a little pale-blue clapboard house in the country just outside the town where Duncan grew up. They had been married now, he guessed, for more than fifty years. He recalled seeing them when he was home, out shopping at the town hub—now Walmart, when it had once been Summitville's tiny downtown—and they always seemed like two halves of a whole. He was attentive, and she was doting. Did she even know he was gay? Of course, she did. There was that scandal no one talked much about, years ago, when Uncle Carl had been arrested out at the rest stop on Route 6.

So Aunt Eleanor knew, and Uncle Carl knew she knew, but yet they had weathered the storm and stayed together.

And now, Duncan's only memories of them were as a happy couple, virtually inseparable. Somehow, they must have made it work.

"But look at the two of them," Duncan said. "Have you ever seen a happier couple? They never do anything separately. They're so close. They're like—"

"Brother and sister?" Scout asked, finishing his thought for him. She had a nasty habit of doing that.

Duncan sighed. "I suppose." He paced around the houseboat, not saying anything for several moments. Finally, in a voice that was a little weak and sad, he said, "I'm tired."

"What?"

"I said I'm tired."

"Well, go back to bed."

"You know that's not what I mean. I'm tired of looking. I'm tired of disappointing first dates. I'm tired of feeling like I'm always the one trying to make something meaningful out of a relationship, when the other guy is just thinking about how to get in my pants."

Scout snorted. "Sounds good to me. I wish Bud would think a little more about getting into mine these days," Scout said wistfully, referring to her husband.

Duncan let this last remark slide. He didn't mean to be selfish, but he needed this conversation to be about him. "I'm tired of waiting and hoping for my Prince Charming to come along and he never does. I've had so many relationships and some of them even had a spark, but in the end, none of them ever worked out—for one reason or another. He was a cheater, or I was too needy, or we didn't click on what we liked to do, in bed or out. He was an alcoholic. That one wore toenail polish in secret. I'm nearly forty, Scout, and yet I can't say I've had one decent relationship with a man."

This last revelation caused Duncan to stop suddenly, a kind of despair filling him, making him understand exactly why he wanted to go against the gay grain and marry a woman.

"I want to be like you and Bud. Like Jem and Vince. Like Mom and Dad. Hell, like Uncle Carl and Aunt Eleanor. Maybe the man/woman dynamic just works better. It's the only dynamic I've seen work well."

"Oh come on, now, don't you have friends who are happy gay couples?"

Duncan did. There was the lesbian at school, Sandy. She and Mary were like yin and yang, but they were a real family, devoted to each other. *They* were planning a June wedding. There was Mike and Pete, whom Duncan knew when he used to belong to the Front Runners, a gay running group. The pair of them even looked alike—both tall and gangly with Nordic features. You never saw them apart. But Duncan couldn't figure out how they had done it. "Yeah, yes. I know gay people who are happily partnered." He thought then of watching the long line outside city hall in downtown Seattle just after midnight, when gay couples could first apply for marriage licenses. All *those* people had found someone, hadn't they?

Rather than giving him hope, though, this thought of happily united gay couples only made him feel more alone, as though he were on the outside looking in, unable to understand some fundamental truth about what made the gay dynamic work.

And from his sad history, he really wasn't sure at all that he would ever make that discovery.

"Well, there you go. You just have to be patient, little brother. There *is* someone out there for you, just the right guy. And he's handsome and sweet, sexy, and he'll make chicken soup for you when you're in bed with a cold or the flu."

"Oh, I wish." Duncan tried to picture such a man, but all he could come up with was a faceless cipher.

"You know," Scout said, "Love often comes along when you give up, when you least expect it."

"Oh, honey, I gave up a long time ago," Duncan snorted. "And *still* my prince hasn't come."

Scout was quiet and then finally said, "You know what's in your heart. And that's what really matters."

"Yeah?" Duncan wasn't exactly sure what he knew, only that Marilyn had made him happier, at least outside the bedroom, than any man had ever been able to. And maybe that's the problem, Duncan thought, you're looking for a man to make you happy, and no one can do that for you. You have to do it for yourself. He shrugged away the thought. "Wait until you meet her, you'll see why I'm so crazy about her."

"I'm sure she's a lovely person," Scout said. "Bring her home soon."

"Really?"

"Of course."

"And you'd welcome her even if she were, even if she were...my wife?" Duncan couldn't believe he had uttered those last two words. He honestly believed those two words would never have come out of his mouth, unless he was referring to the play *I Am My Own Wife*.

"Duncan, we all love you. And we trust you. I don't claim to understand what you're thinking. Hell, I don't really claim to even understand same-sex attraction, but you've always been the smart one in the family. The one with his head on, you should pardon the expression, straight. If this woman makes you happy and you think you can make a go of it, then who am I to say you shouldn't? There are, I suppose, all different kinds of marriages out there. Who's to say this couldn't work?" Scout drew in a breath and then said, "You have my blessing. Not that you asked for it. And I give it with the caveat of what I said earlier—love comes along when you least expect it, so bear that in mind—but I do give it. I am happy for you. And I support you no matter what you do. I'll throw rice at your wedding whether you have a bride or a groom at your side."

Duncan felt himself choke up and wiped the tears out of his eyes. He gave himself a moment before he spoke, composing himself, but also reveling in the simple support he had from his sister. He was blessed.

"I'm gonna do it," he said softly.

"Good. I hope she makes you happy. And if she doesn't, you let me know and I'll come out there and kick her 'voluptuous' ass."

They both laughed.

Scout said, "Listen, I gotta run. I have to get the sauce on, or it won't taste right."

"Of course, it's Sunday." For as long as Duncan could remember, his Italian-American family had always had pasta on Sundays. The ritual was Mass in the morning, and then Mom would come home and put the sauce on, and let it simmer all day and fill the house with the aroma of simmering tomatoes, basil, and garlic, buoyed up by the richness of the pork and meatballs she would poach in it. "I understand that."

"So, talk to you later?"

"Sure." Duncan felt near tears again, and cursed himself for being such a softie. When he could speak again, he said, "I love you, Scout."

"Aw. I love you too, sweetie. You take care."

They hung up.

Without giving himself much time to think, Duncan then punched in Marilyn's number.

She picked up after three rings. She sounded like an eighty-year-old heavy smoker. "I am so *not* up for Bloody Marys this morning."

Duncan laughed. "I'm not surprised. How many shots of tequila did you do last night?"

"Don't ask. Were you calling for something else?"

"Yeah. I want you to come over for supper today. We have to celebrate our impending nuptials."

"Yeah? What's on the menu?"

"Spaghetti and meatballs. A family tradition."

Chapter Nine

Three weeks passed. Three weeks in which Duncan seesawed back and forth about his marriage to Marilyn and finally, at the end of that time, he absorbed the reality of it and accepted what his future held.

He would be like the rest of the world—a married man. Perhaps, if they could get the turkey baster routine worked out successfully, even a dad. He pictured a Craftsman home in some family-friendly neighborhood on Seattle's north side, someplace like Green Lake or Phinney Ridge, with a broad back porch that would overlook water or the mountains. Dark-haired children would caper in the yard, chased by a barking Boston terrier or French bulldog. He and Marilyn would sit on the porch, watching them, occasionally yelling out exhortations to be careful or be more gentle with Ethel, or whatever they would wind up naming the dog. He and Marilyn would sit in contented silence, hands linked casually, and wonder what to have for supper. Should they have a drink—maybe a gin and tonic—before dinner?

It was scenes like the one above that buoyed him, that made him think that his admittedly outlandish plan was a real possibility, a sustainable roadmap for a future that, although not perfect, would be solid and good. Strong. A comfort as he and Marilyn grew older in that house, the memories of Christmases and birthdays piling up like photographs, the years and their children's milestones always giving them something to look forward to.

Thoughts of the hole in the center of his being, his perhaps wayward eye when a handsome guy crossed his path (and just how far he would take such notice), Duncan pushed away, forcing himself back on the path of domestic bliss, that dream he had always wanted to come true.

He and Marilyn didn't talk much about the kind of fantasies he was having, and she, in fact, might have a completely different kind of imaginary future floating around in her head. Maybe she thought of them on Queen Anne Hill, overlooking the Space Needle and beyond: Puget Sound, dotted with ferries crossing the water, and the ethereal majesty of Mt. Rainier rising up. Yeah, like they could afford such a view on a teacher's and receptionist's salaries! But perhaps she did imagine them in an apartment, one filled with cats and stacks of books and DVDs, cleared just enough so one could move without tripping. Perhaps she didn't imagine children, but simply feline babies and weekends in the bars, rating guys and drinking up.

Duncan needed to talk to her soon, he supposed, about her expectations for the future.

But for now, their lives were beginning to be consumed by a more immediate future. They had set a date for the last week in May, Memorial Day weekend actually, because Duncan wanted it to be easy for his family to travel from Pennsylvania.

They agreed they would have the wedding outdoors, a small affair, maybe fifty to seventy-five people, maximum. String quartet and hydrangeas in vases. Lemon meringue tarts on tiers in place of a wedding cake.

Across the water from Duncan's houseboat in Eastlake, was Blue, a combination culinary school and event center, right on the Lake Union waterfront. Duncan had been there before for a work party and was charmed by its rustic elegance, its old oak beams, distressed brick walls, and exposed ductwork. Of course, the floor-to-ceiling windows fronting the water were really the main attraction. And the large dock outside would be the perfect place for Marilyn and him to say their "I do's."

Luckily, Blue had an opening for the Sunday afternoon before Memorial Day. They would have to have an early wedding and reception because there was another party booked for a four o'clock service.

He and Marilyn had taken it, counting themselves lucky for finding such a sweet venue so late in the game. The bonus of Blue was that it was a culinary school, and they could get a buffet thrown in as part of the package, so it was one less thing for them to worry about. And Duncan knew from his past experience the food would be amazing—all locally sourced and organic.

Now, as they sat in Marilyn's apartment on a chilly and rainy Sunday night, they were talking, as they often did these days, about their wedding. They had just finished a casual supper of Pagliacci pizza on paper plates, Chianti in plastic cups, and—Marilyn's concession to health—a bagged Caesar salad Duncan had brought over from Metropolitan Market.

Mike lounged on the couch between Duncan's legs, and Duncan scratched him behind the ears as he purred.

Bridesmaids was queued up in the DVD player.

Marilyn had just finished doing the last of the dishes, i.e., throwing everything into the trash, and came in to sit on a faux-zebra-covered easy chair across from Mike and

Duncan. "So I wanted to talk to you about this wedding planner guy again."

Duncan rolled his eyes. "I told you, I don't see the necessity of someone like that. We can handle it all ourselves and save a lot of money. Or keep our credit card bills from going into the stratosphere, since neither of us exactly has the funds for this shindig anyway."

"It won't be that much more, and he might just save us from making some costly mistakes. Besides, I don't need the stress of planning all that stuff out. I mean, I don't even know where to start looking to find a printer for invitations, or music, or flowers. Do you?"

Duncan had to admit he didn't, but he thought that would be part of their fun over the next few weeks. Marilyn had raised the idea of the wedding planner early on, and Duncan hadn't exactly been wild about the idea, but she kept coming back to it. She knew the guy she had in mind, Peter Dalrymple. He was a client at the vet's office where she worked. "A sweeter guy you would not want to meet. He has, like, three rescue dogs, and he's like big papa to them. I always treat him especially well when he calls or comes in, so I wouldn't be at all surprised if he cuts us a deal on his rates."

"No," Duncan said, sighing. "I really don't know how, or where, to shop for wedding particulars."

"There you go then. Enter Peter Dalrymple."

Duncan snorted. "That sounds like a bad porno. Enter Peter Dalrymple." He laughed again.

Marilyn rolled her eyes, but she was smiling. "Can we just sit down and talk to him? I'm sure a consultation will be free. Maybe you'll see how much time and stress he can save us, and you'll understand why he might be worth it."

Duncan shrugged. "I suppose. It can't hurt to just talk to him. I don't think I've ever met a wedding planner before. What kind of job is that?"

"One you'd probably love!" Marilyn said.

"So when do you want to do this?"

Marilyn grinned and a hint of slyness, maybe mischief, twinkled in her eyes. "I already made the appointment for tomorrow afternoon."

Duncan huffed. "Sure of yourself much?"

"Always. I made sure to give you a couple hours after school before we see him, and as you know, I'm off."

"Something I've known right from the beginning."

Marilyn let the slight pass unremarked. "Good. Then you know what you're getting yourself into. Can we start the movie? I want to see Melissa McCarthy crap in the sink again. That always cracks me up. 'Look away! Look away!'" Marilyn started laughing now, simply at the prospect of the brilliant comedienne and actress debasing herself.

"Sure. Should I meet you at Peter's office, assuming he has one?"

"Yes, yes. Start the movie. I'll get you his card before you leave."

*

The next day after school, Duncan went home and took a quick shower. They were in that long stretch of endless gray and drizzly days that marked Seattle winter, so he didn't bother changing from his school clothes—khakis, duck boots, blue and yellow plaid shirt underneath a navy fleece vest. He ran a brush through his hair and wondered why he bothered. He kept it so short the brush made not a whit of difference. The same went for hair product, which he applied. He had a bathroom drawer full of mousses, gels, and waxes and needed those as much as he needed the conditioner in the shower. But what was a gay guy without hair products? A pretty pathetic creature, indeed.

He took a last look in the mirror, decided he looked good enough for his meeting with the wedding planner, and set out with the thought that the wheels were really in motion and turning back was becoming less and less of a possibility.

*

Marilyn waited outside Peter Dalrymple's office on Capitol Hill. Duncan knew she didn't see him at first, and he took the moment to regard his future wife. There was something plaintive in her expression as she stood under the red awning waiting, an expectancy on her features that was kind of sweet.

Duncan hoped he would never hurt her.

He was touched to see she had dressed differently for the meeting, not wearing the black and heavy sterling silver jewelry she usually favored. Today, she had on a long gray flannel shirt, topped with a bright red V-neck sweater and a black motorcycle jacket over the somewhat staid ensemble (she was, after all, Marilyn). Black tights and a pair of black low-heeled pumps completed the look. She wore little makeup and even her hair, a little flat from the rain, looked a bit more tamed than usual.

She smiled when she saw him coming up the brick walkway. Her face actually lit up and Duncan wondered, not for the first time, if her expectations about this marriage were realistic. In spite of all the m/m romances she read and her haunting of gay bars, he worried that rings on their fingers might somehow give her some absurd hope that theirs would become, like magic, a more traditional union.

He hoped not. He had never lied, not even in his Craigslist ad, about who he was and how gay he was, which was 100 percent.

"Hey there!" Duncan greeted her. "You look so good I almost didn't recognize you."

"Bitch. Come on. We're five minutes late." She tapped her chunky red watch. In spite of all her Bohemian airs, Marilyn was a stickler for punctuality.

She pulled open the plate-glass door, waiting for Duncan to precede her. Marilyn was never much for traditional gender roles. He walked into the cool lobby. The building had been converted from a Georgian redbrick house, with green shutters and cream trim on the outside.

Inside, it felt homey and comfortably worn.

"His office is upstairs." Marilyn took Duncan's hand and led him up the wide staircase, bordered on both sides with elegant carved wooden railings.

Peter Dalrymple was obviously also a believer in being on time, since he waited for them at the top of the stairs, just inside his open office door.

Duncan paused halfway up the steps, taking the man in. If he had any doubt that the man was gay, it was erased immediately by the beautifully tailored and screaming-hot-pink sport coat he wore, beneath which was a crisp bright-white shirt adorned with a red-and-silver bowtie. He wore dark denim jeans, rolled, and a pair of what could only be described as fabulous distressed leather brown wingtips. A bit of shocking-pink sock peeked out in the space where his jeans didn't quite meet his shoe tops.

Yet the man was a contradiction. His clothes belied a man that could only be described with "b" words: butch, burly, built, broad-shouldered, barrel-chested. Beautiful. In spite of all the pink, manliness radiated off him like pheromones. His red hair was shot through with silver and was thick enough to fashion a sweater from. His red-and-silver beard made him look warm and the twinkling dark-brown eyes that gazed down upon Duncan were welcoming.

There was something immediately sexy and (paradoxically?) homey about the man, setting upon Duncan the almost irresistible urge to grab him and envelop him in a bear hug. Duncan gripped the bannister for a second; he couldn't remember the last time simply viewing a man for the first time had so charmed him. He had never been one for bears, although Peter was certainly one, yet there was a comfort about his muscular bulk that made Duncan want to sink into it, like a great feather bed.

And those eyes—those damn dark eyes—drew him in and, for just a second, made everything around Duncan go dark, so Peter Dalrymple stood alone before him.

"Hello young lovers!" Peter called down the stairs, and Duncan wondered if Marilyn had laid out their "situation" to the man or had simply left it open to interpretation. He knew most people would interpret a male/female couple visiting a wedding planner, an *engaged* couple no less, as straight.

He wondered for a moment why the distinction should matter.

Did it?

Peter's voice was yet another contradiction to the brilliant-pink jacket. It was smoky, deep, velvety, and seemed to wrap around him, then sink into him.

Duncan was enchanted.

But *young lovers*? Seriously?

Marilyn shouted up the stairs, snapping Duncan back to reality. He had forgotten she was there. How much time had passed anyway? It seemed like an hour, but Duncan knew it had only been seconds.

"Hey Peter, how've you been? It's so good to see you again."

Peter took Marilyn in his arms and gave her the kind of hug Duncan had envisioned only moments ago, casting a glance at Duncan over her shoulder and smiling at him. The smile made him go weak in the knees, and he hurried up the remainder of the stairs, lest he tumble back down.

Marilyn turned to Duncan and held out her hand. Nervous, shy, and not understanding at all why, he grasped Marilyn's hand. "And this is Duncan, my fiancé."

Duncan wondered again if Marilyn had told Peter what their marriage was really all about.

"Duncan!" Peter's eyes shone, and his smile widened. "Great name. You a hugger or a handshaker?"

"I'm half Italian."

"Come here then." And, rapidly, Duncan was pulled into Peter's embrace. The feel of his hard, manly body pressed against his own set off a kind of fireworks display within him that erupted immediately. Heart rate, respiration, and blood pressure quickened appreciably, probably soaring into danger zones. Duncan hung on for dear life, glorying in the feel of the man and the scent too. Peter smelled clean, like soap, undercut with something unidentifiable, but undeniably masculine. No cologne for this boy!

Little as he wanted to, Duncan jerked away, not only because he feared Peter would sense the erection that had sprouted in his khakis, but also because, for the first time since he was about twelve, he feared he might come in his pants.

This was crazy. Just lunacy.

Duncan turned and stared down the stairs, trying to rein in his thundering heart and near-hyperventilating respiration. When he turned back around, he hoped he was more composed. He forced himself to smile and to meet Peter Dalrymple's gaze.

"Why don't you guys come on in." Peter gestured with his arm, indicating they should precede him into his office. As soon as Duncan stepped into the generously sized room, though, he realized that office was the wrong word for the place. Warren, den, man cave—all those descriptors would be more apt.

First off, there was no desk in the room. The furniture looked as though it should be in some sort of sportsman's club. There were two leather loveseats, the fabric worn and distressed, facing each other in front of a white-painted brick fireplace where a real wood fire danced. The couches looked inviting, kind of like Peter with his arms open, beckoning him into them. They seemed to be saying, "Give us a hug and, in return, we will give you succor."

The floors were hardwood, old and scratched, with a dull matte sheen. Persian rugs were scattered throughout the room, some overlapping, varying in age, hue, and design, yet they all seemed unified in presenting a front that was warm and reflected their owner as a man of taste. Floor-to-ceiling bookshelves lined the walls and Duncan would have liked to peruse titles, but Peter was getting them settled onto one of the couches, while he bustled around them, gathering up a fountain pen and a sheath of paperwork.

"Get you anything? I have water, coffee, and all different kinds of tea."

"Got anything stronger?" Marilyn asked.

Duncan shook his head, wondering if one day he would have an alcoholic wife. The thought morphed into seeing them as George and Martha from *Who's Afraid of Virginia Woolf?* The vision was not enticing because he feared it perhaps veered too close to the truth, so he forced it away. Yet he did linger on how much Marilyn reminded him suddenly of Liz Taylor in that raucous portrait of a dysfunctional marriage.

Enough! "I'd love a cup of coffee." Duncan said.

"Marilyn?" Peter asked. "Beer, wine, cocktail?"

"How about just a glass of vodka with a few ice cubes for color?"

"Done." Peter moved to a rolling cart positioned at the side of the room and busied himself getting their refreshments. As he did, Duncan couldn't help but admire the broadness of the man's back, the way it tested the seams of the sport coat, and the lovely way it tapered down to his waist—all man.

He felt himself growing aroused again and looked at Marilyn. He was shocked to see her staring down at his crotch. He looked down and could see that his happiness at meeting Peter Dalrymple was only too obvious. He shifted and crossed his legs, hoping to hide the bulge.

"Pervert," Marilyn whispered.

Duncan giggled.

Peter turned around. "What? Let me in on the joke."

Duncan watched as Marilyn leaned forward, poised to open her mouth. Duncan pushed her back and quickly spoke up. "I was just chuckling because Marilyn said you should add ice 'for color.' What a card, huh?"

Marilyn cut him a look out of the corner of her eye.

Peter came over and handed Duncan a mug of coffee. "Is black okay?"

Marilyn answered for him. "Oh no, not for our Duncan here. I think he wants you to give him a little sugar." She grinned. "And a squirt of your cream." Marilyn looked utterly composed as if she had no idea everything she was saying was a double entendre.

But Peter caught on and he raised an eyebrow at Duncan, which caused Duncan to swipe at his forehead, where beads of sweat had popped up. *When did it get so hot in here?*

"Cream and sugar, please. Yes. Ignore her." Duncan held his cup out, and Peter took it, their hands brushing as he did so. The simple touch sent a jolt of electricity through him, a tingling all the way up his arm, as well as farther south. He didn't know if he could make it through this session.

Peter handed Marilyn her drink. "I added a splash of olive juice to it and a couple bleu-cheese stuffed olives. I know you like it dirty."

Marilyn thanked him and got to work on sucking down her drink.

Finally, everyone had their refreshments (Peter taking only a glass of tap water) and were settled on the twin loveseats.

"That's a gorgeous view you have," Duncan nodded to the windows on either side of the fireplace, which showed the top of the Space Needle. Behind it, the snow-capped blue-gray range of the Olympics had managed to peek out from a bank of clouds, looking almost unreal.

"It never gets old." Peter set his water on the floor at his feet and smiled at them. "So, let's get started."

"I'm gay!" Duncan blurted, having no idea he was going to utter the sentence, but knew that it came from somewhere deep within, a part of him, uncensored, that wanted desperately for Peter Dalrymple to know he preferred "sausage over pie."

Peter grinned and then did his best *Saturday Night Live* Church Lady impression, "Well, isn't that *special*?" he grinned.

Marilyn stared at him, dumbfounded. Her mouth hung open. "Let's hear it for the boy," she said, voice loaded with sarcasm. She clapped slowly, once, twice, three times, all the while staring at her fiancé.

Duncan could feel the heat rise to his face and knew even his olive complexion must now be displaying a shocking crimson hue. "I'm sorry. I just thought you should know our situation. I didn't want you to get the wrong impression."

"God forbid," Marilyn said, under her breath.

Peter nodded. "I know, sweetie. Marilyn told me all about you two when she called." He shrugged. "I don't play by any rules as a wedding planner; you should know. My only rule is to bring the couple a happy, memorable day. What the two of you—or what anyone, really—does with their marriage after that is out of my hands." He cocked his head. "But since you brought it up, can I ask why?"

Duncan shifted, crossing and uncrossing his legs. Was this to be his lot in life going forward—fielding questions about why a gay man would choose to marry a straight woman? Should he just compose a bulleted list of talking points and blurt them out whenever he was confronted with this question? Perhaps he could have the reasons printed out on a little card and just hand it to whomever asked the question?

Finally, though, he thought it best to be direct and simple. He looked Peter in the eye as he said, "Why does anyone get married?" He then looked over at Marilyn, grabbing her hand and intertwining his fingers with hers. "Love. I love Marilyn. She and I get along great. Like two peas in a pod." The words felt hollow even as he spoke them, but he hoped the breath and conviction he put behind them would make them real to everyone, including himself.

Marilyn leaned forward. "Yeah, who says our marriage has to be like everyone else's? We're playing by our own rules."

"And we will win the game," Duncan smiled at Peter.

Peter sat back in his chair, a tentative smile on his face. "Well, to each his or her own, I always say." He handed them each a sheet of paper. "That's my questionnaire. Each of you can fill it out at your leisure and then get it back to me. It's just so I have an idea of your likes and dislikes, what you imagine your special day will be like, your budget, particulars like number of guests and so on. You can take it home and fill it out and mail it back to me or just stop by and drop it off." He smiled at Duncan.

"No online editable form?"

Peter laughed. "I'm an old-school Luddite, sweetie. I don't even have a website. But no worries—I do have a computer and know how to get *your* wedding website set up, and I can do lots of the legwork for your wedding online. It's just that for me, I don't want to make it too easy for folks to avoid face-to-face. I like to understand my clients, so I can really give them what they want."

Duncan couldn't help where his thoughts went; Peter talking about giving him what he really wanted started all sorts of images flowing in his head. *What I really want is you to come over here, stare into my eyes with those incredible almost-black ones of yours that contrast so wonderfully with your red hair and... What I really want you to do is come over here and straddle me, so our bodies are pressed close together, so I can feel your beating heart against my chest. What I really want is for you to then lean forward slowly, your lips slightly parted, as you swoop in for our first kiss. What I really want is to taste your mouth, feel the pressure of your beard against my face, our tongues dueling. What I really want is to reach up with my right hand and find the back of your neck, drawing you even closer to me, so close our bodies, our lips, our tongues almost merge, becoming one. What I really want is to feel you shift on my lap and feel your excitement, hard, as you press against my own, the aching need like something combustible between us. What I really want is to hold you...*

Duncan? Earth to Duncan." Marilyn was in his face, practically close enough to kiss, even though kissing her was, obviously, the furthest thing from his mind.

"Did you even hear the question?"

Duncan felt as though he were swimming up through dark waters, fighting his way through a fog. He had disappeared in the last several moments, maybe not bodily, but completely in spirit.

"What was the question?"

Marilyn said, slowly, "If you could have any three people, dead or alive, over for dinner, what would you eat?" She snorted with laughter.

"What?"

"That's not what I asked." Peter shot Marilyn a look. "You were a thousand miles away, buddy. Penny for your thoughts?"

Duncan shrugged, the heat rising to his face belying his answer. "Who knows? Work, I guess."

"Oh, okay. I was just asking what's a good time for us to meet. Since the wedding is coming up very soon, we'll have to hustle and I think it's a good idea for us to meet every week to check in and make sure we're on track. Of course, we can keep in touch through the phone, email, texts. I'm here for you."

Again, a quick image of Peter on his lap came to him prompted by his "here for you" comment. Duncan banished it and admonished himself to get his mind back on point. Thoughts like he was having would not help the wedding planning.

He shrugged. "Uh, I don't know. I'm usually home from school around three or four in the afternoon. Would five be too late?"

"Could you do 4:30? I usually like to get out of here by 5:00 if I can."

"Somebody to hurry home to?" Duncan couldn't stop himself from asking.

Peter only grinned in reply. "What do you think?"

"You mean about the time?" Duncan asked.

"Yes," Peter replied.

They all agreed that 4:30 on Wednesdays would be perfect. Duncan was already looking forward to next Wednesday.

For the rest of the meeting, Duncan forced himself to pay attention as Peter outlined how he would go about things. He asked them if they wanted input on every single decision or if they just wanted to trust him to make some decisions for them, based on the questionnaires he had given them at the start of the meeting. Duncan and Marilyn both agreed that things would go more smoothly if they relied on Peter's expertise, especially once he got to know them better.

Duncan managed to not jump on top of Peter Dalrymple for the remainder of the meeting.

*

Outside, the rain was coming down hard. Under the red awning, Marilyn said, "So I don't think I need to ask how you liked Peter. It was obvious how you liked Peter. I guess I shouldn't be surprised since you never made it a secret that you were a *peter lover*." Marilyn looked down at the damp pavement, then back up again. "I guess I just didn't expect you to be so smitten."

Was that hurt in her eyes? Jealousy? How could it be? Duncan had never given Marilyn any reason to think he was anything other than what he was—a proud, all-American, flag-waving, red-blooded homo.

Except, he answered himself, *you agreed to marry her*.

He decided a light response to her statement would be best. He grinned and poked her in the side. "Why? Jealous?"

She slapped his hand away. Hard. "Of course not. But I do think it's weird sitting in a meeting with our wedding planner and having you eyeing him like you're some kind of starving pit bull and he's a T-bone steak!" Marilyn snorted.

"Was I that obvious?"

"Honey, if you were any more obvious, we would have needed some paper towels to mop down the front of your drawers." She looked away from him. "I suppose I should get used to this. It's just that we go out to all the bars; we watch gay movies, even a little porn here and there, and your attention rarely strays from me." She winked. "Except for when we watched that one porno. What was it called? *Dawson's 20-Load Weekend*?" She laughed.

"I was staring because I was scared."

"Right. And I am the queen of Romania."

Marilyn had her back slightly turned to him, and Duncan moved up behind her and placed his hands on her shoulders. "Look, I'm sorry. I didn't realize. He is a cutie. Such a sweet face!"

"Pull yourself together, man!"

"Right. I was apologizing. It was disrespectful to you, and for that, I'm sorry."

Marilyn turned to him, and he was stunned to see tears standing in her eyes. What did she think? What was she expecting? Had he ever really known? "It's okay, I guess. You were just doing what comes naturally. This Peter, though, he really sends you, huh?" Marilyn's eyebrows came together, as though she feared his response.

"I don't know. He's a handsome man."

"Are you sure you want to do this?" Marilyn asked plaintively.

Duncan didn't allow himself time to ponder. "Of course I am. I love you, sweetie."

Marilyn grinned. "We will have to have the talk eventually."

"Huh?"

"Well, you know, about sex."

Duncan didn't say it, but he thought: *Oh Lord, you don't expect sex. Tell me you don't expect sex. I thought that much was clear. I couldn't do it.* "Okay. You want to go get a drink? We can still make happy hour at R Place."

Marilyn shook her head. "No. Mike will be hungry, and I'd just like to get home, put my feet up, and watch a little TV. I have several *Kitchen Cousins* recorded I haven't watched yet."

"You want I should come? We can stop at Whole Foods and pick up a rotisserie chicken and some salad. Easy peasy."

Marilyn put her hand on his chest. "Honey. Are you dense? As Greta Garbo said, 'I want to be alone.' Okay?"

She didn't wait for Duncan to respond. She simply turned and walked away from him, the rain pattering down on her. Duncan watched, debating whether he should run after her, but he knew what Marilyn was like. She always wanted to appear strong, confident, needing no one's help. She would perceive his running after her as pity.

He did feel sorry for her. But he knew her well enough to know she needed her space.

He watched her until she turned a corner, then turned himself and gazed up at Peter Dalrymple's window. The light was still on, warm and butter yellow against the bruised sky. *What are you thinking, Mr. Dalrymple? If my display of attraction was so obvious to Marilyn, was the same true for you? Were you thinking something along the lines of: look at this pathetic couple with the groom all pie-eyed for me? Or were you thinking, maybe, the attraction was mutual?* Duncan wondered this last part because he was a sensitive sort, and he had picked up on certain signals Dalrymple may have not even been aware he was giving off. Things like how their gazes connected, holding just a second or two longer than what was proper, or how Peter's same stare seemed appraising when he looked at him, or maybe, most telling of all, how Peter seemed to be speaking more to him than Marilyn? Or was that simply wishful thinking on Duncan's part?

He didn't think so. Gay men are eloquent with their eyes, maybe even more so than their straight brethren, and he had seen the signals passing between him and Peter because he had seen them all before—from a casual glance in a bar or even on a bus, to the stares that ignited one of Duncan's doomed love affairs.

What did it matter if Peter reciprocated his feelings of attraction? Duncan was getting married, for crying out loud. And that talk Marilyn had mentioned? Duncan knew it was about how they'd handle outside sex (not outside as in a public park, for heaven's sake!). But even he thought it was too soon, and quite unsavory, to ponder having sex with his wedding planner.

What kind of ass would that make him?

So why was he thinking of running back inside and gathering Peter in his arms in some great romantic gesture? Why was he clearly seeing himself pushing Peter back against his office door and covering his face, eyes, neck, and ears with kisses? Why could he hear echoes of sighs, groans, and murmurings of pleasure in his mind?

Should he do it? Should he dash back inside, like some romantic comedy movie, and profess his sudden and complete attraction for this man?

He had taken three steps toward the front door when he stopped and turned.

He flipped the collar on his jacket, jammed his hands into his pockets, and, shoulders hunched, started into the rain.

The cold water immediately beating down on him felt good, cleansing. It would be a long walk home.

Chapter Ten

Peter Dalrymple watched from his window as Duncan headed into the rain. He saw his own reflection dimly in the glass and observed a man whose gaze was plaintive, longing.

And he didn't like it.

Duncan was a client, for crying out loud. He was one half of a couple for whom Peter was tasked to plan a wedding and reception. How unprofessional!

In the job he was in, Peter acknowledged that he ran across many young and very good-looking men. It came with the territory. Most of his clients were at their peak physically. Even the men who were a little overweight or on the plainer side were always kind of beautiful just because they were young. Youth and vitality were powerful attractors.

But Peter had always managed to keep things professional, and although his gaze might linger over some hunky groom-to-be, it had never crossed his mind to do so much as even fantasize about him. That wasn't who Peter was. If his mind ever did stray in a carnal direction over a client, he only need think of the bright-eyed-and-trusting bride-to-be seated next to the man in question.

So he'd never been too tempted by a client. Not really. Nothing more than an internal *hubba hubba* at some faded and ripped jean-clad Adonis in flip-flops and a tight T-shirt.

Until now.

It wasn't just that Duncan was gay. Even today, when gay marriage was in all the headlines, debated by the pundits and showcased on TV, Peter still saw the occasional closet case come in with his fiancée. Such an appearance always made Peter sad, rather than igniting his libido. Those men were unsure of who they were, in deep denial (even if their gayness was painfully obvious), and their fiancées had drunk a tall glass of cluelessness, deliberately or not.

He helped those people pick out flowers, choose a DJ or band, decide on a wedding cake, and so on, but his heart always ached for the eventual confrontation that loomed in such couples' futures, sooner or later. He knew one couldn't make the gay go away, even by doing something as deeply committed as getting hitched. Hey, he knew from personal experience—his own parents had broken up when he was six because his father came to terms with being gay.

But Duncan was different. So was Marilyn. This was not some closet case and his beard, running from a painful truth, hiding behind society's tacit blessing. Duncan was gay and, from what Peter could tell by his eyes and body language, quite smitten with him.

Peter didn't think that because he was conceited. Even he would admit that he was not everyone's cup of tea. He was burly and bearded. While such attributes were definitely attractive to a certain gay subgroup, namely bears, he was not the gay male ideal of miles of smooth, ripped muscle. But his assessment of his own appearance was not what told him Duncan was attracted.

Duncan told him himself, not with words, but with his stares, which lingered for far too long, especially when he wasn't even aware he was doing it. And where those stares went! Well, let's just say they were *not* confined to chaste areas like his face. He had been worried that the burning intensity of Duncan's stare at some points might burn a hole in the crotch of his jeans.

Duncan reminded Peter of some lovesick puppy dog, mooning over his master with a fierce kind of loyalty and devotion. Peter would have been thrilled, if he weren't made so sad by it.

We can't help who we're attracted to. God knows Peter knew that, and the sad thing was that Duncan knew he was attracted to men. He got the impression Duncan accepted it, took it for granted really, as simply a fact of his life.

Peter felt sad for him—and even sadder for Marilyn, who, although she put on a front that said, "Isn't this a hoot what we're doing? Flaunting society's conventions and writing our own rules?" seemed to be hiding a hope for something her head knew was impossible, but that her heart persisted in believing.

Peter couldn't recall, in all his years of being in this business, another couple quite like Marilyn and Duncan. While he would have liked to believe their line that they loved one another and were simply creating the marriage that felt right to them as individuals, their body language, the things their eyes told Peter, made his heart go out to the pair. He hoped they would be able to make a go of it. He really did.

But he doubted it.

Duncan *was* smitten with him. Peter would have bet his life on it. And it was a shame, too, because the feelings, in spite of being highly unprofessional, were returned.

Peter couldn't remember the last time a man had so turned his head. Duncan was good-looking, sure. There was no denying it. He had a nice lean build, with broad shoulders and a narrow waist. Amazing green eyes. His skin was smooth with a Mediterranean cast, and his close-cropped dark hair inspired thoughts of running his fingers through it, just to feel the prickle of its spikes. The same held true for the five o'clock shadow on Duncan's face.

And his smile! It simply melted Peter, made his heart lurch with both joy and remorse because this man, this gay man, was marrying a woman.

And he was a client.

It wasn't simply Duncan's physical attributes that stole Peter's heart. It was the sense of decency, of warmth, that radiated off him. Peter had long believed in the power of first impressions and how we can get a good sense of a person often right away—within minutes of meeting them. And he could tell, as soon as he hugged Duncan, that this was a good man. Caring. Nurturing.

And it was stuff like the latter that Peter *really* found sexy. Intoxicating.

But, he had a job to do and he would do it. This wedding would be a hard one to plan. For one, it was planning a ceremony and party for a marriage Peter wasn't sure really had any hope of long-term survival. But, sad as it was to admit, that much was true for many couples who came to him, even those who were 100 percent straight. Peter's practiced eye could quickly size up those couples who would make it and those who would not. But he didn't try to think that way. Weddings were his business, marriage was the business of the couple committing to one another.

The other reason this wedding would be hard to plan was that Peter knew he would be jealous. Wasn't that silly? He moved about his office, turning off lights and then shrugging into a hoodie, over which he donned a fleece jacket. He caught sight of himself in the mirror just before shutting off the overhead light and thought he was dressed for the rain—Seattle style. No umbrellas for this guy.

All the way home, through the rain, for the several blocks it would take to get to his condo on Broadway, he thought of Duncan, of his smile, of his body. Of how, for that one moment when they first met, their eyes connected in a way that left Peter feeling almost shaken. Sometimes the connections eyes made were more powerful than any words, or maybe even any touch. Sometimes we actually do, as poets said, see into the other's soul.

When Peter looked at Duncan and Duncan returned the look, there was a kind of communion, a deep knowledge that came from—what? Instinct? Telepathy? Peter shrugged, sucking rainwater from his moustache. How, he wondered, could he feel he knew someone so intimately when they had just met? Yet, he had seen it happen time and again. The people he loved, the people who mattered, even the ones he didn't care for so much, he had always known right away, long before logic would have dictated a reason for his liking or disliking.

He liked to think his heart had a better and truer eye than his brain.

At last, he reached his condo, at the north end of Broadway, close to St. Mark's Episcopal Cathedral. It was a small building, redbrick, and quiet. He had lived here since he bought the place four years ago. As he shook the rainwater from his hair and beard in the vestibule, he remembered moving in, the happiness and promise of that day in August.

So why did thinking of it make him frown? It was a sweet memory, but it was a memory of something past, a memory of *someone* past.

Peter checked his mailbox, finding a bill from the electric company, a sampler pack of coupons for local businesses, and a postcard telling him he had a dentist appointment the following week. Peter was old enough to remember when he would get the occasional letter—sometimes handwritten—or postcard, and it made him wistful for days gone by.

But there was no time now to be wallowing in nostalgia or even how meeting his latest client had filled him with conflicting emotions.

He knew three girls, upstairs, waiting by the door, who were impatient for him. They would not cater to his conflicts or his memories. They had a schedule that needed adhering to, and Peter knew there would be hell to pay if he deviated.

Smiling, Peter dashed up the stairs, mail in hand. Just the thought of his three rescue pit bull mixes waiting for him filled his heart with gladness.

They heard him too. They scratched at the door, anticipating the sound of his key in the lock. They were whimpering, and the sound of them running around inside on the hardwood, jockeying for position, each of them wanting to be the first to cover his face with kisses, made him grin wider.

The dogs were definitely demanding, but it was this reception he got whenever he came home—whether it was from taking the garbage out or from a long weekend—that made all the sacrifices, expense, and trouble worth it.

He opened the door and the three girls bounded out, barking and jumping up on him, practically knocking him down. He knew he shouldn't encourage the behavior, but it just made him so damn happy to be greeted with such joy. His homecomings had to be some of the best ever. He cringed, laughing, as long tongues swiped his face, went into his ears, swabbed his neck.

"Girls! Girls!" he cried. "There's plenty of me to go around."

He let them have their moment, patting a head here, scratching behind an ear there, and finding it hard to stop laughing.

Finally, Daisy, Mary Jane, and the regal all-black Butterfly calmed down, taking seats right there in the hallway, their wagging tails thumping against the floor. They knew it was time for their walk.

"You don't care that it's pouring outside, do you?" They stared at him, as if they understood and agreed. Daisy, the smallest of the bunch, a lovely lemon-white mix with one ear that stood up and one that drooped flat, cocked her head at him, as if seeking more clarity.

"It's raining cats and dogs out there—and that's just fine with you ladies, isn't it?" The tails went faster. "Well, maybe not the cats," Peter withdrew their leashes and harnesses from the hooks by the front door and got them saddled up.

A mass of man and beast, they headed down the stairs and into the downpour, happily.

Once back inside, with business taken care of, Peter set about making dinner for the girls.

"Are you *hungry*?" he asked. "You want your *supper*?" Hungry and supper were part of the girls' limited vocabulary and at the mention of the words, all three heads cocked simultaneously. They began running in circles and panting in anticipation. He got this same reaction every night, and every night it delighted him.

He heated up the food he had made for them in a big batch earlier in the week, a mix of ground chicken, cubed sweet potatoes, broccoli, and brown rice, and grabbed their bowls from the floor. Once the food was at room temperature, he took it out of the microwave and distributed it, topping it with a good-quality commercial kibble for crunch. He filled water bowls and, at last, set the bowls down on the floor.

It was as though the girls had not been fed for weeks instead of mere hours. They descended on the food in a frenzy, and for all of maybe thirty seconds the only sounds in Peter's small yellow-and-white kitchen were snorting and gobbling.

"You didn't even taste it!" Peter admonished, after a minute had gone by and his dogs sat looking up at him as though to ask, "What's for dessert?"

When they realized no more food was in the offing and walks were most likely out of the question until bedtime, they all wandered into the living room to take up their places on Peter's weathered couch.

They never left any room for him.

He set his iPhone in the music speaker dock and brought up his Oscar Peterson jazz station on Pandora, drowning out the sound of the rain against the windows with wondrous jazz piano.

He had in mind to start his own dinner, a salmon fillet, baked in the oven with a little Dijon, garlic, dill, and butter, and some roasted brussels sprouts, but he realized he was still thinking about Duncan Taylor. The man's face was an image that had been burned upon his brain.

Dinner could wait. It would take only a few minutes to throw together anyway.

For now, he needed to talk out these conflicting feelings he had, and there was only one person who would understand—his best friend, who also happened to be his dad—out in the Chicago suburb of Evanston.

He took his phone from the dock and brought up his father in his contacts. He touched the screen to connect.

His father's voice coming through the phone was like a balm on Peter's soul. Not only did it have the same velvety quality Peter's voice had, which was comfort enough, but Peter had always had a close relationship with his dad. Even as a child, Peter could talk to him, probably because Dad never talked down to him. Even though Peter's father and mother had divorced when Peter was six, and he had grown up living with his mom, his father had always played a major role in his life, seeing him every weekend and often a weeknight as well. His dad had spent many years working in a job that paid the bills (insurance underwriting), but his real passion had been the theater. Peter had spent a multitude of opening nights in his father's company at the many theaters around Chicago, witnessing everything from Broadway touring companies, to innovative little storefront theater productions, to musicals, dance recitals, and, yes, even Shakespeare at the gorgeous Shakespeare Theater on Navy Pier. Dad wrote a weekly review column for one of the gay newspapers in town and got free tickets to everything. Peter was his favorite guest. Sometimes, Peter wished he were still in Chicago, if only to be nearer to his dad.

"Hey, Dad, what's up?"

"Retirement is up."

"Still loving it?" Peter asked. His father had retired from his job the year before.

"Oh yeah. I have never understood these people who say they're bored after retiring. What's to be bored with? You're free! I'm seeing more theater now, reading more books, seeing more movies, and I have the luxury of taking a nap every afternoon at four. I'm also taking a fast-track French class up in Wilmette before my trip to Paris this summer."

"Seeing anyone special?" Peter asked. Since Peter's mom and dad had divorced, his dad had been forever playing the field. As a good son *and* a wedding planner, Peter always had the hope, in the back of his heart and head, that his father would find that special someone to settle down with.

"You kidding? I just told you I'm free, son. As in footloose and fancy-free. Thanks to good genes and a certain little blue pill, I have more guys than I can handle."

"Oh, Dad, TMI, TMI!"

"What? You get all the men and your father is supposed to ride off into the sunset with the glory of past conquests to comfort me in my dotage? No thanks. I am seeing this hot forty-five-year-old attorney from Kenilworth. Not only cute, but rich." His father laughed.

It had been a point of interest among many of Peter's gay friends that he had a gay dad. They marveled at the automatic bond the pair must have, but the truth of the matter was that while both of them being gay did provide common ground, it was the least of what drew them together. Their sense of humor, their love of the arts, their passion for cooking—all these things were way ahead in reasons Peter and his dad got along. Probably most important was their worldview, which was based on kindness and effortlessly putting their fellow men and women first.

"No, I'm happy for you. I just don't need to hear about how Viagra is your friend."

"Well, son, at your age the concept may be a bit foreign to you, but for me, it's a blessing. Men of my dad's generation probably gave up and turned to canasta." He snickered.

"Well, the lawyer from Kenilworth sounds like a good catch."

"He's in love with me; that's for sure. Absolutely smitten. He left a red rose on my windshield last week."

"That's good!" When his father said nothing, Peter asked, "Isn't it?"

"Well, we have a fun time together. I won't get into too much detail because of my son's delicate sensibilities, but let me tell you this: the first time I went to his house, his gorgeous four-bedroom fieldstone house with a gazebo in the backyard, I looked around. Looked all over the place. The guy had every high-tech device you'd want, sixty-inch plasma screen, desktops and laptops and tablets and sound docks and whatever was new on the market. The place was decorated like a photo shoot for *Architectural Digest*. But in all that looking around, you know what I *didn't* find?"

Peter knew but he asked anyway. "What?"

"Books. Not one book in the place."

"Maybe he reads on his tablet, or his Kindle."

"Nah. He told me he doesn't have time to read."

Peter knew this would be a major character flaw to his dad. What he told Peter next sealed the deal that Mr. Rich Attorney would never be Peter's new daddy.

"And I took him recently to see a wild production of *The Misanthrope* at Lookingglass, directed by none other than Mary Zimmerman. It was wild, brilliant, insanely funny. One of my picks for the week."

"Let me guess. He didn't like it."

"Didn't like it? How would he know? He was asleep after the first fifteen minutes! And this is the guy who watches that real housewives crap on his big screen with rapt attention." His father sighed. "When I told him the play was Moliere, he said, 'Who?' I'll get bored with him and move on."

There was something sad in his father's voice that Peter was kind enough not to point out. His dad certainly played the *bon vivant* and carefree bachelor, but Peter knew the man had always hoped he would one day find the companionship and easy comfort he had had with Peter's mother, only in the form of a male. His father and mother had joked they had always had the world's most perfect union, if it weren't for the unsettling fact that they both liked dicks.

Peter thought it was kind of ironic and fitting that he was calling his father now, about the couple he had just met.

They said nothing for a few moments. Peter was smart enough to know that empty platitudes on his father's dating life would be not only inappropriate, but unwise as well.

"How's your love life, kiddo? Seeing anyone special since that heel dumped you last Christmas?"

"Dad! He wasn't a heel. Marco was a good guy; we just weren't right for each other."

"Ah. He cheated on you." His father's wrath toward Peter's ex came clearly through the phone. Peter knew that Marco hurting Ray Dalrymple's son was an unpardonable act. Even though Peter had (sort of) come to terms with how Marco had betrayed him and (sort of) forgiven him, the memory of their time together and the belief that that time would be forever continued to haunt him.

"Yes, he did. But I wasn't calling to talk about Marco."

"Oh, you met somebody new?"

"Very perceptive, Dad. And I kind of wish I hadn't."

"What?"

"It's all wrong."

"Come on, Pete, don't tell me you fell for another straight guy again. How many times do I have to tell you? You can't change them! Oh, maybe for a quickie here and there, they'll become 'gay for you' or even 'gay for pay' but they always go back to women."

Peter had once had a crush, in college, on his freshman roommate, a lacrosse player with legs to die for. His father had never let him forget it.

"No, it's a gay guy."

"Well then, what's the problem? He doesn't like you? You want your dad to give him a call and tell him how foolish he's being? Tell him he's missing a guy with brains, good looks, wit, charm, and a heart as big as the ocean."

Peter felt heat rise to his face, knowing his father meant every word. It was embarrassing. And sweet. "Nah. It's okay. I think he likes me—a lot."

"I'm not getting this then. Tell me."

And Peter did.

His father listened as Peter laid out the story of his latest clients and their rather unusual situation. When Peter stopped talking, his father said nothing for a while. "Wow. Are they sure they want to do this? I mean, when I got married, it was supposed to be the right thing to do. That's what men my age did, they grew up and got married and, believe me, a lot of men I've come to know followed that path whether they were gay or straight. But today? People don't have to do that anymore."

"They say they know they don't *have* to do it; they want to."

"Why?"

"He says he loves her."

"Yeah? I love your mother, with all my heart. That woman is as dear to me as, well, you. And Petey, you know how dear you are to me!" He chuckled and Peter knew he was just trying to cover up the mush. "But that doesn't mean I want to be married to her. I tried that. It didn't work. And I knew that, as much as for me, a divorce was for her, so she could be free to meet a man who would love her in *every* way. It took her a long time to understand that, but she eventually did. And we're happy now. We go to dinner at least once a week. She calls me or I call her almost every day. We talk about our wonderful kid and commiserate that he's chosen to live so far away from us.

"But we both know that however much we love each other, marriage isn't in the cards for us. If times had been different when we were younger, it never would have been."

"I know. I know all this. It makes me sad to see. I think the guy's screwed up and has gotten a lot of raw deals along the way."

"He must have. You gonna try to stop this thing?"

"Oh Dad, I can't do that. They came to me as clients. It's my job to plan their *wedding*, not their *marriage*." Peter sighed. In light of his attraction to Duncan Taylor, an attraction he felt pretty strongly was 100 percent reciprocated, a part of him thought stopping this sham of a marriage was really the right thing to do, almost a moral obligation.

"I think you need to shove that bitch out of the way," his father said softly, and they both burst into laughter. Peter felt like his dad had, as he often did, read his mind.

"As much as I'd like to, I can't. He, she, they have to come to their own realizations themselves."

"You could gently sabotage things. Make the wedding so stressful and difficult that they give up."

"I know you don't mean that. Besides, that idea sounds like some bad situation comedy."

"I know. I guess all you can really do is be a good wedding planner for them."

Peter sighed. "That's the goal. But why does life throw curve balls like this? I mean, I have wanted to meet a nice guy now for months. And I *have* looked! I go out on dates. I post a personals ad. I go out to the bars now and then, even though I'm not such a fan, and I always come up empty-handed."

"A guy who looks like you? Really?"

"Well, maybe not completely empty-handed, but I never meet anyone special. And then, when I least expect it, *he* walks into my life and sets off bells and whistles inside, fireworks behind my eyelids, leaving me thinking sappy thoughts like 'Oh dear Lord, he's the *one*.'"

"Maybe you'll feel differently next time you see him?"

"No way. I felt something, a connection, almost the minute we met."

"Sparks?"

"Yup."

"They're real, son. Don't let anyone tell you different."

"What am I gonna do?"

"I wish I had an answer for you. But I do have a quote, from Moliere, no less: 'the greater the obstacle, the more glory in overcoming it.' He also said, 'We die only once and for such a long time.' Keep *those* things in mind next time you see your young man."

"Thanks, Dad. Or not. No, really, it was good to talk to someone about this." Peter looked out the window; the rain had stopped. Perhaps, after dinner, he'd take the girls on a long walk through Volunteer Park. "How's Mom?"

"She's good. Why don't you call her? She'd love to hear from you."

"Trying to get rid of me?"

"Actually, Peter, I am. I have a date in less than an hour, and I still have not showered or shaved my balls."

"*Goodbye*, Father."

Chuckling, his dad professed his love and hung up. Peter turned toward the living room, where all three dogs looked up at him, as if to ask who he was talking to and what the topic of conversation was.

Peter shook his head. "He doesn't have any answers either." He set about making dinner for one, wondering when he would next see Duncan Taylor again. The salmon he was preparing reminded him that he would most likely incorporate this Pacific Northwest staple into the reception dinner. Salmon showed up everywhere.

Kind of like love—when the timing was all wrong.

Chapter Eleven

"We have to charge you the extra money. Think of it as combat pay." Marilyn faced the perfectly coiffed, dressed, and made-up African-American woman who hugged her Persian cat, Matilda, to her chest protectively.

"Combat pay? How dare you! For this little darling?" Dravus Bell scratched the cat behind its ears. It growled. "Sh, sweetie. I know. Did these people give you a hard time?"

"Anyway," Marilyn continued. "It's ten dollars extra when we have to do a toenail trim on a fractious cat."

"Fractious?"

"Fractious. As in Miss Matilda here left claw marks on our vet tech that will probably require stitches. I'm sorry if you don't understand the policy. Would you like me to speak to one of the doctors or the clinic administrator? Perhaps we can get them to waive the extra fee for this little sweetheart here." Marilyn, unwisely, reached out to pat the cat's head and was rewarded with a lightning-swift claw to her wrist. In spite of just having her claws trimmed, Matilda still managed to leave a bright red line on Marilyn's forearm. As Marilyn looked down in horror, the blood started beading up.

Dravus Bell smiled and Marilyn suspected she could see pent-up laughter behind the smile. Sometimes, Marilyn hated her job at the vet clinic. And right now, she hated this woman, but being a professional "client specialist," she simply smiled back, as if clueless that the woman was amused that her cat had just scratched Marilyn.

"She doesn't like strangers," Dravus explained, as if that excused Matilda's aggression.

"I'll be right back." Marilyn went in the back, washed the scratch with Hibiclens, and applied a smear of Polysporin. She counted to ten and returned to the front desk.

"We'll just charge you the usual for the toenail trim," Marilyn said, staring at the computer screen, typing as she adjusted the woman's bill. "But next time, there will be the surcharge." She looked into Dravus Bell's amber-colored eyes. "I'm just noting that we had this little talk here in your record, so we don't forget next time Miss Matilda comes in."

"Thank you," Dravus Bell said, producing an American Express card from her Ferragamo handbag.

Marilyn took care of the payment, smiled at her latest clients, and gave them their receipt.

"Have a nice day!" she called brightly as they waltzed out the door, the woman kissing the top of the cat's head. "Bitch," she whispered under her breath once the door had closed behind them.

Marilyn shook her head. "Who can I help next?"

It had been one of those days, the clinic so busy Marilyn hardly had time to think. Her former best friend, Hannah, had quit the week before to move to St. Paul with her new husband, and that only made things worse. Even though the friendship wasn't the same between the women since Hannah had found herself a man, she was a great team member and really helped out at the front desk. Today, Marilyn was stuck with Chanel Keiger, a pretty young thing who was as dumb as a box of rocks, except when it came to craftily avoiding work of any kind. Right now Chanel was busy at one of the other computer monitors, looking for a new job or apartment on Craigslist.

Marilyn glared at her, but it made no difference. It never did.

Marilyn looked up just in time to see something that had the potential to brighten her day. She witnessed Chanel's gaze move from her computer screen as the very handsome stranger entered the clinic. The younger woman quickly stood and headed toward the day's appointments, their files arranged in chronological order just below the counter.

Marilyn put her arm across Chanel's chest. "I've got this one," she said softly.

Chanel glared, mouth open.

Marilyn smiled. "I just saw how busy you were. Trust me, I'll take care of him."

Marilyn turned to their latest client, a broad-shouldered blond with the piercing blue eyes of a young Paul Newman. Marilyn shivered and thought, *I know this guy*, but she could not recall where she had ever met such a delicious number.

He was walking an all-black French bulldog on a leash. The dog wore a studded leather collar and waddled.

Marilyn may not have remembered her latest client, but to her surprise, he remembered her.

"Marilyn! I didn't know you worked here."

"Hi," Marilyn smiled, cocking her head and furiously trying to put that handsome face to a name or even a memory of when their paths might have crossed. Probably because she was trying so hard to recall, the answer stayed elusive.

"You don't remember me, do you?" He yanked at the leash to pull his dog back from pawing at the counter. "Behave, Onion." He looked back up at Marilyn. "It's okay. It's been a few weeks since I ran into you."

Marilyn laughed, giddy. "Oh, that's right. Where was it again?"

"Dinette. You were there with my buddy, Duncan."

And then it all came back—completely. This was Ben McBride, brother of Tucker, the man who, as a Christmas present to Duncan, dumped him when he had the nerve to propose marriage.

Marilyn snapped her fingers. "Right. Right! You're Ben." Marilyn shook her head. "Sorry, it's been the day from hell around here. I've been so busy I don't know my ass from a hole in the ground," Marilyn snorted and then felt heat rise to her face when Ben only stared at her. "Anyway, you're here to have us look at little—what did you say his name was?"

"Onion. I named him that because his farts make your eyes water." Ben boomed out a big laugh and Marilyn joined in. Even Chanel looked up from what appeared to be Amazon and chuckled.

"That's good." Marilyn looked down at the dog, which was the picture of innocence. "You want a treat?" Marilyn dug a dog biscuit out of the fish bowl on the counter and held it out to Onion. He sniffed it curiously, then turned his head away.

"He's picky," Ben explained.

"So have you been in before?" Marilyn keyed McBride into the computer and an Elizabeth came up, so did a Ryan, but no Ben.

"No, we just moved over this way and our last clinic wasn't leaving Onion and me impressed, so we thought we'd make the switch. Onion here is due for his rabies shot and a checkup."

Marilyn nodded, speechless for a moment, as she stared into Ben's blue eyes. Stared was perhaps not a strong enough word—fell would be better. She snapped herself back to reality and gathered up a clipboard that had the new patient forms attached to it and handed it to Ben, along with a pen. "If you could just do me a big favor and fill these out, I'll get someone right out to bring Onion back."

Marilyn watched as Ben and Onion took a seat in the waiting area. The weather was beginning to get warmer, and even though the sun was shining, Marilyn knew that today's high would be only in the midfifties. Still, Ben was a true Seattleite, wearing a pair of olive-green cargo shorts, a black T-shirt with some sort of bright green and pink robot on the front, and a pair of battered Keen sandals. She wondered if he knew the rule around the Pacific Northwest was that such footwear was to be worn with socks, white preferably.

But it was not his sandals that had Marilyn, for the moment, shirking her responsibilities. It was Ben—all of him. She couldn't help but notice, up top, how Ben's broad shoulders and chest tested the cotton T-shirt's seams. The shirt did not hide that Ben had two very firm pecs beneath its cotton. Marilyn restrained herself from pointing at his chest and saying something witty like "You came to the right place, honey, because those puppies are sick."

But that would have been very unprofessional.

Peering down lower, Marilyn felt her pulse quicken as she took in Ben's very shapely calves, dusted with golden-brown hair. It looked as though someone had secreted a baseball, or perhaps a grapefruit, underneath the skin.

Chanel nudged her and whispered, "Girl, careful you don't drool all over that keyboard."

Marilyn started and then let out a high-pitched giggle that was completely uncharacteristic. Onion barked.

Chanel said, "I thought you were taking care of this one. I'll get a vet tech to bring Onion and Mr. Studly there back."

Marilyn was glad for the chiding. It gave her more time to moon over Ben.

"So how have you been?" she called from the counter.

Ben looked over at her and smiled, which caused her to melt just a little more. She was glad she'd worn pants, lest there be a puddle on the floor beneath her stool. This man was having a serious effect on her. She might just have to go home after work and take out her dearest friend when she got lonely, a Mr. Jack Rabbit.

"Oh, good. I've been busy with work."

"What is it you do again? You work at Swedish, right?"

"No, that was my ex, Marta. She was, is, a nurse there."

"Your ex?" Marilyn gave Ben an ear-to-ear grin, which was completely at odds, she quickly thought, with how someone should respond to the news that someone had a new ex. She couldn't help herself. Damn it. She forced herself to appear solemn, even though the grin continued to radiate inside.

"Uh, yeah. But I work over at Ba Bar? I'm a baker. I make macaroons that you would die for."

"Ooh. A handsome man who bakes cookies? How is it you're still single?"

Before she got an answer to her question, Sheryl Fujimura, one of the vet techs, emerged from the back.

"We can see Onion now. You want to come on?" Sheryl smiled at the dog and let her gaze flicker briefly up to Ben. Marilyn wondered how the woman could look at the dog first when this luscious morsel of masculinity was sitting right there in front of her, legs spread invitingly.

The phone started ringing and Marilyn picked it up, watching longingly as Ben followed Sheryl back to an exam room. He looked as good going as he did coming. *You could balance a tray on that ass*, Marilyn thought.

"This is Marilyn. How may I hurt you? I mean, help you today?" Marilyn rolled her eyes. She couldn't recall the last time a man had left her so shaken—and she admired a lot of men! But almost all of them were gay, so her admiration was at a remove.

Marilyn made an appointment for a schnauzer to be neutered the following week. When she got off the phone, Chanel was grinning at her.

"You have been struck by Cupid's arrow. You're blushing like a school girl."

"I am not!" Marilyn busied herself with a stack of files, her hands trembling ever so slightly.

Chanel crossed her arms. "Aren't you supposed to be getting married?"

Marilyn slapped one of the files open, trying to force her eyes to focus on what one of the vets had written there. "That doesn't mean I'm dead."

The phone rang again. "I got the last one," Marilyn snapped.

But Chanel had a point...damn her.

Later, as Ben settled up with Chanel for that day's visit and Marilyn, fuming, took care of another client, Ben looked over at her.

"You know, when I saw you and Duncan last, we talked about getting together. Think that'll ever happen?"

Marilyn finished with her client and turned her attention to Ben. "I think I can arrange that. What are you and Onion here doing this Friday? Maybe you guys could swing by the houseboat?"

"I'd love that. And Onion here has never met Duncan—or been on a houseboat."

"I'll see if I can set it up. Shouldn't be a problem."

Ben grabbed a Post-it from the front counter, scribbled something on it, and shoved it toward Marilyn. "Email and number. Give me a call if it'll work out."

"I will! You betcha!"

She could practically see, in her mind's eye, Chanel rolling her eyes as Ben left.

Chanel shook her head. "You're gonna get yourself in trouble."

"Oh, what do you know?" Marilyn snapped. *And what do* you *know*? Marilyn wondered to herself. *What the hell are you doing?*

She watched Onion and Ben through the plate glass front windows of the clinic with the feeling that she both wished they had never come in and the reality that she was completely thrilled that they did.

What's it gonna be like? You, your fiancé, and Ben?

Chapter Twelve

Friday night found Duncan straightening up the houseboat, which meant, for Duncan, giving it a thorough cleaning. He had mopped the hardwood floors, dusted every available surface, polished with an old sock and a bit of Pledge where necessary, cleaned the bathroom and set out a stack of hand towels, and made sure all his kitchen surfaces gleamed.

In the kitchen, he checked the fridge one final time, noting the bottle of sauvignon blanc chilling on one shelf and six bottles of Mac and Jack doing the same on another. On the counter were bowls of olives, a plate of two different kinds of crackers, and an assortment of cheeses: a bleu, Brie, and Seattle's own Beecher's Flagship.

It had been so long since he had entertained. He looked forward to seeing Ben again. He had been surprised when Marilyn called earlier in the week to tell him that Ben and his Frenchie, Onion, were the clinic's latest clients and she had invited him for cocktails. "At your place!" she added. "I hope you don't mind."

"What's wrong with yours?" Duncan asked.

"Mike, for one. He'd scratch Onion's protruding eyes out, then waltz away as the dog lay there screaming. If that's not enough of a reason, I remembered when we ran into him at Dinette a while back how much he liked your houseboat."

"I guess you had no choice."

Now Duncan was glad. The place was so clean it practically sparkled, and it would be good to have the company. The last time Ben had been here had been with Marta and Tucker, for Thanksgiving dinner. That seemed like such a long time ago and, except for Ben, peopled with the cast from a movie rather than folks whom he had once known and cared about.

He supposed he was making some progress getting over Tucker.

He set the *hors d'oeuvres* out on the coffee table and went to shower and dress.

*

Marilyn made her way down the wooden walkway toward Duncan's. She lugged along a Metropolitan Market cloth grocery bag filled with one of the few things she could make: angels on horseback—oysters wrapped in bacon. She also brought some cocktail napkins left over from some long-ago party at her apartment. They had a picture of a frowning, very pregnant woman with the legend "I should have danced all night." She thought Ben would get a kick out of it.

A bottle of vodka from her freezer completed the bag's contents. Marilyn mused that within the bag were really all the staples one needed for a happy life.

She paused near Duncan's houseboat to admire how the setting sun bathed the Eastlake neighborhood across the water in golden light. The boats moored in the marina, the houseboats, and the buildings rising up the banks of Lake Union all appeared almost to be glowing.

She and Duncan hadn't discussed where they would live once they got married. She wondered if it would be here. She could picture herself sitting on his deck, enjoying this view on a summer's night with a beverage in her hand. What she couldn't picture were the sleeping arrangements within, because the houseboat had only one bedroom. She also found it difficult to imagine herself ever leaving her bachelorette pad on Capitol Hill, which she had lived in for more than a decade. Even though it was only a rental, it was home.

She shrugged and was just about to head inside when she heard a voice call from behind her, "Well hello, stranger!"

Marilyn turned to see Ben and Onion traipsing down the pier, Onion stopping every so often to peer over its edge at the lapping dark water. Ben grinned. "I swear he'd jump right in if I didn't have him on a leash."

Marilyn smiled and squatted down so the dog would come. Dragging Ben behind him, Onion bounded over and jumped on her, almost knocking her flat on her ass. He began to cover her face with kisses.

"Onion! Down! Stop!" The dog chose not to hear his master's commands, and Marilyn could only giggle, then shut her mouth quickly as the dog's tongue dipped inside. She struggled to get up from the excited pooch, who was snorting and was now licking her legs. When he grabbed one of Marilyn's calves to begin humping, Ben swopped him up in his arms.

Marilyn laughed. "What a little horndog!" she cried, straightening her clothes.

"He gets it from me," Ben said. "Never could resist a beautiful woman."

"So are you gonna stick your tongue in my mouth and hump my leg?" Marilyn asked, hoping she sounded like she was joking.

"Don't tempt me." He looked down at the bag she carried. "Help you with that?"

"Sure." Marilyn handed him the bag, and he peered inside. "Looks like a party. You're a girl after my own heart." Ben grinned at her.

"Yeah," Marilyn said and then added, reluctantly, "and don't forget—this girl is engaged to be married in just a few weeks."

Ben cocked his head. "You're really going through with that?"

"Well, yeah."

"I thought you guys were pulling my leg."

Marilyn's good mood evaporated quickly, much as the sunset, now complete, had plunged Eastlake across the dark water into a murky shade of gray, so different from the gilded light only moments ago.

"No, we're getting everything ready. We even have a wedding planner." Marilyn felt a slow burn rise to her face and she didn't want to ponder why. "We should go inside."

Marilyn hurried into the houseboat, leaving the door open behind her so Ben could follow. "We're here!" she shouted too loudly and too brightly.

Duncan emerged from the bedroom, looking like he belonged in the dictionary next to the term "clean-cut." His dark hair was still wet from the shower, and his skin glowed with radiance and vitality. He was clean-shaven and his emerald eyes sparkled. He wore a pair of faded jeans, ripped in the knees, and a rumpled yellow linen shirt that brought out the olive of his skin and made a wonderful contrast to his dark hair. He was barefoot.

Suddenly, Marilyn was filled with an odd sort of tenderness for this man, a kind of relief at him appearing, and the genuine joy in his smile when he saw her. She hurried over to him and gathered him up in her arms, squeezing tight. She held on to him, kissing his neck, and for a reason she couldn't quite understand, or couldn't quite face, wanted to cry. "I love you," she whispered in his ear.

"I love you too, sweetie," Duncan sounded sincere—if not a little confused. He gently disengaged himself from her as, presumably, Ben and Onion stepped onto the houseboat.

"Hey, man, good to see you!" Ben called.

By way of introduction, Onion lifted a leg and pissed on Duncan's kitchen cabinets.

"Oh fuck, I'm sorry, man. Bad dog!"

"Don't worry about it," Duncan said. He gathered up a handful of paper towels from a roll over the counter and swiped the urine away. "I do the same thing when I'm in a new place."

Ben chuckled. "Yeah. All us guys—we have to mark."

Marilyn was glad for the distraction. It gave her a chance to pull herself together. She was not quite forty, but she wondered if she was starting to go through the change her mother had warned her about. Her emotions lately had been all over the place. She thought of herself as a tough broad, but yet suddenly she cried like a baby at the slightest provocation. Yesterday that damn Sarah McLachlan TV ad for some animal rescue charity, with its montage of sad and damaged dogs and cats, had set her to blubbering as though her heart was breaking.

"That dog's a menace to the community. I'm taking him to the sheriff and make sure he's destroyed," Marilyn said in her best Myra Gulch impersonation.

"Destroyed?" Duncan cried. "You can't! You mustn't!"

Marilyn grinned. It figured that the gay guy in the room could match her in *Wizard of Oz* quotes.

"You guys," Ben said, shaking his head. "This is Onion, Duncan, and no one's destroying him. He's a bad boy."

"Just like his daddy," Marilyn quipped.

"Not at all like his daddy," Duncan said softly. "He's the good one."

The room grew silent for a moment as Marilyn assumed they all knew Duncan was making a subtle dig at Ben's brother.

Duncan clapped his hands together, perhaps to dispel the mood. "Well, let's get this party started!" He hit the play button on his iPhone screen to bring up his "Favorite Females" playlist, a compilation of Ann Hampton Callaway, Ella Fitzgerald, Nina Simone, Bonnie Bramlett, Etta James, and Sarah Vaughan. He took a few steps into the tiny kitchen area.

"What do you guys want to drink?"

"Beer, whatever you have on hand," Ben said.

Marilyn said, "I'll have what he's having."

Duncan cocked his head and grabbed three bottles of Mac and Jack out of the fridge. "Beer? You, Marilyn?"

"Why not? I don't have to worry about bloat for another few weeks. I want to be one of the boys."

Duncan handed them each a cold beer and asked if anyone required a glass. "I thought we could have a couple drinks here and nibble a bit and then walk over to Fremont for dinner. I was thinking Revel?"

"The Korean street food place?" Marilyn asked.

"That's the one," Duncan said.

"Never heard of it," Ben said. "When in Fremont, I usually go to Norm's."

Marilyn grinned. "That would be the better choice. That way, we could bring Onion." Norm's was a bar with decent food and one of the only places in the city that allowed dogs. Marilyn recalled her first time there and how amazed she had been seeing a Rottweiler sitting in a booth with his or her human pack, just like a person. The place usually had more dogs than a dog park, yet everyone seemed happy. Maybe the dogs ingested the beer fumes and it made them mellow.

"That sounds like a great idea," Ben said. He nudged Marilyn with his shoulder and she giggled.

*

Duncan watched Marilyn and Ben and wondered what was going on. For one, Marilyn generally hated beer, unless she could have it mixed with tomato juice and a squeeze of lime, on the rocks. She had told him the drink was called a Michelada. But straight out of the bottle? That was not his girl at all. And, as big an animal lover as Marilyn was, she also was not one to frequent a place like Norm's. The food there was passable, maybe even good bar food, but he and Marilyn usually liked to visit the more esoteric eateries in their city. Duncan had been looking forward to some of Revel's green onion pancakes, or a rice bowl topped with mustard greens, daikon radish, and braised short ribs.

Now home again, Marilyn sat next to Ben on the couch, their bodies touching. Duncan wondered if she realized how much the two of them looked like a couple. When he had run into Ben at Dinette a while back, he would have never pictured the two of them together. Ben's girlfriend Marta—and what was the story with her, anyway?—was rail thin, tall, and blonde, a woman you'd see prancing down a runway, eyes straight ahead, with a sour expression on her Cupid's bow lips.

Yet now, as he observed Marilyn and Ben together, there was something almost right about the two of them. There was a sort of yin and yang going on, his gruffness complementing her generous femininity.

If things had been different, he might have thought at that moment of fixing them up, but he wondered if they would even need his help. The way Marilyn was casting quick glances at Ben, over and over again, thinking she was being sly, told Duncan a story that made him uneasy, causing him to wonder once more if he was doing the right thing in marrying this woman.

Even though Duncan had not one iota of sexual feeling for Marilyn, he knew he loved and respected her, which was why he supposed it took him a moment to identify the giddy queasiness in his gut as jealousy.

"Hey Ben. Why didn't you bring Marta? She working tonight?"

Ben looked over at Marilyn. "You didn't tell him?"

"I haven't had a chance."

Ben took a swig of beer and said, "She dumped me."

"*She* dumped *you*?" Marilyn asked, incredulity written all over her face and open mouth.

"Oh don't flatter me. I'm not the easiest guy to live with. Like Onion here, I snore, I eat too fast, I get way too excited when a female goes by, and my farts are epic."

"Okay, I don't think we needed to learn that last part. And here's me feeding you beer and cheese. Let me see if I have some cabbage in the fridge," Duncan said, rolling his eyes.

Ben snorted with laughter. "Oh come on, Duncan, you know refinement is not exactly my middle name."

"So, what? You kept your more sterling qualities hidden from Marta?" Marilyn wondered.

"Not really. Like many women, she was charmed at first by the beast in me, the cute *guy*, you know what I'm saying? Aw, he left the toilet seat up, isn't that sweet? Aw, look, his dirty jockstrap is hanging from the bedroom door. Precious!"

Duncan watched as Marilyn crossed her legs at the mention of Ben's dirty jockstrap. She also couldn't hide the flush rising from her chest to envelop her face. He knew she was excited by the image it conjured up, knew because he was, a little bit, too.

Ben took a swig of his beer, belched, wiped the foam from his upper lip with the back of his hand. He took a piece of Beecher's Flagship, put it on a rye cracker, and popped it into his mouth. Shifting the food to one side, he continued. "But when we moved in together, those same things that she found so delightful began to annoy her. One Sunday, when I had been watching a little too much ESPN, she decided she'd had enough. Things had reached a kind of critical mass, I guess." He swallowed and washed down the cheese and crackers with another gulp of beer. "That girl should become a lesbian. I don't think she really ever liked men. I'm sure she's with one of her gal pals now, crying about how insensitive I was."

Duncan heard what Ben was saying and it all sounded, yes, very *guy*ish and devil-may-care, but he could see the hurt on Ben's face, the stiff way he held his upper lip as though he were holding back tears, the faraway look that came into his eyes when he talked about Marta.

He supposed Marilyn could, too, because she leaned in even closer to Ben and said, "You loved her once, though, huh?" She patted his shoulder.

Ben stared straight ahead for several moments and didn't answer, which in a way was an answer. He shrugged. "Yeah. She had a hot bod."

Marilyn punched his arm. "You know there was more to it than that! I can tell from the look in your eyes."

"And what look is that?"

"Sad. You look sad, you big marshmallow."

Ben chuckled, shaking his head. He pointed a thumb in Marilyn's general direction and turned to Duncan. "You're gonna have your hands full with this one here, brother. You sure you don't want me to take her off your hands?"

"As if you could handle me!" Marilyn said.

Duncan watched as they both collapsed into laughter. He remembered a saying his mom always had, which was something along the lines of "in all kidding, there is some seriousness."

He sipped his beer and continued to watch. He felt as though he were on the outside looking in.

The rest of the evening went much the same, with Duncan feeling like a third wheel. If he didn't know better, he would have said Marilyn and Ben had flirted with one another the whole time. When they had walked over to Fremont from the houseboat, with Ben and Marilyn in the lead, Onion tugging them along on his leash, and Duncan bringing up the rear, he heard their laughter dimly and tuned out their conversation, pretending instead he was interested in the view from the Fremont Bridge and the lights of Capitol Hill in the distance.

Dinner was more of the same. Duncan didn't say much, yet no one seemed to notice.

Which was why it surprised him, once they finished at Norm's and walked back to the houseboat, Marilyn tapped his shoulder and motioned for him to come close so she could whisper in his ear, "Can I stay here tonight?"

Duncan looked at her with surprise, honestly at a loss for words. The request was the last thing he would have expected to come out of Marilyn's mouth. He had time to stall, since Ben was making his goodbyes. He hugged Duncan and thanked him for a great night and made Duncan promise they would all get together again soon.

Of course they would.

Duncan and Marilyn watched as Ben and Onion moved off into the darkness, presumably headed for their car, which he had mentioned was parked in the lot running along Westlake Avenue.

Marilyn turned to Duncan in the shadows, the only sound right now the wind in the budding trees above them and the water lapping at the dock. Duncan stared into her eyes, feeling a paradoxical mix of amusement and melancholy.

"Did you hear my question?" Marilyn softly asked.

Duncan had all sorts of things to say back, chief among them why she wanted to spend some sexless night here with him when he knew for a fact she had lusted for Ben throughout the entire evening. But all he said was, "Yeah. I heard you. And of course you can stay."

She took his arm. "I want us to sleep in the same bed," she said softly.

Duncan started leading her toward the front door. "You know it's just sleep, right?"

"Don't flatter yourself," Marilyn said. "I know." She stopped and stared up into his eyes. Duncan noticed Marilyn's eyes were shining. "I just want to be close to you," she whispered, her voice so soft he could barely hear her.

Duncan only nodded and led her inside.

Chapter Thirteen

The wedding day was hurtling rapidly toward him like some heavy object, growing larger and larger, as if it would crush him once it arrived. He actually dreamed of such images and chose not to consider the symbolism. He was happy to let the dream remnants scatter and die amidst the sound of children's voices in his classroom.

He and Marilyn continued their courtship. Yet things weren't the same, not with her and Ben flirting when the three of them got together. And they were now a trio most every Friday night. Yet, in spite of all the flirting, at the end of the evening Marilyn continued to shyly ask if she could share Duncan's bed. None of them ever acknowledged the flirting; it was simply there, and Duncan supposed they were all aware of it. Yet to comment on it, even in a joking way, would seem, to his mind, threatening. The nights he and Marilyn spent together sent a mixed message, especially the way she wanted to spoon with him after being with Ben, whispering sweet nothings in his ear, which all revolved around telling him how very much she loved him and how glad she was he was so much more sensitive and caring than Ben.

The two of them had had a couple of appointments with Peter Dalrymple, and Duncan tried to force down his attraction and feelings for the man, but it was an almost impossible task, like trying to stuff the trick snakes back into a can of gag peanut brittle. So when he was with Marilyn and Peter, he stayed quiet, letting her make all the decisions, which she was only too happy to do. So far they had decided on a menu that consisted of three options: beef tenderloin, poached salmon, and chickpea cakes on a bed of spinach for the vegetarians among their guests. They had opted for jazz and Big Band music at the reception, with a little modern, funky stuff thrown in for the younger folks: Adele, Pink, Black Eyed Peas. Floral arrangements would be simple—local wildflowers.

Their ceremony was to be performed by a friend of Duncan's from school, a teacher who had once been ordained as a minister in the United Church of Christ. They wanted to keep things short, simple, and traditional, and both had agreed that in place of vows they would read a favorite poem to the other.

Today Duncan trudged up the walkway to Peter's for one of their final meetings. Almost everything was in place and what most surprised Duncan was how easy it had been to put it all together—and so fast. Of course, Peter knew what he was doing and even had all the right connections, so he could call in a few favors to get things done in a hurry for the couple.

The days were lengthening, and as Duncan waited outside Peter's office for Marilyn to show up, he noted how the air itself was making predictions about the coming summer. Beneath the damp and chill there was an undercurrent of warmth. The sun sitting low in the sky was unimpeded by clouds and foretold a brilliant sunset, the kind that would be imbued with orange and violet. The trees now were almost all green, as if they too anticipated summer.

What would this summer be like for Duncan, his first as a married man? He had promised Scout he would be out to visit in August, at their annual family reunion, so he could introduce Marilyn to the extended family who would not be coming for the wedding at the end of this month.

He remembered how Scout had laughed when he told her of his plans.

"What's so funny?" he had asked.

"Don't get me wrong, little brother, a visit from you is always cause for celebration, but I am imagining some of the confused looks on the family's faces when you introduce your new *wife!*" Scout had collapsed in laughter again. When she reined in her mirth enough to speak, she sounded as though she had run a marathon. "I mean, they've thought of you as the gay one in the family for years now. Hell, remember when you brought what's his name that one year?"

Duncan had rolled his eyes at the memory. "Quentin."

"Oh God, nice guy, but when he showed up in a wifebeater, construction boots, and Daisy Dukes, I thought I'd die. If anyone had any doubts about which way you swung, Quentin's appearance at your side erased them."

"I was hoping they'd be happy for me," Duncan had said.

"Oh, and they will. I'm just saying the idea may come as a bit of a shock, all things considered. You have to allow them that. You're the token homo in the family, even though we all know about cousin Jeanne and her 'roommate,' Pat."

Duncan guessed it would come as a something of a shock to his extended Italian family and they *would* wonder if he had done the impossible and gone straight, or if, as his nana had said when she found out Duncan was gay, "Maybe he just hasn't met the right girl." Perhaps they would all think Duncan had finally met the right girl, the one who could turn him. Whatever they thought, the plus side to all this was that they were Italian, which meant they pretty much loved anyone in the family no matter how weird they were, simply because family was foremost in all their minds—they had all been brought up the same.

He shook his head and glanced down at his watch. They were now five minutes late, and the "right girl" still hadn't shown up. Weird. Duncan could always rely on Marilyn to be punctual.

Just as he was thinking about Marilyn's punctuality, or lack thereof, he heard the distinctive ringtone he had given her—"Power of Two" by the Indigo Girls—from his cargo pants' pocket. He pulled the phone out and looked at Marilyn's face smiling up at him as he pressed the screen to take the call.

"What's up? Are you okay? It's not like you to be late."

Marilyn's breath came through; it was choked. Was she sobbing?

"Honey? What's the matter?"

She sniffled and drew in a big breath. "I'm still at work. I got called in to help with a Labradoodle that got hit by a car over on Green Lake Way. We were short a vet tech today; Sheryl called in sick. Anyway, the little guy didn't make it, and I've just been trying to comfort his owner. She only had the dog for three months. She's heartbroken."

"Aw. I'm sorry. And I understand." Duncan looked up at Peter's office window. "You want to me to see if we can reschedule?"

"You're already there, aren't you?"

"Well, yeah."

"Then you go ahead and handle things. I trust you. I think all we have left now is looking over the seating chart for the reception. Just don't put my mother anywhere near my father, unless you want to turn this thing into a prize fight."

Marilyn's parents had been divorced for five years, but they still did not get along. Marilyn's mother had never gotten over her rage at Marilyn's father for leaving her for another woman. To add insult to injury, he didn't even leave her for a younger model, as the story usually went, but for a woman three years his senior.

Duncan chuckled. "Okay. I'll make sure. Anything else?"

"No. I gotta get back to my client. I may have to drive her home. I mean, she's really taking this hard."

"You're all heart, Marilyn."

"Ah, screw that. I'll talk to you later." She hung up.

Duncan turned and went inside to meet with Peter.

*

The seating for the reception was all sorted. Peter had made little adhesive-backed people that they could move around on the diagram of the tables that would be set up at Blue. It was very simple and Duncan hoped the arrangement would promote both harmony and synergy.

It was strange being here alone with Peter. It was the first time Duncan had had the experience, and the nearness of him made him tongue-tied, causing his brain to function in only fits and starts. It certainly increased his heart rate, respiration, and blood pressure when Peter came close and leaned over him to position the adhesive-backed figures in a new location.

Peter eyed Duncan and Duncan noticed again the way the man's eyes seemed to cut right into him, as if he could view the depths of Duncan's soul. Duncan cast his gaze away, almost embarrassed at how Peter's look affected him, especially when they were all alone here in this cozy and close office. Duncan couldn't stop himself from imagining what it would be like to touch Peter, what his skin would feel like, the coarse hair of his arms bristling under his hand. He imagined a lot more, and it made his face feel hot, made him worry that somehow his thoughts were being telepathically broadcast to Peter.

If they hadn't already come so far with Peter, Duncan would have suggested backing out. But Peter had already put all the wheels in motion for their wedding and reception, and they had already paid him. If he had any common sense at all, Duncan would have pulled away from Peter after their very first meeting. He had known then he was drawn to him, known he harbored secret fantasies, ranging from blissfully romantic to downright filthy. These secret mental interludes came into play every time he and Marilyn met with their wedding planner. He should have backed out; he thought it after every meeting.

But he hadn't wanted to. Like an addict, he wanted to see Peter just one more time, and then one more time. Each occasion was an exercise in unfulfilled longing, leaving Duncan filled with questions he couldn't bear to answer.

The guilt would rise up easily—he had only to imagine Marilyn sleeping next to him. Duncan would look down at her. Slumber always erased the hard edge to her features. There was something innocent and childlike as she slept that touched a tender part of his heart. She never knew that he would very, very gently stroke her cheek or pull some stray strands of hair tenderly away from her face.

Marilyn loved him. And in his way, he loved her. Their union would not be typical, for sure, but Duncan thought it stood a better chance than he had with the scores of disappointing men he had dated in the past. Hell, he thought they even stood a better chance than many straight couples, what with the divorce rate reportedly running at 50 percent these days.

Still, he knew he should have run as far from Peter Dalrymple as possible the moment he laid eyes on him. Because in that moment he had known that Peter was a man with whom he could fall in love.

If circumstances were different.

But circumstances were *not* different. They were what they were.

"So," Peter asked, "everything look in order to you? Are you getting excited about the day?"

Duncan grinned at him and wondered how the smile made his face look, since it was so at odds with the confusion he felt. "Excited?" he asked.

"Well, yeah."

"I guess I am. Marilyn is a wonderful woman, isn't she?"

"She's an original, all right."

The two lapsed into silence, and Duncan knew he should stand and be on his way. Their business had been concluded, yet here they sat, neither of them making much of a motion to put an end to things.

Outside, the light had died and the room was illuminated by the soft glow of Peter's sole lamp on an end table.

Peter got up from the couch across from Duncan and went to sit at his side, close enough that their bodies touched. Duncan shivered and fought an urge to run in terror from the room, flee from the reality of the erection rising up in his pants simply from the nearness of this man.

Peter leaned forward and turned off the light, plunging the room into a murky half-light, gray, making things shadowy, but still visible. A gentle rain had begun outside and it tapped on the glass.

"You don't have to do this, you know," Peter said softly.

The words hung in the air, suspended, for several moments. Peter could have said just about anything—I killed a man once, I have three penises, I eat dead mice—and nothing would have shocked Duncan more than the simple statement he had just made. Duncan could actually visualize the words floating in the air before his eyes, turning and taunting, a hot neon touch to his fear.

Neither of them looked at the other and Duncan realized, with a kind of instinct, that the darkness Peter had brought into the room was there so it would be easier for Duncan to speak. This kind of thing was one of the attributes about Peter that Duncan loved—Peter seemed instinctively to "get" people. Along with his warmth, there was a caring, an empathy that set him apart from most others.

It, along with his pecs and his red-flecked beard, was very attractive.

"What do you mean?" Duncan finally asked, even though he knew—exactly—what Peter meant.

"I usually try not to counsel the people who come to me for planning. That's not my job." Finally he turned to Duncan and took his hand in his own, intertwining his fingers with Duncan's and squeezing. "But you're different." In the dim, Peter's eyes sought out Duncan's.

"Different how?"

"Well, there's the obvious. Most of the men who come in here are at least straight and most of them are having sex with their intendeds."

"I told you when we first met, that part wasn't what Marilyn and I are about."

Peter nodded, rubbing his beard. "I know. You're all about caring, companionship, supporting one another."

"All that happy horseshit?" Duncan asked.

"Not at all. Those things are too meaningful to put into words." Suddenly, Peter broke their connection by standing and walking to the window. He peered outside. Speaking to the glass, he said, "Don't think I haven't noticed."

Duncan laughed, higher and more nervous-sounding than he would have liked. He felt as though he had been caught with his hand in the cookie jar. The man-cookie jar. He felt like he had been outed on national TV. He knew precisely what Peter was talking about, yet a stubborn little part of him refused to admit it. "I don't know what you mean."

Peter turned toward him. "Yes, you do."

Duncan sat limply, staring at him, feeling like a trembling mound of want.

Peter came back, sat, and put an arm around Duncan. He lifted Duncan's chin so he could turn his face toward him. Duncan closed his eyes, waiting. And then it happened: Peter's lips were on his own. At first the kiss was gentle, like the misty rain falling outside. But then Peter pressed himself closer, his beard rubbing against the skin of Duncan's face, and pried his lips open with his tongue.

Almost involuntarily, as if he had been born to it, Duncan hungrily returned the kiss. He had wanted it for weeks, and both his soul and his body knew it. He reached up to grab the back of Peter's neck, mashing their faces and their mouths together, even though there was now no possibility of them getting any closer.

Everything disappeared around him, save for the feel of Peter's lips, his tongue, his body pressed hard against Duncan's. He wanted to rip off their clothes, fling them to the floor, and do everything his dreams and fantasies had been foretelling for the past several weeks.

But Peter pulled away. He stood and moved hurriedly back to reclaim his place at the window. "The rain's not too bad at all. Maybe you should go."

Were Peter's hands trembling?

"What?" Duncan didn't understand. This was crazy. Lunacy. Devilment. Was Peter simply teasing him? *This isn't fair*, he wanted to cry out.

But he stayed silent.

Peter said, "I want you to remember that kiss."

"Why? Because I'll need it to sustain me through the years with Marilyn?" Duncan clapped a hand over his mouth, stunned by the harsh truth of his own words.

"I hope not. I just want you to think about it. Think about what you're giving up."

When Peter turned to him, Duncan could see the man was hurting. There was a pained expression on his face. The furrowed brow and the compressed lips told a tale of unrequited longing.

But screw that. Duncan was angry. What was this guy trying to do? His pass had been inappropriate in so many ways, Duncan wondered if he could count them all. He felt a rush of emotions—confusion, lust, despair, remorse— and he stood as well, his breath coming faster. He wanted to pummel Peter with his fists.

He wanted to yank his pants down and take his cock in his mouth.

He wanted to slap Peter's face, spit on him.

He wanted to bend over the couch, pants around his ankles, and look over at Peter, on his face an invitation.

He wanted to get the hell out of there. He wasn't sure what would happen if he stayed one moment longer. He might kill the man. He might rape him. Only it wouldn't be rape, he was sure, because the old saw was true: you can't rape the willing.

Finally, Duncan reined himself in enough to know what to say. "I think our business with you is finished. If we still owe you any money, send me a bill, and I'll get a check right out to you."

Peter stared at him. "Is that what you really want?"

Duncan nodded, suddenly feeling the hot rush of tears pricking the corners of his eyes. "That's what I want." He sucked in a breath. Hoarsely, he whispered, "That's what I need."

He turned away, took the few steps that would bring him to Peter's office door. He rushed outside, paused, and then turned back, his body half in, half out of the doorway.

"I can't do this to Marilyn."

Duncan hurried away. He could hear Peter's voice behind him. "Think about what you *are* doing to her. Think about that!"

Duncan headed for the stairs and heard the sound of Peter's door closing softly.

Chapter Fourteen

"I don't know. Maybe I should get out of this business." Peter paced his living room, cell phone in hand. On the other end was Dad, across the country in Evanston. Peter had hurried home after his meeting with Duncan, his emotions in disarray, feeling as though everything he had ever believed about himself was wrong.

Shaken, he had walked the girls, fed them their suppers. They looked at him with mournful eyes, as though they sensed his inner turmoil.

"Why? Because you're falling for one of your clients?" His father very reasonably asked.

"Of course. It's unethical."

"Son, it's not like this is a pattern. It's not like you're mooning over some straight man who doesn't return your affection. This is about a gay man, who we both know is making a big mistake and who, from what you've told me, is just as attracted to you as you are to him." His dad sighed. "This is silly."

"I know! But he really cares for this woman he's engaged to—and he doesn't want to hurt her."

"And marrying her and divorcing her later isn't going to hurt? Because I will bet you dollars to doughnuts that's exactly what will happen."

Peter barked out a short laugh. "Dollars to doughnuts? You're starting to sound like Gram."

"Shit, Pete, I turn more and more into her every day. It's not pretty."

They shared a laugh and then Peter redirected the conversation to where it had started. "It doesn't matter, anyway. He told me today that our business was done and that he wouldn't need to see me again."

"Really?"

"Yeah."

"Why? Don't your clients usually want you there for the ceremony and overseeing the reception? I thought that was part of your deal."

"It is."

"Then why forego it?"

"Because I did a bad thing." Peter drew in a breath, and then told his father all about the passionate kisses that had erupted just a few hours ago, kisses that left him still feeling bruised with longing and regret, half hard at the memory, powerless to do anything about it. "Do you think I'm terrible?"

"Of course not. Your actions were maybe a tad bit unprofessional, and I'm positive you crossed some ethics line, but your intentions were good, even if I can't quite classify them as pure. But I think what you did was a kindness, if only he would have realized it."

Peter shook his head. He didn't know if he thought of what he had done as kindness or more of a wake-up call for Duncan. But weren't wake-up calls, in their way, a kindness, setting the person in question on the right path?

Oh, who was he to decide what the right path was for someone else? He felt things for this man, deep down, yet he didn't really know him well. And now it was over. Maybe that was for the best. Maybe Duncan's abrupt departure from his office was a wake-up call for *Peter*, letting him know that, this once, he should have stayed mute, stayed professional. Live and let live.

Live and let love.

In his mind's eye he saw Duncan, close-up and blurry, when he opened his own eyes as they kissed.

He wondered if the desire, the sense of lost opportunity, would ever leave him.

"I don't know," Peter said, returning to his mantra from earlier. "Maybe I just need to go out tonight and get drunk."

"Maybe you just need to go out and get laid."

"Dad!"

"Well, sometimes a little oblivion can work in our favor, you know? Like taking a painkiller to smooth out the rough edges of some trauma or sickness."

"You're a weird Dad. But I love you."

"I love you too, Peter. Call anytime. And go out and be restless tonight. Be a tomcat." His father laughed, his voice like a hug surrounding him.

"Thanks, Dad." They said their goodbyes and Peter disconnected.

The dogs looked up from their places on the couch, heads cocked. He chuckled. "Don't worry. I'm not going out tonight." Peter turned from them and headed into his yellow kitchen. The idea of getting drunk, or worse, laid, was anathema to him. There was only one person he wanted to *lay*, and anyone else, no matter how hot or how flexible, or how well-endowed, would simply not do.

One didn't settle for carrot sticks when one craved chocolate.

He pulled out his cutting board, Wusthöf santoku knife, and a wide frying pan, and set to work on dinner. He would bury his sorrow in food. He pulled a chicken breast from the refrigerator and set it to marinating in lime juice, smoked paprika, cumin, and coriander, and then went to work on shredding carrots, cabbage, and radishes. He would have a nice taco supper and with it, perhaps a glass or two of the soave he had chilling in the fridge, uncorked a couple of nights ago.

Hell, maybe he would have three glasses of wine, and follow Dad's advice to smooth out the edges. He deserved it. The wine and the full belly would lull him to sleep.

And then, he thought, knife poised above the cutting board, he would dream of Duncan.

He had dreamed of Duncan almost every night since he had first walked into his office.

What would it take to make that stop?

Peter shrugged and turned to the sound of a dog's nails clicking on the kitchen's terrazzo tile floors. It was just Daisy, the smallest of the pack, with her comical and endearing one-ear-up-and-one-down look, staring up at him with warm brown eyes.

"What? You heard I was making chicken?"

One ear stood more erect at the mention of the poultry.

"You mooch."

Daisy walked over to him and pushed her head against his leg. Peter put down the knife and squatted to scratch her behind her ears. "You always were the most sensitive of the pack. Thanks, Daisy." He hugged her before going back to making dinner for one.

Daisy sat beside him the entire time, watching. Peter knew she was most likely waiting for an errant piece of chicken to fall, but he liked to imagine she sensed his unhappiness and was staying close to comfort him.

Once the chicken was sizzling in the pan, he picked up the phone to call Duncan. He brought up his contact and remembered Duncan's face. He thought of calling to apologize, to tell him what he had done was not only out of character, but also out of line.

He kept the image of Duncan's face in his mind, that sweet face, and set the phone back on the counter.

He would not call. He had nothing to apologize for, nothing to explain.

He had done what he thought was right; and his intention, although selfish, was also benevolent—he hoped to stop a looming disaster from occurring.

And for that, he would not apologize.

Chapter Fifteen

The phone ringing on his nightstand woke Duncan from a sound sleep. He groaned into the darkness surrounding him. He turned, agitated by the ringing phone, forcing his bleary eyes to adjust to the alarm clock on his nightstand. Shit. It was only a little after four in the morning.

A rush of adrenaline coursed through him. Middle-of-the-night calls were never good news. He snatched the phone and looked down.

It was Scout. He chuckled, feeling a little relieved. His sister often forgot about the time difference. It was a little past seven in Pennsylvania. Scout had probably just gotten the kids off to school, poured herself a cup of coffee, and rang up little brother for a chat.

He pressed the screen to connect himself. "Hey hon. Do you realize what time it is on the West Coast?" He laughed, settling back against the pillows.

Scout said nothing. She didn't join him in laughter. He could hear her breath catching on the other end. A sniffle.

He sat upright, his anxiety throttled to full force, clutching at his gut like a physical thing. "What is it?"

Scout continued to stay silent, though Duncan could hear his sister struggling to speak.

"Is everyone okay?" Duncan asked.

"No," Scout finally managed to squeak out, her voice broken.

Silence again, which Duncan was wise enough not to rush in to fill with words, chatter. Something was very wrong, but he had to allow Scout the space to tell it.

If it hadn't been for the sound of her broken breathing, what sounded like sobbing, quiet and tortured, Duncan would have asked if his older sister was still there, so long did the silence continue.

"It's Bud," Scout finally managed to say.

Duncan saw his brother-in-law in his mind's eye and felt a rush of love—and worry. Bud was a big guy, a robust Irishman with green eyes, red hair, and a potbelly that shook when he laughed, which was all the time. He was one of the sweetest men you'd ever want to meet and totally devoted to his sister and Duncan's twin niece and nephew. The last time he was in Pennsylvania, Bud had shared a cigar with Duncan out in the garage, where Bud was working on rebuilding a vintage VW bug.

"Is he okay?" Duncan asked softly, bracing himself.

Scout sighed and the outrush of air sounded quivering, light, as though she could barely find enough air to put behind it. "No. He's dead."

Duncan felt as though the floor had dropped out from under him. His heart began beating too hard in his chest. He lay, unable to move, or even speak, for several moments. Surely, he had misheard his sister. Perhaps she said, "He's red" because, even though it was only May, he had gotten a sunburn. It was possible. Duncan had always teased him about his "fish-belly white" skin and his freckles. Bud would burn after a few minutes in the sun.

Sure, that was it. Bud was red. A sunburn. A bad one, maybe.

"Do you have aloe?" Duncan asked, hopefully, playing into his fantasy, trying to keep the horror of what he knew was true at bay.

"What?" Scout asked. "Did you hear me? Bud passed away last night. Car accident." His sister's usually deep voice came out high, choked. "Over on River Road. Some kid ran his pickup into Bud head-on, killing him instantly. The cops think the kid was trying to kill himself, aiming for a tree, but he was going so fast he lost control of his truck and hit Bud instead.

"I sent him out for milk. We didn't have any for cereal in the morning. He didn't want to go! He said the kids could have toast and coffee. I asked him what kind of breakfast was that for a child. He asked me what kind of breakfast was a bowl of processed sugar for a kid. I made him go. It was all my fault."

Duncan wanted to be there, wanted to take Scout in his arms. He felt so helpless, thousands of miles away. "Don't say that. That's ridiculous."

"Had it not been for me, Duncan, he would not have been out on that road last night, with a fucking gallon of milk on the seat beside him."

"You can't blame yourself."

"Yes I can. And I will. Because when I blame myself, I get mad. And when I get mad, I don't have to feel the pain." She cried for long minutes, and Duncan simply listened, wishing so, so much there was a magic machine that could transport him to Pennsylvania *now* so he could hold her, make it all better for her, as she had always done for him.

Yet he knew, even if he were her, there was nothing he could do to make it all better. All better, if it ever came, was so far down the road for his sister it was for all intents and purposes invisible.

A number of platitudes ran through Duncan's mind to say for comfort. "At least it was over fast. He didn't suffer." But he rejected that; he didn't know. Even if Bud had been "killed instantly" as Scout had said, no one would ever know what the poor man went through in that final instant. Duncan could fall back on something along the lines of the Lord working in mysterious ways, but he didn't believe in such platitudes himself. And his sister, he was pretty certain, would come back with "Fuck the Lord."

Yeah, fuck the Lord. What kind of God took a good man away from his wife and two kids, barely into puberty?

In the end, Duncan knew all he could say was this: "Sweetheart, I'm going to go now, but only so I can hop online and get the first flight out of Sea-Tac to Pittsburgh today. I'll call you back when I have a time and flight number."

"I'll pick you up," Scout said, sounding like a zombie.

"No, you won't. While I book a flight, why don't you call Jem? She should be with you. Does she know yet?"

"I called you first."

And Duncan's heart clenched. She called him first, even though their sister, Jem, lived a few blocks away from Scout. He needed to get home—and soon.

*

"I don't know what the fuck to put on him. He never wore anything but T-shirts and jeans!" Scout flung herself down next to Duncan on the bed she had once shared with her husband. She looked at him with moony eyes, begging silently for help. "The only suit he ever owned was the one he married me in. And he was about thirty pounds lighter back then, the little beanpole."

"Did he have a nice sweater?" Duncan wondered, thinking that maybe suits weren't an absolute must for men being buried.

"He had nice sweat*shirts*. Old Navy. Steelers. Hoodies, stuff like that."

Duncan lay back on the bed, exhausted after his cross-country flight, which even with his bereavement fare, still wiped out his bank account. He wanted to do nothing more than sleep. His nerves felt all jangly and raw.

But he needed to be here for Scout, who was putting up a brave front. Now, she seemed angry, as if she resented the task of putting together her husband's funeral.

Duncan recognized her attitude for what it was—denial. He would have to keep an eye on his sister for cracks in the façade and be ready when they started to appear. He had a feeling that would happen suddenly.

Scout held her head in her hands. Duncan heard her breathing hard. The kids were in the living room, and he could hear the TV going, soft voices, rises of music. He had greeted and hugged Keith and Keira when he came in and knew that whatever was on the TV, they weren't seeing much of it. Their glazed expressions and forced smiles told a tale of shock. Things had yet to sink in, and his heart went out to them. They were so young, too young, to lose such an important figure in their lives. Duncan knew it would leave an unfillable hole they would carry around with them forever.

Jem, his other sister, was due in a bit, but Scout wanted to get the clothes planning over before she arrived. Duncan knew it was because Jem was a control freak, and she would want to take over what Bud wore, from socks to shirt.

Duncan scooted next to Scout and slid his arm around her. His older sister had always seemed so strong to him, bigger than he was. Yet now she felt bony and insubstantial. There was something fragile beneath his fingertips that induced in him an urge to protect. He realized he had been a lot bigger than his big sis for many years, but had never fully taken in that fact until this very moment.

"You know what?" he said softly. "There's no law that says what you have to bury someone in. If Bud was a T-shirt and jeans kind of guy, then maybe you should consider burying him in his favorites—what he was comfortable in."

"Oh, what would Jem say? She's probably headed over here right now with a couple of Vince's suits in a bag. They were about the same size; Vince was—is—a little shorter, but I guess pant legs won't matter in a coffin. They'll cover him with a blanket or something, right?" His sister jumped from the bed and crossed the room to pick up an old bowling trophy of Bud's on the dresser. She turned it upside down, examining it as though she had no idea how it had gotten into the room. She put it down and directed her gaze at her brother. "This all just seems unreal."

"I know. So what do you think? Nice jeans? Favorite T-shirt?"

"Mom and Dad would never approve. And what would the rest of the family say?"

Their parents were headed north as they spoke, from their retirement condo in St. Petersburg, FL.

"It doesn't matter what anyone else thinks. How would Keira and Keith feel about their dad in T-shirt and jeans? Would they be cool with it?"

"Cool is exactly right. I know they'd appreciate seeing their Dad like he always looked." Scout sucked in her breath, suddenly. "Although it's not even gonna be close, no matter what we eventually put on him." She sat back down next to Duncan and grabbed his hands. "He was pretty banged up. But the funeral home said they could fix him up. Even then, they have this netting stuff they're putting over the casket."

Duncan shuddered at the reality of it.

"I had to have an open casket. For the kids. They needed to see their dad again." Scout bit her lower lip, eyes bright with tears she refused to shed.

Duncan put his arms around her, drawing her close.

She pushed him away, blew out a shaky sigh, and laughed. "So you really think T-shirt and jeans?"

Duncan nodded, trying hard to rein in his own tears. "If that's what you and the kids want, go with it. The hell with what everybody else thinks."

Scout smiled at him. "He'd like that." She pulled Duncan to herself and wrapped her arms tightly around him.

They didn't say another world until they heard Jem's bright "Yoo-hoo!" from the other room.

*

It was late evening. Duncan sat alone at last with Scout, on the screened-in porch at the back of the house. Bud had built the addition all by himself when they first bought the place some sixteen years before. Duncan recalled how the trees outside, two maples and a pine, were small when they moved in. Now, they towered over the little porch, making him feel as though he were sitting in a forest with his sister. The new spring leaves on the trees whispered to one another; there was the intermittent chirp of crickets, and the sound of rushing traffic over on the highway a few blocks west.

Duncan and Scout sat in the Adirondack chairs Bud had also made, blankets thrown over them. The night air was chilly; it was still early in the season, and although the day had been warm and sunny, belying the sad occasion, night brought with it a coolness that felt oddly comforting.

Bud was all around them. This little porch was his refuge. He had his TV out here, a couple of recliners, a little workstation with an old Dell laptop on it. In one corner was a minifridge stocked with his favorite local beer, Iron City. On the walls were framed prints of Bud, Scout, and the kids on camping trips, at the Pittsburgh Zoo, on a vacation to Sunset Beach, NC, and various holiday shots. Thankfully, Duncan could see these only in memory, since Scout had left the room dark when the two of them had come out here to sit, after the viewing at the funeral home was over and the kids had gone to bed.

Neither of them said much for a long time. Their hands were loosely linked across the space dividing their chairs and Duncan had the thought that, should strangers look in upon them, they would appear to be a long-married couple, sitting in contented silence.

"You were good tonight. Very strong," Duncan said.

"Ah, shit. You don't know what was going on inside. I felt like someone had taken something sharp and ripped everything in me to shreds. I wanted to scream; I wanted to cry, I wanted to fling myself on the coffin, but I had to think of Keira and Keith. This is tearing them both up inside."

"And it's tearing you up too. You just said. I'm sure your kids understand that their mama is hurting. No one's going to hold it against you if you're weak."

"I know. I know. It's just—weird. Two days ago, Bud and I were bickering about how much overtime he worked and I told him he could never get those hours back. Told him in a not nice way." Scout sighed. "Little did I know then how little time we had left. That's what makes it all seem so unreal. And that's maybe why I haven't yet been able to quite process that he's gone."

Duncan squeezed her hand.

"I mean, I was thinking about growing old together, watching the kids get married, bringing their first grandbabies home. You can't let all that stuff, all those dreams that everyone has, just vanish, can you?"

"I understand," Duncan wished there was something profound he could say, something that would remove the immense pain he knew his sister was quietly experiencing.

"But they *have* vanished. They're gone. And my life—my kids' lives—will never be the same."

"You had a good man."

"That's right. I did!"

Duncan heard Scout's voice go up and knew she was finally starting to cry. Duncan likened his sister's tears to the first patters of rain, when storm clouds have been massing all day, and the release was at last beginning.

"It's not fair. He was my rock. He made me laugh. In the bedroom, we were *still* a couple of kids, like horny teenagers. Maybe it didn't happen as often, but it seemed as though we could never get enough of each other when it did. We used to laugh about it." Scout looked over at Duncan through the darkness. Even in the dim, he could see the tears rolling down her cheeks—one after the other. "I know you don't want to hear about that! TMI!" She barked out a quick laugh, mixed in with her sobs.

"How can it all be gone, Duncan? I keep listening for the crunch of the gravel in the driveway, thinking he's going to pull up and honk the horn to let me know he's home. That never got old, you know. Whenever he came home, even after all these years, I still felt a little thrill, my heart beat a bit faster.

"I rolled over in bed last night and reached out for him and my hands came up empty. Can you imagine how that feels? We never spent a night apart! I don't know if I can do this." Scout drew in a crazy, strangled breath. "I keep telling myself I can. I have to. But I don't know if it's true!"

He listened as Scout sobbed. There was nothing he could say that would offer any kind of succor. Words, at a time like this, were just so much air, good intentions that could never be adequately expressed, because the loss was simply too great to be confined to any combination of letters from a very limited alphabet. So he stayed quiet, holding his sister's hand, something he wasn't sure he had ever done.

Suddenly, Scout snatched her hand away from him. Duncan looked over, surprised.

Scout stood up and he could see her sorrow morph into something else—rage. *Here it comes*, he thought, *she's going to rail against God now for taking Bud away from her, when they still had so much happiness, so many good years before them.*

But what she said shocked him, rendering him speechless, although for a different reason.

"You're an ass. You know that?"

"What?"

"You're a fucking ass." Scout spat the words and turned away from him to stare outside at the dark. A crescent moon peaked out from a bank of clouds, cloaking his sister in silver light.

"Honey, what are you talking about?" Duncan felt his mouth going dry, his heartbeat accelerating, and he didn't know why. Had he done something—or failed to do something—Scout had expected at the viewing tonight? Was he not being enough of a comfort?

But that wasn't what was making her breathing quicken or causing her to clench her fists. "I was going to hold my tongue. You're a smart man, I told myself, and you know best what's right for you. People have to make their own paths. But I can't, I just can't sit by and keep quiet. Not when I've known real love." She let out a hiccup of a sob.

"And *lost* love.

"You, little brother, are a self-delusional ass and I could just slap you for it." And she did. She walked over and casually slapped him across his face. Hard. It stung. Duncan brought his hand to his cheek and his mouth dropped open.

Duncan suddenly knew where this was going and how this rage was taking the place of his sister's grief, offering a weird bit of respite.

He tried to swallow, but he had no spit. He was afraid of what his sister was going to say.

All at once, he pictured Marilyn, sitting with her cat on Capitol Hill. He had forgotten to call her to let her know what had happened.

Even though he knew what this anger was all about, he asked anyway, "What are you talking about, Scout? Calm down. Come here and sit back down beside me. Let's talk."

"I don't want to sit down, not next to a brother who's an idiot!"

"Scout!"

"No, no let me finish." Scout paced back and forth, a hand to her forehead, as though she were struggling to find just the right words.

Finally, she stopped and stood before him. "What the *fuck* are you doing?"

"What do you mean?"

"Oh please! You know what I mean. Marrying this woman! This Marilyn! Why? Because you've been unlucky in love? Because maybe, just maybe, you think that by following your head instead of your heart, you can have what Bud and I did? A family?" She dropped to her knees and clutched Duncan's hands in her own. "You're lying to yourself, little brother. You're spinning out this cockeyed fantasy that's only going to hurt you—and *her*, whether she knows it or not."

Duncan felt weird inside—all giddy and sick at the same time. "I know what I'm doing," he whispered.

Scout shook her head. "Uh-uh. I'm not gonna let you say that. You *don't* know what you're doing. If you knew, you wouldn't do it."

Duncan stared off into the darkness. Was that a raccoon out there? Foraging by the trash cans?

Scout slid back into the chair beside him. She didn't look at him as she continued. "I know you didn't get lucky like I did. Bud and I met when we were teenagers. I didn't have the string of heartbreaks I've consoled you about over the years. But I want you to understand something—you can't force love. You can't make a family where there is no love, where there is no passion."

Scout laughed.

"What?" Duncan asked.

"Do you remember that line from *Steel Magnolias*? Oh, of course you do! Look at who I'm talkin' to!" Scout gave a little bark of laughter. "That girl Julia Roberts played, she said, at one point, something like, 'I'd rather have five minutes of wonderful, over a whole lifetime of nothin' special.'"

"I think it's thirty minutes," Duncan corrected.

Scout's head went down and she sobbed in earnest, her shoulders shaking, snuffling and pounding the arms of her chair every few minutes.

"What? What is it?" Duncan cried, his own tears starting to flow now, too, even though he would be hard-pressed to say just what the *hell* was going on.

Scout turned to him. "Don't you see?" she said through her tears, wiping at her eyes and nose with the back of her hand, trying to rein in her hiccupping sobs. "Don't you get it? Dumbass!"

"Stop it. Tell me." Duncan didn't really need to hear the words, because he could have said them for her, but something he didn't yet understand about himself compelled him to carry the charade out to its logical conclusion.

Scout managed to slowly pull herself together. When the tears had slowed to a trickle and her breathing was labored with only the occasional hitch, she said, "Because, by doing this sham of a marriage, you're settling for a lifetime of nothin' special." She shook her head. "And I can't stand to see you do it. Not when I am sitting here mourning my own true love.

"Little brother, you have to get out there and find that man. Find *your* Bud. Don't do this. Don't settle. Find your man." She stood, placing her hand under his chin so that their eyes met. "He's out there. You listen to Scout. You just need to find him."

They stared at one another for a few moments, and then she started toward the house. "I'm going to bed. All of this has taken it all out of me. I feel like I ran a marathon today. I'll see you in the morning."

Duncan watched his sister move through the darkness and enter the kitchen. He listened to the whisper of her footfalls as she made her way to the back of the house and the bedroom she had once shared with her man. He felt something tender inside clutch at him as he imagined Scout turning down the covers and climbing into bed alone.

"Find him?" Duncan asked the empty dark. "Find him? Maybe I already have."

Chapter Sixteen

Marilyn wondered what the hell was going on. She made her way down the rickety steps that led to Duncan's houseboat. For the last three days, she had called and called him and never got an answer. She had left a zillion voice mails. She had texted—over and over again. They were supposed to have dinner. They were supposed to meet with Peter to finalize wedding plans. He had promised to take her to PetSmart up on Aurora to get a new "kitty condo" for Mike.

But all that came back to her was silence, chilling her, and causing a trembling anxiety to rise up in her.

Now, on this so-chilly-it-felt-like-winter afternoon, Marilyn was determined to find out what was going on.

For better or worse.

She only hoped Duncan was not lying dead inside the houseboat, or his bloated drowned corpse was not hitting up against the dock leading to it. *Girl, you need to stop being so morbid.*

But she *was* worried. Duncan was one of the most responsible people she had ever met, and it was not like him to just vanish. She had even tried calling his school and had actually spoken to a woman in the office there, who told her they were not allowed to give out personal information about the teachers.

"Well, shit," Marilyn had said, and the woman on the other end gave a little gasp. "Can you at least tell me if he's still alive?"

"Far as I know. Can I help you with anything else?"

"Honey, you need to help yourself. Go out and track down Miss Patti LaBelle; maybe she can give you a new attitude," Marilyn snapped, just before hanging up.

Now she approached the houseboat with caution, anxiety coursing through her that felt almost electric. She had a key, but she wanted to make sure she wasn't intruding. It had crossed her mind that Duncan, with sudden frozen feet, had gone out and gotten himself a hot trick and was holed up in a haze of passion with some big-dicked Adonis, giving himself his own bachelor party.

She found that thought oddly titillating.

She peered into the windows as she made her way around the outer perimeter of the houseboat.

It was deserted. She was sure. The place was so tiny, really little more than a one-bedroom on the water. She could see into every empty room. Dishes were piled neatly in the drainer. The bed was made. A lamp next to the bed was illuminated, in spite of the fact that it was still daylight. This last fact told Marilyn that maybe Duncan had gone somewhere.

"But why would he go away and not tell *me*?" she wondered aloud. She dug in her oversized bag for her ring of keys and quickly located Duncan's with its green rubber identifier.

She didn't know if she'd find any answers inside, but she had to look. She entered and saw right away at least one answer: Duncan's iPhone sat on his kitchen table. He never went anywhere without it, which was disturbing and comforting at the same time. At least it explained why he hadn't called or answered her calls.

Still, couldn't he have called her from another phone? Wouldn't he have thought she might be concerned?

Marilyn paced the houseboat's small interior, looking for something missing, something out of place that might give her a clue to what had happened. Although she might say that the air felt a little stale, there was nothing else that informed her of anything awry. She opened his closet and saw the usual crowd of shirts, jackets, and pants, all bunched too closely together. Pair after pair of shoes lay in disarray on the floor, along with the stack of Catalina porn DVDs Duncan thought she wasn't aware of.

She checked his desk and saw nothing out of the ordinary—bills to be paid, a pair of glasses Duncan used solely for the computer, a notepad with a grocery list. She eyed his computer and even ran her fingers over its keyboard, but she was not yet ready to take her invasion of privacy to that level.

A footfall on the dock outside caused her to give a little scream and to jump from the desk chair. She turned just in time to see Duncan's familiar visage fill the window of the houseboat's door. Because of the light, Marilyn realized he couldn't see her, and for whatever reason, she slipped back into a shadow, holding her breath. *What's wrong with you? You have a very good reason for being here. What's next? You gonna hide under the bed? Try to slip out when he's not looking?* She imagined the scene, and it seemed like something out of a farce, and she began to giggle.

*

Duncan opened the door to Marilyn's laughter. The scene felt surreal, especially after the weekend he'd had, with all its tears, memories, and loss. He stood, door still open, staring at her, his leather duffel slung over his shoulder. He cocked his head. "What are you doing here?"

"I'm sorry. I hope you don't mind." Marilyn neared him, cautious, as though she were afraid. It was obvious she wasn't expecting him. He wondered if she had done this before.

"What were you laughing about?"

"Nothing important." Marilyn scratched at the back of her head and a blush rose to her cheeks. "Not to sound all June Cleaver, but where have you been? I was worried about you. I called. I texted. You didn't get back to me and it's been *days*, Duncan."

Duncan noticed the worry creasing her features. He closed his eyes, hot shame filling him. He should have called. He should have shared what had happened to him. It should have been automatic, given their relationship.

But, being honest with himself, he had to admit that he'd hardly thought of Marilyn over the past several days. It wasn't until he was on the flight home that he had given this wonderful woman some serious thought. But the days before? He could say he was preoccupied with the funeral, and comforting Scout, along with seeing Jem and his mom and dad, had crowded out thoughts of anything else.

But still... *Shouldn't it have occurred to you to call her*? He looked around the room, feeling caught, feeling heat rise to his face, born of embarrassment and an odd sort of confusion. And a stark realization confronted him, the words rising up like neon in his mind.

It says a lot that you didn't think of her. And none of it's good.

"I'm sorry," he mumbled, fearful of meeting her eyes. He cast a glance around his home, and his gaze lit upon his iPhone on the kitchen table. He hadn't given that piece of equipment much thought either. But he did consider, now, how it would give him at least a feeble excuse.

"There it is!" He stepped farther in, dropped his bag, and crossed the short space to scoop up his phone. "I've been wondering if I lost it. And it was here the whole time." He brought the screen up and saw that the battery was nearly completely discharged. He set it back down. "I would have called you, but I left this here."

Marilyn nodded and he could see that her features were ramping up with anger—her eyebrows coming closer together, her thick lips thinning into a straight, furious line. "And there were no phones where you were? That's why you couldn't call? You were—I don't know—on top of Mount Rainier for the past several days? Or maybe you were on top of *Mr.* Rainier the past several days and too busy to give your fiancée a second thought?"

"Oh, Marilyn, I'm so sorry. I was a jerk. I just didn't think." He sat on one of the little benches next to his kitchen table and invited her to join him. She did. When she was across from him, he said, "I was in Pennsylvania."

Marilyn nodded. "And?"

"And my brother-in-law, Bud, passed away. He was killed in a car wreck."

Marilyn's features morphed from indignation to concern in an instant. "Oh, my God! Scout's husband?"

Duncan nodded.

"Oh, that's terrible. I'm so sorry, Duncan. I can understand why you didn't call."

"No, there's really no excuse. I should have called."

"I'll give you a pass on this one." Marilyn smiled. "That's so awful."

Duncan had been in a fog of confusion all the way home, but he thought it was funny how sometimes life simply blew the fog away, revealing a path. He had wondered if he had a lot to think about, decisions to be made, how everything should be approached when he got back.

And now what he needed to do was there—clear—before him. He gnawed at his lower lip, feeling sad. He didn't want to hurt Marilyn, and yet there really was no other way.

He reached across the table and covered her hand with his own. Their eyes met, and they stared at each other for a moment. "You shouldn't give me a pass," he said quietly. "The fact that I didn't call was inexcusable."

Marilyn cocked her head, a small grin across her features. "Well, now that you mention it... Still, it's okay. Don't worry about it."

"No. No, you don't understand." Duncan looked out the window; all he could see were gray clouds and he had a fleeting thought of how they mirrored his mood. "It's not so much that I'm *sorry* I didn't call, although I certainly am, but it's more what it says about me, about us, that it never really occurred to me to do it." He couldn't look at her; he cast his gaze down to the floor.

When he looked up, he could see her eyes were bright with tears. Perhaps she sensed what was coming. Hell, maybe it had been coming all along, and both of them were simply too blind to see it.

"What does it say?" Marilyn's voice was different. It was soft, almost girlish, as though she were waiting for something, and that something was *not* good.

How could he blurt out the truth? That maybe she wasn't really an important enough part of his life to think to call her in his time of trauma? That maybe their relationship was really too new—that it was natural he hadn't thought of her, since she really didn't know his family, except for a few brief descriptions given in the most offhand way?

The truth of the matter was they liked each other a lot. Maybe even loved each other. But their friendship—and that's really the only term that applied—was too new, still at the laying-the-foundation stage, and it really might not have even been all that appropriate to share his grief with her.

Should that be what you're thinking of someone you're about to marry?

He couldn't say all that to Marilyn though. As nicely as he might be able to couch the words, their truth would sting, nonetheless. So in the end, maybe he just said the words that would also sting, but that might progress them toward something different and ultimately more meaningful.

"I don't think we should get married." He blew out a sigh and, yes, there was sadness, but an enormous sense of relief filled him. It made him feel guilty, sure, but it also endowed him with a sense of liberation.

He looked to Marilyn, expecting to see her lower lip extended, anticipating the tears gathering in her eyes.

But she was smiling. "Do you remember what I wrote to you? Way back when I sent that first email to you in response to your Craigslist ad?"

Duncan shook his head, not sure where this was going. He could remember her sassiness and how that made her response stand out, but he couldn't recall anything more specific than that.

"I said you were a fool. I said you had your head up your ass, if I'm remembering correctly. I said *it would never work.*" She stopped, staring at him, and still the smile had not left her face. Her eyes shone with tears, too, but she didn't look unhappy.

She moved around to Duncan's side of the table. "Scoot over." She nudged Duncan with her hip and sat close to him. She picked up his hand, interlacing her fingers with his. "I still think those things. And maybe I thought them all along."

"Oh, Marilyn, I'm so sorry." Duncan felt an uncomfortable lump forming in his throat.

She waved his apology away with her other hand. "No. No, don't be sorry." She kissed his cheek. "I may not have a fiancé anymore, but I made a good friend. And that means a lot. The sad truth is that I suspect good friends are an even rarer commodity in this world than husbands." She sniffed. "I think, all along, I knew, just like I said right from the start, this would never work. I was living in a fool's paradise. Thought I could have my handsome prince, even if I'd get none of this." She grabbed his crotch and gave it a quick squeeze, and then snorted out a burst of laughter. She sighed. "I think we both want the same thing—the whole package." She turned to him and grinned through the tears now rolling down her cheeks. "And by package, I am not talking about what I just grabbed."

"I know," Duncan said softly.

She reached up and grabbed his face, squeezing his cheeks and forcing him to look at her. "This wasn't a mistake, my sweet man. Us meeting was never a mistake. Don't you dare think that."

"I won't. I couldn't."

"In spite of the wedding being off, I still think you and I are in it until death does us part. In sickness and in health. For richer or poorer? Maybe, as long as you can still afford to buy me dinner at Dinette and several cocktails afterward." She stroked his cheek and lowered her hand. "I love you, Duncan. Marriage isn't the right set of clothes for us, but we're a damn good fit."

Duncan laughed. "How is it you manage to say all the wise words when I was the one who walked in here thinking I was going to end things? Thinking I was going to break your heart?"

"My heart *is* a little broken." She held up her forefinger and thumb, about a half inch apart. "A little bit. I dreamed about us being a family. I liked it in the morning when I would pretend to be asleep and you would touch me so gently, not wanting to wake me."

"You knew?"

"Of course. I'm a light sleeper. Always have been. But the guys I have managed to spend a night with here and there usually wake me up by poking their hard-ons into my butt or grabbing my tits. It was nice to be touched gently...and with such love."

"I do love you, Marilyn."

"Ah, you think I don't know that? That's why my heart is only broken a little bit. We're in this for the long haul, kid." She looked away, and Duncan could tell she was thinking. "Someday we'll both be married, and I bet you our spouses will be jealous of our relationship, because we'll always have a special bond."

Duncan realized she spoke the truth and could see the charm of it. It didn't mean they would have bad marriages someday, only that their relationship would always be unique and special, maybe *because* there would be no sexual chemistry and all the baggage that came along with it.

"I can always tell you everything, right?"

"You better."

"I think I may have fallen for someone."

Marilyn patted his hand. "I know, sweetie."

"You do?"

"I'm not blind."

They laughed and Duncan began to say, "He—"

Marilyn put a finger to his lips to shush him. "No. I don't want to hear about it right now. I'm still a silly girl who needs to lick her wounds. It's right, what we're doing now, but that doesn't mean it doesn't hurt—a dream deferred." She smiled sadly at him. "You know that poem? About the dream deferred?"

Duncan nodded.

"I think, sad as it is, we should let our dream dry up, like a raisin in the sun."

She stood. "I need to go home now. To Mike. To a few glasses of that nice Malbec I have put back for a special occasion. Maybe I'll stop and pick up some Fran's truffles on the way home." She laughed. "Or Ding Dongs."

Duncan didn't have any words, so he simply watched her, understanding her pain, but taking comfort in knowing he would see her again—and again—and again. But he knew she needed time to cope with her dream deferred. He knew because he needed time too.

She opened the door, then paused for a moment, her back to him. Then she turned around and said, "A girl's best friends when a handsome guy dumps her, are chocolate and red wine." She smiled at him and waved, and he knew she was unable to say any more.

And then she was gone.

Duncan lowered his head to the table and wept.

Chapter Seventeen

It wasn't until Marilyn had gotten up over the rise from Lake Union and onto West Lake Avenue that she pulled her phone out of her bag. She brought up her contacts and pressed the one to connect her to the person she needed to talk to.

She got his voice mail and, as she listened to his deep voice, debated whether she should leave a message. Even though her heart ached, there was a sense of something uplifting there too—a new liberation. She decided to leave a message because it was a lot easier than saying what she wanted to live. "Hey Ben! How you doin'? It's Marilyn." She paused. *Do you really want to do this?* She forced herself to say, in a rush, "I seem to find myself free this Friday night." She let out a brief snort of laughter, then said, "Actually every Friday night from now on, if you get my drift, and wondered if I couldn't ask you out on a proper date, since I am now a sexy single once more. Well, I've always been sexy—" The voice mail on the other end cut off with a beep. "Shit," Marilyn whispered and called Ben back.

"Call me," she said, and hung up.

She crossed West Lake and started up the rise of Dexter Avenue and burst into laughter.

*

Duncan allowed himself a good cry. The tears were from sadness and reality catching up to a silly, but earnest, dream. But they were also cathartic. In the back of his mind, he had always known what he was doing didn't make sense and was doomed.

He knew that breaking off the engagement to Marilyn set them both free to find their dream men. He also realized if they had gone through with the marriage they might have eventually ruined the very beautiful and harmonious friendship they'd built over the last few months. And that would have been a shame. But he could see how a gay/straight marriage, even one where both participants entered it with eyes wide open, could slide downhill pretty quickly into resentment and disillusionment.

No, he thought, getting up from the table and wiping his eyes with balled-up fists, this was the right choice; there was really no downside.

Duncan had two phone calls to make. The first he knew would have a positive outcome. The second he hoped and prayed would.

He called Scout first. He was optimistic that his news would shed at least a little light into her darkness. When they'd said goodbye at the airport, she had whispered in his ear, "Don't you dare do it." He had hurried from her car without looking back, stinging. He realized he would have a lot of thinking to do on the plane.

"Hey, Sis. How's things?"

"Oh peachy," Scout replied. "A lot more room in the closet for my clothes!"

Duncan expected her to sob, but she only laughed. He realized in that moment that Scout and Marilyn were a lot alike and his love for Marilyn was born from his adoration of his strong and resilient sister.

"Was that insensitive?" Scout wondered.

"Hey, *Reader's Digest* has always said, 'Laughter is the best medicine.'"

"Oh Lord," Scout cried. "You gonna quote *Reader's Digest* to me now?"

"No. But I know your remark was just your way of dealing with things. I know where you are and what you're going through. Part of the reason I called was to tell you I love you, that I'm here for you, and that I have some news I think you'll like."

"Oh God, you've listened to your sister? You're not going through with the insane plan to marry that gal, Marilyn?"

"Well, you just about stole all my thunder." Duncan chuckled. "You were right. And I think you just brought the truth up out of my subconscious. I knew all along."

"Sure you did," Scout said. "God forbid you should give your wise big sister any credit."

"Oh now, don't be that way." Duncan didn't say anything for a long while. What he wanted to say next could throw them back into another crying fest, and he didn't want to do that. His tear ducts were dry and stinging. He could at least go one night without tears, couldn't he? He drew in a breath and said what he wanted to say quickly, as though speed would lessen its emotional impact. "You want credit? Well, I can tell you this: it wasn't so much what you said that sunk home to me that marrying a woman wasn't a smart idea, but it was the life you had with Bud that really got your point across. I always knew you two were stupid in love with each other and seeing you with the kids, standing there at his casket in the funeral home saying goodbye...well, I knew then that the magic of true love can't be forced. Not with logic.

Not with good planning. Hell, not even with common sense. It's what I said—magic. And I know you had that with Bud.

"I want it too."

"Of course you do," Scout said softly. He couldn't hear any sobs, but he knew there were tears coursing down her cheeks, even if that hadn't been his intention. He had some on his own face again too. His eyes burned.

"I won't say you'll be okay. But Bud will always be with you. And you can always take comfort in the fact that you and Keira and Keith gave him a very happy and fulfilled life, even if it was cut short."

"Damn right. He was lucky to have me."

"Damn right." Duncan brushed the tears away and tried to smile. "Listen, I should go. But you take care—of yourself and those babies. And you call me—every day, okay? I want to know how you're doing."

"We'll see," Scout said, laughing. "No. Thanks, Duncan. Talk soon. Love you. 'Bye."

They hung up. Duncan's next call induced in him an almost trembling anxiety. What if this next call resulted in another disaster for him, yet another disaster in a long line of them in what he called his "love life"?

"Well, buddy, nothing ventured, nothing gained." He brought up his next contact and touched the screen to connect.

*

Peter had just finished bringing the dogs in from a long walk through Volunteer Park. They were happy, contented, and worn out. All three of them curled up on the couch as he gazed at them, almost resenting their togetherness and closeness.

Why couldn't he have a little of what they had? He realized he did, in a way, because he was part of the pack. But dogs, wonderful as they were, did not make for a life complete.

He sat in the easy chair next to the couch and picked up the remote. He had gone through his HBO channels and his DVR list and thought he'd spend the night in front of the TV, counting himself lucky if he made it through the first of them without falling asleep.

Just as he pressed play on *Pitch Perfect*, looking forward to a few laughs and a lighthearted movie to ease the sadness he had been feeling since Duncan Taylor walked out of his life, presumably for good, the phone rang.

He picked it up and glanced at the screen.

Duncan.

His heart lifted and a smile spread across his features. He couldn't help it.

"Hey, Duncan," he answered.

"Hi Peter. I hope I'm not interrupting your evening, calling after work hours and all."

"Not at all. Your timing is perfect. I was just about to start watching a movie I had recorded."

Duncan was quiet for a while, and Peter wondered why he had called. After all, the last time he had seen him, he had said they were through, both professionally and, Peter had to presume, personally.

To break the silence, Peter asked, "So what can I do for you? Everything okay with the wedding plans?"

More silence and then Duncan said, "Actually, that's what I wanted to talk to you about."

"Oh?"

"Yeah. It's a long story, and one I hope to share with you sometime, but I guess you could say I came to my senses."

Peter's heart lifted a bit. "Yeah? How's that?"

"Marilyn and I have decided not to get married after all."

Peter didn't want to rejoice, or at least didn't want his happiness at the news to show. He didn't know why Duncan had "come to his senses" but maybe what he hadn't said was that it was Marilyn who had reached that point and she dumped him.

"Oh, I'm sorry to hear that. Is everything okay between you two?"

"Don't be sorry. It's the right choice and maybe one I've known all along. I just needed to have the veil lifted from my eyes, so to speak."

Peter nodded and then, because he knew Duncan couldn't see him nodding, said, "Okay."

"As I said, I'll tell you all about it, just not right now. Right now, I wanted to let you know professionally that the wedding is off and tomorrow you should go about canceling all those plans you made for us."

"I'll get on the phone just as soon as I get in."

"And if there are any fees—as I'm sure there will be—just let me know what they are, and I'll take care of them."

"Don't worry about that," Peter said. "What? You think I'd pay them?" Peter laughed.

"Of course not. And if you have any further charges you need to make to do the 'tear down,' so to speak, you just let me know. I'll gladly pay you. It's only fair."

Peter didn't say anything and his heart sank a little. So this was why he was calling? For professional reasons? *Well, of course, Peter. Why should you expect anything more?*

"Is there anything else?" Peter asked, trying not to sound too hopeful.

"Well, yeah." Duncan went silent for a few moments, and Peter wondered if he was gearing up to say something significant. Maybe something along the lines of "Thank you for all you've done for us, and I wish you well in the future."

But what Duncan said was "Um, Peter, I don't think either of us can deny there's been, um, a certain attraction between us."

Peter chuckled. "I'd be the last person to deny that. And, don't take this the wrong way, but I'd be lying if I didn't say there was a little glee on my part when you told me your news."

Duncan went on. "Anyway, I'm wondering if you might want to explore that a bit more." Duncan laughed nervously and blurted, "That kiss was *hot*!"

They both laughed this time. "Yes, yes it was," Peter said.

"Maybe that tells us something," Duncan said, and Peter thought it was cute how nervous he sounded. His spirits rose again because he realized now that Duncan was probably calling not just to cancel the wedding plans but also to ask him out.

"I want to explore it more too," Peter said. "What should we do about it?"

"Dinner this Friday? Maybe we could head down to the International District and find some good Vietnamese? You like Vietnamese?"

"I love it," Peter said, catching a glimpse of himself in the mirror above the fireplace. He was beaming, grinning from the proverbial ear to ear. "What time?"

"You say."

"Seven?"

"Can we make it six? I get off from school, and I can't wait that long to eat. I have voracious appetites."

"I think that bodes well for this Friday night."

"I bet it does. Should I pick you up?"

"You know where I am?" Without waiting for an answer, Peter told him his address.

"I'll see you on Friday, then," Duncan said.

"I can't wait."

"Neither can I. Bye."

They hung up. Peter turned to the dogs, who had raised their heads as one and were now staring at him. Daisy had her head cocked. It was almost like they knew what had just transpired.

He told them anyway. "Guess what, girls? Your daddy has a date!"

They weren't impressed. All three lowered their heads, curling back into sleep. One farted.

"Well, gee," Peter said. "Is it asking too much for you to be happy for me? Or is the jealousy already setting in?"

The dogs stayed mute.

Peter crossed the room to sit on the floor next to them, his back against the couch. He started up the movie and under the opening credits, he told the girls, "Don't worry. He's gonna love you just as much as I do."

He thought about calling his dad but decided against it. In spite of his joy at this recent turn of events and his dour mood being turned on its head with a single phone call from a sexy man, Peter had had his share of false starts in the romance department. Well, probably more than his fair share.

He thought it would be prudent to wait until after Friday to call Dad. Then, maybe he'd have a little better clue if Duncan Taylor was a false start or a new beginning.

He didn't credit psychics or foretelling the future, but he had a strong inkling it would be the latter.

Chapter Eighteen

"Would you mind if we didn't go out?" Peter opened the door wider to admit Duncan. He drank in the sight of Duncan like a man lost in the desert who had just seen an oasis. Duncan looked somehow bigger outside the confines of his office. Bigger and a whole lot better.

Tonight, Duncan was clad as many Seattle men would be when the rain was pouring down: a pair of old jeans, worn thin and faded in all the right places—Peter wondered if he qualified as a lecher as he took in the eye-catching and hard-on-inducing basket, where the denim was worn so thin Peter wondered if Duncan had taken a rasp to the jeans—a purple University of Washington hooded sweatshirt, and a pair of sandals beneath which was the ubiquitous pair of white athletic socks. Peter couldn't help but snicker as he stared down at the socks.

"What's funny?" Duncan asked, following him inside.

"Nothing. You a Seattle native?"

"No. I grew up in small-town Pennsylvania, just outside Pittsburgh. Why do you ask?"

"Never mind," Peter blew out a puff of air and made sure his face wore its most welcoming grin. He was trying to remember what his agenda was here, what he had asked as he had opened the door to this hunk of tall, dark, and handsome. Who was it who said there was no such thing as a great dark man? Peter couldn't remember, but he suddenly felt the line was pretentious and had no connection to reality because his (he hoped) great dark man stood right here before him, rainwater dripping down from his great dark hair, making his great dark skin look oh-so-touchable and soft.

Peter's mind had gone blank, and all he could do was back up farther as Duncan entered his apartment. It was weird having him here, as if some fantasy man had been breathed into life and deposited at his front door.

It was Butterfly who jarred him out of his reverie. She made him realize he probably appeared to Duncan like a man who had not only lost the power of speech, but the power of thought. Through the lens of Duncan's eyes, he most likely looked like some hungry, drooling pervert intent on raping him.

Peter had to admit to himself that the assessment was not that far off base. But his dad had taught him some manners.

Butterfly came up to Duncan and thrust her blunt nose into his crotch, sniffing intently.

The blush that rose to Duncan's cheeks only made him look that much more fetching. "I hope she's not gonna bite off my junk."

"Butterfly! Behave!" Peter said in a loud, commanding voice. The dog slinked away. "She better not. I have some ideas for that junk." Peter raised his eyebrows and grinned.

Duncan laughed. "Well, aren't you the forward one? And the confident one too."

Peter shrugged. "Optimistic is more like it. I'm the guy for whom the phrase 'hope springs eternal' was written."

Duncan looked around the apartment. "Nice. I like it here. It feels homey and comfortable."

"A combination of thrift store finds coming together with the charm of a vintage building. Either it works or it just looks cheap."

Duncan stepped closer to Peter and touched his chin. "You look a little cheap," he said hoarsely. "Your home is sweet." He gulped in another view. "It's the kind of place just made for long, rainy afternoons with a good book, Saturday naps, and meatloaf or beef stew suppers. It's the kind of place I suspect people picture when they think of the word 'home,' regardless of what kind of home is actually in their own histories."

Peter was aware they were standing less than a foot apart, and the closeness of Duncan and the heat radiating off his body was inducing in him once more that temporary amnesia, that inability to coordinate tongue and brain to form words. Perhaps it was because all the blood that kept his brain working under normal conditions had abandoned ship and headed south. The words that finally tumbled from his mouth were born of simple need. "If I don't kiss you right now, I think I'll die. Literally. I think my heart will simply stop."

Duncan's green eyes stared for a moment into his own. "Well, in that case, you better kiss me." And he closed his eyes. His lips were moist, parted, waiting.

The kiss lasted forever, so long that the dogs, feeling left out and miffed at not being properly introduced, began to whine and pace about the apartment.

Peter barely heard them. He was too busy savoring Duncan, something he knew he wanted to do since the moment he first laid eyes on him. The kiss in his office a few weeks before had been merely an appetizer. This was the main course.

Peter tasted rainwater, something herbal, like basil, and something else he couldn't describe, something elemental found only on Duncan's lips, his tongue, his inner mouth. He mashed his mouth harder against Duncan's, feeling his dark stubble pressing against his skin. He brought his hand up to the back of Duncan's neck to draw him even closer, if that was even a possibility.

He felt almost as though he were floating. It was like the two of them were merging into one being, and that was just fine with Peter. Butterfly and her damn probing nose burst the bubble when she stuck that nose into Peter's ass. Peter at last broke the kiss and whirled to look down on the all-black dog, who returned his gaze with utter and complete innocence.

"Demon," Peter whispered, breathless. He felt as though he had just come back to earth and the landing was not an easy one. He looked back at Duncan, who he was pleased to find looked as flushed and breathless as Peter himself felt.

Duncan said, "When I came in the door, you asked if I would mind if we didn't go out."

"Oh yeah. I did say that, didn't I?" It all came back. He had thought, what with the rainy, cooler-than-average weather, it might be nicer if he cooked for Duncan, rather than heading to the International District, as they had planned. He thought a night at home—a little wine, a little beef stew, some nice music—would be preferable to hoofing it around the ID, the rain pattering down on them, the chill seeping beneath their clothes. A quiet dinner at home would be the antithesis of that experience.

He then remembered he had a nice chuck roast just about finished in his slow cooker on the kitchen counter. The aromas, which had always been there, suddenly alerted him to the fact that he had made dinner for the two of them. There was the smell of beef, underneath which were the aromas of a cabernet sauvignon, tarragon, and garlic. Peter had thrown onions, carrots, and potatoes in the pot.

He looked back at Duncan and shrugged. "I went ahead and made a meal for us, since it was raining so hard out there. We don't have to stay in if you really had your heart set on dim sum or pad Thai, but I thought it might be nice. I can eat what I made myself later, take it to work."

"It smells wonderful." Duncan cocked his head, grinning. "Do you think we'll get much eating done?"

Peter liked the question, to which he thought the only logical response was "If we build up the proper appetite."

Should he be forward? Should he grab Duncan by the front of his sweatshirt, pull him into the bedroom, and begin ripping off his clothes? Once the clothes were off, should he drop to his knees in supplication before Duncan and tease the head of his cock with his tongue, dipping the point of it into Duncan's piss slit to taste the precum surely building up there? Should he pause to savor the clear nectar, swirling it around in his mouth like a wine taster, but never, oh never, spitting it out, only letting it slide down his throat like the finest Pacific oyster? Should he then form a tight ring around the corona of Duncan's cock and slide down on it, ever so slowly, so that the man felt he was being embraced by the world's wettest, hottest, and tightest grip? Should he proceed to bob up and down, tongue swirling, teeth so gently nibbling, building the rhythm until he felt a trembling in Duncan's spread and hairy thighs? Should he pause only then to pull away and look up at the ecstasy he had wrought on his lover's face?

Should he slide his head between Duncan's thighs to take his furry balls into his mouth one at a time?

Should he, when Duncan's breathing indicated he was begging for release, lean back on the floor and, eyes never disengaging with Duncan's, slowly strip from his body every inch of clothing he had on? Should he save the black Papi briefs he had worn in oh-so-naughty anticipation for last? Should he pull them down and away slowly so his hard cock popped out at last, rising up to slap against his own belly?

Should he spread his legs in a kind of welcome, grabbing his ankles, so his hole would be an obvious target? Should be breathe harder as Duncan sank to his knees between his spread thighs and made to insert his precum-dripping, hard-as-concrete cock between his ass cheeks? Should he scoot forward on the floor to gobble up that cock with his ass?

Oh, God, yes. He should.

Peter felt faint. He sat down suddenly on the floor, and Duncan grinned down at him, as though he knew the thoughts that had been coursing through his head, as if he knew how those thoughts morphed into blood, lengthening, thickening, and hardening Peter's cock beyond dimensions he even thought possible. It was as though Duncan read his mind.

*

Duncan had no idea what was going through Peter's head. He wondered if he needed some kind of medical intervention, sitting on the floor before him as if dizziness had taken hold so completely his legs could no longer support him.

He had never seen Peter like this. The Peter he knew, from his visits to the wedding-planning office, was professional and organized, in control. Sure, he had a kind of light, easygoing touch, was maybe a bit quirky in his clothing choices, yet he never acted like this.

"Are you okay?" Duncan asked, squatting down beside Peter. He touched the back of his hand to Peter's forehead. "You don't feel warm."

"Yet I'm burning up." Peter looked up at Duncan with eyes that Duncan could only describe as "pleading."

"You are?"

Peter drew in a deep breath and then grinned sheepishly up at Duncan. It was, almost instantly, as though he emerged from a trance. He laughed and took in several deep breaths. Slowly, he got to his feet. When Duncan held out a hand to help him up, he motioned it away.

"If I even touch you, I don't know what'll happen," Peter said. "I may spontaneously combust." He laughed.

"Okay," Duncan responded, his head cocked in wonder. "I think it's a good idea if we stay in for dinner."

"Right." Peter's laugh was sheepish. "I'll get us some wine. Some of the same cab I used in the stew, okay? It's a nice one, from western Washington. Very blackberry-y. Is that a word?" Peter scratched his head.

"I get your meaning." Duncan nodded. "That sounds great."

Peter backed away from him, and then hurried into the kitchen. Duncan could hear glasses being taken down from a cabinet, the muted pop of a bottle being uncorked, the *glug-glug-glug* of wine being poured into glasses. He could already taste the notes of blackberry in the deep red wine. Peter called from the kitchen, "Why don't you put some music on? The hi-fi is in the corner by the window."

"Hi-fi? Seriously? What is this? An episode of *Mad Men*?" Duncan turned and moved toward the window, beneath which was an old console stereo, the likes of which he hadn't seen since he was a little boy and his mom and dad had a similar model in their living room. It was a relic even then.

"I'm old school," Peter yelled out to him. "There are records in the compartment underneath the turntable."

Duncan moved to the console and squatted. He slid aside a maple wood-grain panel to reveal a row of albums neatly organized alphabetically. He noticed one of his favorites, Oscar Peterson, and found several selections. "Oh! You have the *Paris Concert*!"

"One of my faves. Put it on! Put it on!"

"Are you sure you don't mean put it in! Put it in!"

"Later, Tiger!" Peter yelled from the kitchen.

Duncan had to look at the turntable controls to refamiliarize himself with how it worked. Once he thought he had it, he slid the record from its sleeve and watched as the record slid down to the turntable and the arm moved automatically over to land on the black vinyl. There were a few scratches and pops and then the music began. Duncan closed his eyes in rapture as the first song on the disc began, "Please Don't Talk About Me When I'm Gone." It was a great song, but he knew there was one further along that would even more perfectly suit the mood of the evening. He snatched the arm up off the vinyl, eliciting a groan from Peter in the kitchen and a cry of "Don't pull it out!" that made Duncan roll his eyes.

He counted the grooves and replaced the needle on the twelfth song, "Lover Man (Oh Where Can You Be?)". Its smoky plaintiveness brought a lump to Duncan's throat. He stood and switched out the lights, harkening back to Peter's darkened office not so very long ago.

"Would you get out here?" Duncan called. "I want you to dance with me."

Peter hurried in to join him, bearing two balloon wine glasses, filled with dark-red liquid. Grayish light spilled into the room from outside and Duncan thought of them suddenly as two characters in some black-and-white movie from the 1960s.

Peter set the glasses on the table and came to Duncan. Duncan wrapped him in his arms and pulled him close. They began making slow progress around the living room, and their feet tangled together. They tried to move in smaller circles. Duncan tripped. Peter laughed.

And then they were kissing and everything, the pale light, the piano music, the sound of one of the dogs snoring, vanished as Duncan became aware of only Peter's body pressed against his own. He would swear he could feel the beat of Peter's heart against his chest. He didn't think there was an inch of free space between them anywhere. He took in the smell of Peter's hair (clean), and the aromas wafting from his skin, which were a combination of sweat, garlic, onions, and red wine. Cataloging the scents in his mind, Duncan thought they sounded gross, and yet he couldn't imagine anything more delicious.

Peter's red beard rested against his own cheek, scratchy, yet impossibly soft. He wanted to fall asleep on that beard.

Peter kissed his ear softly, flicking his tongue inside and then licking his lobe, finally surrounding it with his tongue. The attention was making Duncan's knees weak. He growled, "I swear to God, you keep that up and I am going to come in my pants."

Peter chuckled, his breath hot in Duncan's ear. He whispered, "That would be such a waste. I can think of far better places for it to land than a field of cotton. Should we go into the bedroom? I put clean sheets on the bed."

"Seducer! You are so cocky," Duncan said.

"It's on account of my big cock," Peter said. "Wanna see it?"

And Duncan paused, the erection in his pants throbbing, his blood pressure somewhere in the stratosphere, his breath coming like a dog's on a hot summer day. He just stopped. He pulled back. Although he wanted nothing more than to follow Peter into the bedroom, to rip off his clothes and do whatever popped into his head to do (several times), he knew one thing that marked the past few decades of having men in his life (or as Mae West might say, life in his men) was the consistent action of jumping into bed with all of them at the first opportunity. Now, while he could not deny that such jumping (and hopping, and thrusting, and rubbing) was fun, he wondered if it said something about why he was still alone at almost age forty.

He and Peter had really only had a few times together. And even though there was nowhere else Duncan would rather be *right now*, he wondered suddenly, through the fog of lust and the throbbing of his cock, if maybe it wouldn't be wise to slow things down a bit.

Tucker, his last disastrous sojourn into the waters of love, had been at first a hook-up culled from the Adam4Adam website. They had spotted each other online, chatted briefly, and ended up in bed. It was only after they had each come a couple of times they had exchanged names.

He didn't want Peter to be another Tucker, or another Matt, or Tim, or Ron, or Christian. He wanted Peter to be more. He knew he could fall in love with him, if he hadn't already.

So, firmly but gently, he put his hand against Peter's chest and pushed him back. Peter's face darkened in confusion, and he took a couple of awkward steps back. His mouth opened in surprise.

"What's the matter?" Peter asked.

"Nothing at all. Would it surprise you if I said I wanted to wait? That I think we might have the beginnings of something special here?"

"How old-fashioned. It's sweet."

"Are you making fun of me?"

Peter moved closer, kissing Duncan tenderly on the cheek. "Not at all. I respect it." He stepped back and Duncan noticed the furtive grope Peter gave himself and saw how his khakis tented out in front. He smiled.

Peter turned to head toward the kitchen. "I need to get dinner ready. If I don't remove myself from you, I won't be held responsible for my actions. You rip all the sense clean out of my brain, mister. You make all the blood in my body flow to one place," he snorted. "So I am going to finish up with dinner." He veered near the door, where the dogs' leashes hung on a hook. Peter pulled them down and held them out to Duncan. "And *you* are going to take the girls for a walk. Volunteer Park is just a couple of blocks over, and if you take them there, I swear they will love you forever. And that's a prerequisite for any man in my life. Hold on tight, though, if they spot a squirrel. You may get your arms ripped out of their sockets, but you will save a squirrel's life."

Duncan took the tangle of leashes and harnesses from Peter's hand. He squatted to begin putting them on the girls, who knew what was up. They were already circling him excitedly, whimpering and barking.

"You sure you trust me with them?" Duncan asked, once he had the dogs tethered and clawing at the door.

"I trust you implicitly."

"And yet you hardly know me."

"I know you well enough to trust you. And really, what is trust other than faith in a clever disguise? And trusting you with these gals? Honey, there's no better way I could say I care about you." Peter smiled and looked down at the dogs. "These dogs are my heart."

"I'll keep them—and it—safe."

"I know you will. Now, scram!" Peter opened the door and, whether he wanted to or not, Duncan was tugged by the pull of three pit bull mixes right out the door and down the stairs.

The rain had abated to a fine mist. Duncan recalled a poem he'd once read comparing a misty rain to being kissed, and the thought made him smile. Outside, dusk was approaching through the gray clouds. Shafts of golden light illuminated the droplets of mist as though they were dancing in the slight breeze.

The air felt cool and refreshing over the heats-of-many-sorts inside Peter's apartment. He noticed how the trees were greening. Before he knew it, summer would be here.

Where would he be? With Peter? Alone? It seemed like only minutes ago he had envisioned a weeklong trip back east with his new bride, the saucy Marilyn, in tow. The thought made him winsome, a little sad. Even though he knew a marriage between them was the wrong thing to do, he still loved her and wanted her in his life—always. Wasn't that the kind of desire that brought two people together in holy matrimony?

The dogs charged forward, gleeful to be outside, their olfactory senses in overdrive with the smells of pine, fresh-cut grass, and who knew what else.

Duncan was not having second thoughts about Marilyn, but that didn't mean he couldn't long for her, couldn't feel the lonely pull of regret over what might have been, no matter how delusional the plan was.

He sat on the steps outside the Asian Art Museum. Before him was a view of the Space Needle through a circular sculpture. All three of the dogs looked back at him, as if to say, "Hey, what are you stopping for? Whose walk is this, anyway? Yours? Think again, buddy."

But when their looks didn't rouse him from his seat on the damp steps, they too settled down on their haunches, staring forward, waiting. Perhaps, Duncan thought, they were also admiring the view.

He pulled his phone out of his pocket and without thinking much about it, called Marilyn.

She answered after three rings. "Hey stranger."

She didn't sound sad; she sounded the same: cheerful, maybe a little cocky. Duncan grinned.

"What are you doing?"

"Got my hair up in pink foam rollers and am just stuffing cotton between my toenails in preparation for painting them. I have a wicked shade of red called Cherries in the Snow that's bananas."

"Foam rollers? Do they still make those?"

"I don't know! I'm kidding, at least about that. I *am* painting my nails though."

"Bored?"

"What? You think I'm sitting over here pining for you? Working my way through a box of Fran's salted caramel truffles? Maybe watching *Stella Dallas*? The Stanwyck version, not the Midler."

"Uh, no. I just wondered how you were doing. I was thinking about you." Duncan looked off into the distance; the golden light had vanished, forced away by a bank of clouds that looked heavy with rain. He and the dogs would be getting wet very soon. "I miss you," he said softly.

"Aw, sweetie, I miss you too. Can we do dinner next week?"

"Sure." He shifted, considering letting the dogs run free for a few minutes and then thought better of it. "Everything okay?"

Marilyn said nothing for several moments. "I have news," she said, her voice teasing.

"Really?"

"You won't be mad at me for completely rebounding off you, like you're some sort of trampoline?"

Duncan chuckled, rolling his eyes. "A manpoline. No, I won't be mad." He grinned. He knew what Marilyn was about to tell him, but wouldn't take away the joy he knew she would take in the telling, so he waited.

"I'm getting ready for a date. Me, Marilyn Samples, an honest-to-goodness, no Dutch treat, pick-me-up-in-his-car date." She giggled, sounding girlish for a change. "I got a man coming for me." She paused. "That sounds dirty doesn't it?"

"Delightfully so. I hope you do. Later."

They both laughed into the phone.

"Who's the lucky guy?" Duncan already knew. He'd known when he first introduced them at Dinette. That dinner seemed so long ago. It had been when Marilyn had proposed to him. How much had changed!

"It's Ben! Ben McBride. Can you imagine? Can you believe he's interested in pleasingly plump, quirky old me? I mean, come on, his last girlfriend looked like Heidi Klum. I better grab hold tight before he realizes what a dud I am! I am not worthy!" Marilyn laughed.

"Listen to yourself," Duncan chided. "You're beautiful, Marilyn. Inside and out. Don't you know that?"

"Honey, all I know is what I see in the mirror—over the hill and overweight."

Duncan shook his head. "I don't think Mr. McBride sees the same things. I suspect he sees a voluptuous, confident woman whose sense of self is so strong it exudes this funky kind of sex appeal."

"Oh what you do you know? You're just a big old homo!" Marilyn cried.

"You know what I think, Marilyn? We gay guys can actually appreciate, truly appreciate, beauty in a woman, even more than our straight brothers. We don't have any of the sex stuff mixed in, so our appreciation is more pure."

"Ah, what a lot of hooey," Marilyn said, but he could tell from her tone that what he had just said pleased her very much.

"Well, it's my theory and I'm sticking to it."

They were quiet. The dogs were up now, tugging rudely to let him know they wanted to continue with their walk. Duncan considered telling Marilyn where he was and what he was doing, but decided it could wait.

"You guys have a good time tonight. And you make sure he treats you like the lady you are."

"Fuck that. I want him to honor my inner tramp." She snorted. "I have no problem putting out after dinner. Honey, I want a big old man blanket to cover me tonight!"

"May all your dreams come true, sweetheart."

He was just about to hang up when Marilyn said softly, "You know I love you, don't you?"

Duncan nodded and whispered, "Yeah. Me too."

"No matter what, you always have a special place in my heart."

Duncan was a little choked up, so all he could manage in return was, "Likewise."

They were quiet for a moment, and then Duncan thought of something. "Those words sound like goodbyes."

"They are," Marilyn responded. "The good thing is they're hellos too."

"Hello," Duncan said.

"Hello," Marilyn replied.

And they hung up. Duncan started off with the dogs knowing that everything would be all right.

*

Peter hurried to finish up with the table setting when he heard their footsteps on the wooden stairs outside. The dogs were not running, which was a good sign; it meant they were tuckered out.

His prediction came true when Duncan opened the door and the dogs sauntered in ahead of him. They allowed themselves to be unleashed, then wandered into the living room and hopped onto the couch, taking up their customary spots. It took only minutes before a chorus of snores rang out.

"You done good," Peter said. "It takes a lot to wear that powerhouse out." *And it would take a lot to wear me out*, Peter thought winsomely. He had decided, while Duncan was out, to slow things down, to rein in his lustful impulses if he could. He may have been coming on a bit too strong earlier. *A bit?* Peter laughed at the thought. Besides, he agreed with Duncan. A quiet dinner with some good conversation would be nice, whether or not it was a prelude to a more physical dessert. He eyed Duncan, who was soaking wet. The rain had returned with a vengeance. It beat against the windows with a rhythmic tapping, making Peter feel warm and cocooned inside.

"You want to dry off?" he asked, noticing Duncan was shivering ever so slightly.

"That would be great. I'm soaked through to the bone."

"Hey, we're about the same size. Feel free to go in my bedroom and raid my closet and drawers." He guffawed, unable to resist adding, "Especially my drawers."

"I just might do that," Duncan said. He disappeared.

When he came back, Peter was seated at the table waiting for him. Low bowls were filled with steaming stew, the rich scent wafting up in the steam. He retrieved their glasses of wine and set out a cutting board with a loaf of Peter's beer bread.

He grinned at Duncan, wearing a pair of old sweats and one of his T-shirts, a turquoise-and-pink affair with the Elephant Car Wash logo emblazoned across the front. *You are such a dirty old man,* he mentally chastised himself when he noticed the swing of Duncan's cock in the sweatpants. He must have shed his underwear too. Peter felt like doing his best Ethel Merman and breaking into "Everything's Coming Up Roses."

"Hope you're hungry," Peter said. "I made lots."

"I'm starving." Duncan met Peter's eyes with his green-eyed gaze, which left Peter to wonder if his reference to starvation was a double entendre.

Duncan sat. They ate. Duncan marveled over the food, the subtle layers of flavor in the stew, how the wine complemented each one. Peter told Duncan how simple it was to make beer bread.

"Oh, I know all about beer bread. My sister Scout swears by it. She puts dill in hers." Duncan lowered his head, and Peter was surprised to see, after a second, a tear drop to the surface of the table.

"What is it, Duncan? Are you okay?"

Duncan raised his head to smile. His eyes were bright with unshed tears. "Just mentioning Scout. I haven't told you what happened."

"Oh?"

"Yeah, see I really love my sister Scout, and I just saw her. I was out in Pennsylvania for a few days."

"I didn't know. Is she okay?"

"She is, but her husband Bud..." Duncan's voice trailed off and he looked away, breathing hard. Peter noticed his knuckles whitened where he gripped the table.

"Hey, buddy, it's okay to cry. Let it go."

And Duncan did, for a minute or two. He then sniffed, drew in a great breath, and blew his nose on his napkin. He held it up, laughing. "Sorry."

"It's okay. I have a washing machine." Peter leaned back and waited.

"Bud got in a car accident and was killed."

Peter got up from his chair and came over to Duncan. He squatted a little so he could wrap his arms around Duncan's chest. "I'm so sorry. You were very close, weren't you?"

"Yeah, but more than that, I grieve for Scout. She and Bud were high school sweethearts, and they were still as crazy in love as when they were teenagers. It kills me to think of her going to bed each night alone now." Duncan looked to his left to give Peter a sad smile.

"I'm sure it helps she has a brother who loves her so much."

"And who's something like three thousand miles away," Duncan scoffed. "But she has the twins and our sister, Jem."

"Your sisters are named Scout and Jem? Seriously?"

And the question lifted Duncan, if only briefly, out of his misery. He laughed. "Yeah. Mom had a *To Kill a Mockingbird* fixation. I guess I should be grateful she didn't call me Atticus."

"I think it would be kind of cool, actually." Peter let go of Duncan and went toward his own chair. "More wine?"

"That would be lovely."

Peter refilled their glasses and as the candles on the table flickered, they shared their lives with one another and had the kind of heart-to-heart conversation that usually only comes after people have known one another for a very long time.

By the time the words ran out, the apartment was almost completely dark and the music had stopped. There was a lonely rush of wind outside.

Peter thought about asking if Duncan wanted to stay. He thought that the dogs needed to go outside for a final walk. He guessed the table needed clearing, the dishwasher loading.

But all of that could wait. He stood and took Duncan's hand. Duncan let himself be led back to the bedroom.

In the darkness, Peter moved to turn on the light, a small lamp he had on his bedside table that gave the room a warm, rosy glow.

"Wait," Duncan's voice came out of the darkness behind him. "I like it like this."

And Peter had to agree. The rain still tapped softly on the window and the night sky gave an almost-silver glow to the bedroom. "It feels safe, doesn't it? Like we're the only people in the world."

*

Duncan thought that was *it*, what Peter had just said. He felt like they were the only people in the world and right now he needed that solitude. He wanted to be away, for a time, from the worries about his sister, his disappointment over Marilyn and things not working out as he had hoped, from wondering about how the rest of his life would be spent.

It had been a long time since Duncan had actually been intimate with another guy, truly intimate and not just sexual, and he felt that time was now upon him. Oh yes, it aroused him, filled his veins with a kind of lust that quickened his breathing and heart rate, but it also felt different, more special, as if in their aloneness now, they were one.

He moved closer to Peter and drew him near. He wrapped his arms around him, one hand at the small of his back and the other at the nape of his neck. He kissed him, tentatively at first, and then with more passion as their tongues connected and they merged into one.

The rest, once they exchanged their first passionate kiss, was familiar and new all at the same time. The motions were so practiced they were born of a kind of easy familiarity. They fumbled with each other's clothes. Duncan was certain Peter felt what he felt—that impatience, that hunger to reveal more and more skin, so he could taste it, revel in the unique flavors of this wonderful man who had been in front of him for so long, tastes that would be uniquely Peter's. They both struggled to pull back the bedclothes, Peter laughing when, in their haste, both comforter and top sheet landed on the floor in a heap at the foot of the bed.

When they collapsed together on the bed, it was like coming home. It simply felt right. And even though there was passion there, great, great passion, there was also a kind of comfort that Duncan realized he had never felt with another man before. Oh sure, he had this kind of desire previously. Many, many times. But none of his erotic encounters in the past had included this familiarity, this succor, this sense of his having found a place in the world. They were about to make love, for sure, but it also seemed like they were joining hands together to leap off a cliff that neither knew the height of. But that was okay, because their hands were joined, and they were doing it *together*.

Duncan spread himself out on Peter's cool sheets. He couldn't discern the color of them in the dark, but he imagined them as pale blue and already thought ahead to the morning, when he would see the wonderful contrast Peter's red hair would make with their pale, summer-sky color.

He flattened himself against the mattress and pulled Peter on top of him, his heart pounding as though it would beat clean out of his chest. He didn't care. He grasped Peter's body so hard it was as though he wanted to make them into one body. His hands ran up and down Peter, as if they couldn't touch *everywhere* fast enough, couldn't draw in the experience of him, the reality of him quickly enough.

They were kissing and it truly was like their lips, tongues, and mouths were working in a kind of hungry harmony, almost independent of conscious thought. There was a desire in both of them, Duncan was sure, to draw the other inside, to keep him, to travel to a place that was safe and warm.

A place that was only for them.

They did all the things their bodies dictated to them that they should do in this moment. The kissing morphed into licking, sucking, tasting—and at one point Peter had Duncan teetering on the edge of orgasm, using his hot mouth and tongue in ways Duncan wasn't sure he ever knew were possible.

He did the same for Peter.

But Duncan knew neither of them wanted things to end, at least not this time, with what was possibly the world's best blow job. Duncan wanted something more. "Come back up here," he whispered frantically, thrusting his hands into Peter's armpits and pulling him up so hard he worried he might hurt him.

When Peter was on top of him, spread out like some heated, furry blanket, Duncan raised his legs, positioning himself finally so that his calves rested on Peter's shoulders. "I want you inside me, so, so bad."

Peter whispered into his ear, "Me too," and then he bit Duncan's earlobe, laving his ear and making Duncan shiver. "But shouldn't we think about the practical?"

For just a moment, the passion waned ever so slightly. Duncan thought briefly of the long dry spell he'd been through lately, of how safe sex had been the watchwords of his adult sexual experience from as far back as he could remember, and how his last checkup, three months ago, had yielded, not surprisingly, a negative result.

He was as sure as he could be that he did not pose a threat to Peter.

Peter's cock was poised at Duncan's ass, the head of it throbbing at his sphincter as though demanding entrance. Duncan wanted nothing more than for Peter to slide it in bare, to feel Peter inside him without any barrier and the bliss that would come when he knew Peter was shooting deep inside, burying his seed within him.

Duncan had never, never, in all his years, done it bareback and he was amazed at himself right now, how willing he was, knowing that lust and passion were erasing the practical, common sense way of thinking that usually made up all his decisions.

Duncan whispered, "I don't want to be practical."

Peter said, "Are you sure?"

Duncan wriggled his ass forward, so that the tip of Peter's cock slipped inside. "God, yes. Fuck me."

Peter paused for a moment, there above him. "We can never be 100 percent about anything, but I promise you, you have little to fear from me." Peter leaned back and opened the nightstand drawer. "In spite of that, let's just play by the rules for now. Okay?"

Duncan looked up at him and nodded, disappointed, but knowing they were doing the right thing. He watched as Peter bit the condom wrapper open and then unrolled the latex sheath over his gorgeous dick. Duncan had to concede that it looked very sexy.

And it was taking too damn long!

"Now please, please, for the love of Christ, fuck me."

And that's just what Peter did. And all of Duncan's hopes, wishes, and wants were confirmed, delivered like a blessing, in the half hour or so that followed.

When they lay spent and sweating in one another's arms, Duncan whispered the words that he knew were way too soon, but that he felt so strongly in his heart, his very core, he thought he might burst if he didn't tell Peter, "I love you."

He felt compelled to add, since they were so new, "Please don't let that scare you off. I'm not usually like this, but something about you, about us, just feels so right. I thought of it earlier as coming home."

Peter turned to him and ran his fingers over Duncan's stubbly head. *Oh God*, Duncan thought, suddenly in the cold grip of fear, *here it comes. He's going to say he's very fond of me. He'll tell me we should take things slow, see where this is going.*

But all Peter said was, "You wore me out, Duncan. I can barely breathe, let alone think." He sighed deeply and Duncan was already consoling himself with the fact that this was okay. Peter didn't have to reciprocate his pronouncement right at this very moment. There was every reason to think that one day he would.

Peter sat up.

"Where are you going?"

"The girls. They don't care that I just had the most incredible sex of my life. They just need to pee, and they are very selfish bitches." He laughed and Duncan made a game attempt to join him in the laughter, but inside, his heart felt a little broken, because his "I love you" was lying there by the side of the bed, like a cast-off sock.

"I'll be right back. Keep the bed warm."

"I will," Duncan said softly.

He listened as Peter struggled back into his clothes and crossed the room. He opened the door and then paused in the doorway, a shaft of light from the living room throwing his form into silhouette. "Duncan?"

"Yeah?" Duncan was prepared to hear him say something like "I don't sleep very well with someone else in the bed. Would you mind?" Duncan braced for it.

"I love you too. I fell for you the minute you and Marilyn walked into my office. Maybe we're just a pair of romantic fools." He crossed the room quickly, back to Duncan, and planted a soft, quick kiss on his lips. "And that, my sweet man, is what makes this so wonderful and so promising. We. Are. A. Pair."

He moved away.

"Hurry back."

"Try to stop me."

With that, Peter was gone. Duncan listened to the clink and clatter of the leashes and harnesses being brought out, the anxious clicking of canine toenails on hardwood, an impatient bark from one of the girls.

He lay back contented, knowing this was the beginning of something he had always wanted. He had no doubts.

He couldn't wait to fall asleep next to Peter and to wake up in the morning and do what they had just done, over and over again.

"Hurry back," he whispered to the air, certain that Peter always would.

Epilogue

The houseboat glowed. Two Christmas trees—one adorned only with white lights, red bows, and candy canes, and the other, dressed in the traditional style Duncan remembered from his childhood, with colored lights, tinsel, icicles, and ornaments weighing down almost every branch—were positioned in each corner of the houseboat's common area. Strands of pine garland stretched all around the perimeter of the ceiling.

On every surface candles flickered, smelling of cinnamon and vanilla. From Duncan's little portable music player the jazz riffs of Duke Ellington's *Nutcracker Suite* filled the room with the sound of Christmas magic.

"Oh Lord, this is like Santa's Village," Marilyn whispered to Duncan, struggling to fasten his boutonnière to his lapel. She poked him with the pin, and he yelped, causing the assembled guests to look up as one.

Duncan whispered, "I just wanted the day to be magical, like Christmas morning was for us as kids."

"Well, I don't know about that. I'm Jewish."

"You are? You never told me," Duncan whispered.

"Would it have mattered? Still want me as your, er, best man?"

Duncan giggled. "Of course. And no, it doesn't matter." He grabbed her and hugged her quickly. "I can't believe this is happening."

And Marilyn, for once, was at a loss for words. She simply smiled at him, her eyes brimming with tears. Duncan pulled his best friend close again, holding her to his chest. He said in her ear, "It's all thanks to you. If we had never made plans to get married, I never would have met Peter."

"And I, Ben." Duncan watched as she looked back at Ben, seated on Duncan's couch, looking both sexy and uncomfortable as hell in a dark blue suit, white shirt, and red tie adorned with mistletoe. *Only a straight man,* Duncan thought, *would wear that tie.* And then he thought about what was immediately below the point of the tie and thought it wasn't such a bad idea, considering where kissing under the mistletoe would lead.

"I'm so happy for you. Maybe one day soon I can return the favor and be *your* best man."

"Maybe. We'll see. He's a wonderful guy; he even rivals Mike for my affections. And that's saying a lot."

"I'll be your best man when the time comes," Duncan repeated.

"Fuck that," Marilyn said. "You'll be my maid of honor. Or, I guess it would be matron of honor. How do you look in taffeta?"

"You two about ready?" Peter interrupted them. "People are starting to get impatient. Besides, everyone is wondering what you two are whispering and giggling about like a couple of school girls." Peter rolled his eyes.

"Yes, yes," Marilyn said. "I am as ready as I'll ever be."

Duncan eyed her. Over the summer and fall, due a strict regimen of nightly and daily rigorous sex with Ben (and Duncan knew because Marilyn couldn't wait to kiss and tell every time), she had shed about twenty pounds. Today she looked amazing in a simple black sheath, a rope of pearls, and a pair of Christian Louboutin black pumps that probably cost more than her wedding present to him and Peter. She had recently dyed her hair a rich shade of magenta and it suited her. She carried a single white rose.

Duncan's gaze moved around the room and the small group assembled couldn't have been nearer to his heart. Scout, of course, was there, along with her twins, Keira and Keith, each beaming and so happy and proud for their uncle. Jem and her husband, Vince, had made the trip; Vince looked like he was afraid some man in the houseboat might propose to *him*, the way he kept looking anxiously around. Duncan's mom and dad couldn't make it from Florida, although they had wanted to. His father had had a heart attack in the fall, and although he was nicely recuperating, cross-country travel just wasn't a good idea. There were several fellow teachers from his school, there not only because they had been good friends but also because Duncan wanted them to bear witness to something he was sure they believed they'd never see. Peter's dogs, Butterfly, Mary Jane, and Daisy, were also in attendance, wearing ropes of gold tinsel garland around their necks and behaving amazingly well, sitting as one beside the couch. There were a couple of Peter's good friends from his long time in Seattle.

The real guest of honor, though, stood at the front of the room, which just happened to be the houseboat's kitchen. Peter's father, Ray Dalrymple, looked nothing like Duncan would have imagined him. Peter got his red hair and freckles from his mom, who was now sitting in Peter's TV-watching recliner, sobbing into a handkerchief. She had started when she walked in the door and not stopped since. Duncan could only hope they were happy tears.

Ray Dalrymple looked every bit his sixty-plus years, but that didn't mean, at all, that he was not a head turner. His hair was buzzed close, which only served to highlight Ray's strong bone structure and amazing dark eyes. He wore a small salt-and-pepper moustache and goatee and the effect was sexy without trying too hard. He had outfitted his trim physique in a perfectly cut dove-gray suit, pale-lavender tie, and a pair of suede wingtips that matched his tie. Who knew where a man could find lavender wingtips? Duncan could see where Peter got his sartorial sensibility.

Duncan recalled the conversation he and Peter had had the night they got engaged. That night would always be clear in his memory.

It was early July and they were sitting on the deck of his houseboat. This time of year, the sun did not set until very late, close to ten o'clock, and the pair were having a contented moment on Duncan's vintage aluminum deck chairs, watching the sailboats float by, marveling as the seaplanes landed and took off, and taking in the Seattle Ducks, the land/water vehicles that looked like nothing more than white buses that had taken a wrong turn and ended up on the water.

Their hands were loosely linked and earlier they had opened an Alsatian Riesling that had left them both very relaxed, much like Peter's three dogs, who lounged at the end of the pier, looking into the water, on the rare occasion when they deigned to open their eyes.

The air was warm, a balmy-for-Seattle seventy-five degrees and it was crisp and dry. It was the perfect summer night.

Duncan had not been expecting anything that night other than to draw Peter inside the houseboat, whistle for the dogs to join them, and then collapse into bed with him once night had fallen. They could have fireworks sex or fall asleep in each other's arms. Duncan realized it didn't matter that much to him either way, as long as they were together. Well, maybe he hoped it would be both.

As the sun set behind them, Peter leaned over and said, "When are you and I going to get married?"

"How 'bout tomorrow?" Duncan replied. "We'll go down to city hall and pick up the license and then we can get married three days after that." Duncan took a sip of wine, all cool, calm, and collected, but inside, it felt as though everything were shaking. Had he fallen asleep out here on the deck? Was he dreaming?

"So that's a yes?"

Duncan looked at Peter, taking in the expectation in his eyes. This was for real. "You're proposing?" Duncan just wanted to be sure. He figured that one day they would take this step. He wanted it. He knew Peter wanted it. Yet, it just seemed like there was no hurry; they were so happy.

"You want me to get down on one knee?"

Duncan quipped, "I want you to get down on your knees, but let's wait until we're inside." Duncan winked. "Don't want to alarm the neighbors."

"I'm sure they've seen worse, knowing the string of men you've probably had parade in and out of here over the years."

"And yet you still want to get hitched to this old whore?" Duncan snickered.

"With every breath of my being." Peter smiled and squeezed Duncan's hand. "Will you be my husband?"

Duncan leaned forward and tenderly kissed Peter on the lips, the neighbors be damned. When they pulled away from each other, their faces still close, Duncan said, "Now, that's a yes."

Peter sat back in his chair. Even in profile, Duncan could see a broad grin stretched across his features. He looked like a little boy who had just won the biggest stuffed animal at the carnival. "But not tomorrow, okay? I mean, I'm as eager for this as you are, but I'm a wedding planner, for Christ's sake. We have to have at least a little do."

"Punch and cookies in the church reception hall?"

"What? And ruin my reputation?" Peter turned to him. "How about we have it here? I can't imagine a lovelier setting."

Duncan had never thought about his houseboat as the place where he would one day marry. Sure, he hoped he might live here one day with a mate. But the notion of having a wedding here had never crossed his mind.

The plan, however, seemed perfect. He gazed out at the serene blue waters of Lake Union, dotted here and there with a sailboat, as though it were primping itself for a postcard moment. Across the water was Eastlake, the neighborhood rising up the bluffs, green mixed in liberally with the houses and apartment buildings. At the shore, houseboats and regular boats were moored.

He could see it. "I think that would be perfect. It would have to be small though."

Peter nodded. "Small is good." Peter gazed out at the water. "One more thing I'd like."

"I know you want the dogs to be flower girls."

Peter laughed. "I hadn't thought of that. But it's not a bad idea. No, the other thing I'd like is to ask my dad to officiate."

Duncan cocked his head. "You didn't tell me he was a minister."

"He's not and we'd have to get him a license. But hey presto! Thanks to the Internet, we can get that accomplished in no time." Peter was quiet for a moment. "You haven't met him yet, but there's always been a special bond between me and my dad. It would mean a lot if he could unite us. More than some minister we don't know. And I know it would mean the world to him."

Duncan said, "I think that would be lovely. I look forward to meeting him."

Now Duncan looked admiringly at his future father-in-law and could see he was just as jittery as he was. Ray stood near the kitchen counter, sorting the papers upon which he had written the simple ceremony, moving them restlessly back and forth. Duncan was sure he was not seeing them.

He leaned over to whisper to Peter, "I think we should get started, before your dad gets any more nervous."

"I think we should get started so I don't have to wait anymore to be your husband."

"That too." Duncan squeezed his hand.

Peter moved to the portable music player and pressed "pause." The sudden silence was so abrupt that it was as though he had rung a gong. "Everybody?" He turned toward the guests. "We're going to get started." He turned back to the portable player, pushed some buttons, and the first strains of Pachelbel's Canon in D began. Cliché, yes, but the piece just screamed wedding, happiness, and two hearts united.

Marilyn quickly stepped to the back of the houseboat, then turned and made a slow procession toward the kitchen. The walk was only a few steps, but she made the most of it, holding her rose like a bouquet, smiling, and blinking back tears.

Next, Peter squatted down and reached out with his hands to the dogs, making a soft kissing sound. The girls, their parts rehearsed many times, rose as one and made a dignified trot to the kitchen, where they knew their favorite beef liver treats awaited them. When they reached Duncan and Peter, Peter handed them each a treat. They lay down on the floor with them, knowing they were about to be part of something important.

Ray gestured for Scout to cut the music and she hopped up. She looked down at the music player with consternation. "I don't know how to turn this damn thing off!" she whispered, and everyone laughed.

Duncan went to help his sister, and they finally silenced Johann Pachelbel. Marilyn sat down. Peter's mother let out a sob and blew her nose loudly.

Ray stepped closer to the couple, who now faced toward him and away from their guests.

"I'm so glad you could all come today," Ray began. "I have to say first off that I am a big crybaby from way back, so if I get through this without tears, it'll be a miracle. So bear with me and witness the real miracle—the joining of these two beautiful young men.

"I remember when Peter came out to me. You'd think I'd have known, being gay myself, but I hadn't a clue. But when I spied that hickey on his neck when he was a freshman in high school—" Ray had to stop here to allow for the guffaws and titters that swept through the room. "I had to ask him if Caitlin, the girl he was spending all his time with, had given it to him.

"And I guess that was my son's cue to finally come clean. He told me that, no, Caitlin had not given him the 'monkey bite' as he called it. They were just friends. The culprit, he said at last, unable to meet my eyes, was Jake Solomon, his best friend.

"At first, I wasn't sure what to think." More laughter. "But it dawned on me, finally, that he was telling me something significant."

Ray beamed at the crowd, and there was a hint of sheepishness in his expression. "'You're gay?' I asked him. He nodded. 'Are you sure?' I said, knowing even then I was asking the stupidest question a father—let alone a gay dad—could ask.

"He nodded again, and he couldn't resist adding a little eye roll. It took some adjusting to this new facet of my son; he was not the person I had thought he was. Of course, I loved him just the same." Ray looked away for a moment, breathing fast, eyes bright. "But one of the thoughts I had—and this might surprise you because it wasn't really all that long ago—one of the thoughts I had as I processed my son being gay like me was this one: *I'll never dance at your wedding.*

"See, back then, it just didn't seem possible. And yet, and yet—here we all are today." Ray stuck a foot in the air, displaying the suede lavender wingtips. "And I've got my dancing shoes on."

Ray waited for the laughter to die down and dabbed at the corners of his eyes, rolling his eyes at his own vulnerability, and returned his gaze to his son and future son-in-law. "Peter and Duncan, we're all gathered here today, not as separate units, but as one. We're a community coming together to join in the promise of the future, the promise of love. All of us in this room support you, stand beside you, and wish for you only good things as you join hands to travel the road of life together.

"The striking thing to me today is not the differences between this 'gay' marriage and the straight ones I've attended but the commonalities." Ray turned back to the assembled crowd. "This wedding, this joining of two people in love, is no different than any other wedding I've attended, regardless of gender.

"We have two people in love, their hearts reaching out to each other with the fantastic and optimistic hope that they can be one thing for each other for the rest of their lives: *family*. We have two people in love who want to build a future together. We have two people in love who will celebrate, argue, take care of one another, be there for the other on holidays and birthdays, make chicken soup when the other is sick... In short, as I said, we have two people in love.

"And isn't that all that's required for taking that leap of faith known as marriage? Two *people*, not one man and one woman, but two people. Gender is not the operative word here, love is.

"Peter and Duncan have chosen, in place of vows, to share a special poem with the other.

"And being a parent, I can't resist adding my own two cents to their decision. So I'll just ask them both, real quick: Do each of you take the other for better or worse, for richer and poorer, in sickness and in health, in good times and bad? Do you promise to love unconditionally, to support each other in your goals, to laugh and cry with each other, and to cherish one another, as long as you both live?" Ray said the vows breathlessly, racing to get them all out before, Duncan guessed, Peter stopped him. The vows were not part of the plan, but Duncan was glad Ray had inserted them. He was going to be a good father-in-law.

"Yes, Dad," Peter said, prompting laughter from the guests.

"Duncan?" Ray turned to him and Duncan felt he already loved this man.

"I do," Duncan said softly, cleared his throat, and then said it again, louder.

"Go ahead, read those poems to each other." Ray nodded to the guests. "Get out your hankies."

Peter turned to Duncan and grasped both hands in his own. Duncan had a moment, again, where he felt he was dreaming as Peter looked into his eyes with an intensity that made his knees weaken and his heart flutter. "Duncan, I chose this poem for you because I think it says most clearly what I think will carry us forward for our life together."

There was a moment of silence and then Peter began. Duncan was amazed that Peter had memorized his poem. He didn't even have a sheet of paper as backup, just in case his nerves got the best of him.

"This is 'How Shall I Woo?' by Thomas Moore." Peter cleared his throat and then, looking only at Duncan, recited:

> "If I speak to thee in friendship's name,
> Thou think'st I speak too coldly;
> If I mention Love's devoted flame,
> Thou say'st I speak too boldly.
> Between these two unequal fires,
> Why doom me thus to hover?
> I'm a friend, if such thy heart requires,
> If more thou seek'st, a lover.
> Which shall it be? How shall I woo?
> Fair one, choose between the two.

Tho' the wings of Love will brightly play,
When first he comes to woo thee,
There's a chance that he may fly away
As fast as he flies to thee.
While Friendship, tho' on foot she come,
No flights of fancy trying,
Will, therefore, oft be found at home,
When Love abroad is flying.
Which shall it be? How shall I woo?
Dear one, choose between the two.

If neither feeling suits thy heart,
Let's see, to please thee, whether
We may not learn some precious art
To mix their charms together;
One feeling, still more sweet, to form
From two so sweet already—
A friendship that like love is warm,
A love like friendship steady.
Thus let it be, thus let me woo,
Dearest, thus we'll join the two."

The assembled crowd was quiet, save for a bit of sniffling here and there. Duncan wanted to cry, too, but it was time for his own moment, and as much as was possible, he didn't want to mar it with tears or outright sobbing.

He leaned in and, even though it wasn't time, kissed Peter deeply on the lips, and then whispered, "Thank you."

Hands shaking, he reached into the pocket of his sports coat and pulled out the sheet of notebook paper upon which he had copied the sonnet he had found for Peter. For just a moment, he took his eyes from his soon-to-be husband and looked out at the two women who meant so much to him, who served, really, as his inspiration and port-in-a-storm. Scout and Marilyn both shared the same posture and look. They were upright, a little stiff, eyes shining, with smiles that said, "Go ahead. Do it."

He and Scout's eyes connected for a moment, and Duncan could see the happiness there, the simple joy. He had asked her, once he and Peter had committed to the other, if *she* would be his "best man." She had declined, saying it was too soon, and she wanted to be free to sit back, with her kids, and watch the brother she loved more than almost anyone find his "thirty minutes."

That memory gave him the courage to still his trembling voice and say, "For you, Peter, I have 'Shakespeare's Sonnet Number 116.'" And he began:

> *"Let me not to the marriage of true minds*
> *Admit impediments. Love is not love*
> *Which alters when it alteration finds,*
> *Or bends with the remover to remove:*
> *O no! it is an ever-fixed mark*
> *That looks on tempests and is never shaken;*
> *It is the star to every wandering bark,*
> *Whose worth's unknown, although his height be taken.*
> *Love's not Time's fool, though rosy lips and cheeks*
> *Within his bending sickle's compass come:*
> *Love alters not with his brief hours and weeks,*
> *But bears it out even to the edge of doom.*

*If this be error and upon me proved,
I never writ, nor no man ever loved."*

Peter kissed him and held him tightly. Duncan heard Peter's breath catch, and he squeezed him hard, whispering, "Courage."

Ray moved forward. "Well, I was going to do the bit about 'You may now kiss the groom,' but the boys here stole my thunder." Everyone chuckled. "But should we have them do it again? Just for tradition?"

They all clapped and Peter and Duncan, husbands at last, leaned together for a kiss. The applause grew louder, lifting them higher, higher.

When at last they pulled away, Duncan stared at Peter, at this man he loved with all his heart and mouthed, "We did it."

And Peter kissed him again.

*

Later, when most of the guests had left and darkness had fallen upon the water, making it an obsidian sheet, Duncan stood outside on his deck, alone. He was a little tipsy from all the champagne and wine he had imbibed and, even more, drunk on love, and more than ready to return inside to the man he loved and to have their wedding night.

The last guest came out. It was Marilyn. She walked a little unsteadily across the pier in her heels, leaving Ben behind her, a tall silhouette in the light from the doorway.

She clutched Duncan's elbow. "Hey, I'm happy for you."

"Thanks," Duncan whispered, turning to her and meeting her eyes through the darkness.

"We have to go."

"I know! I know!" Duncan said. "I was thinking you'd never leave. I have a wedding night ahead of me, you know."

Marilyn snickered. "All you think about is sex."

Duncan looked out at the water, wistful, and said, "How easy life would be if that were really true."

Marilyn moved behind him and slid her arms around his waist and laid her head upon his shoulder. "You'll still be there for me, right? I mean, we'll always be good friends."

"The best." Duncan squeezed the hands wrapped around his waist.

Marilyn pulled away. "That's good. Because Ben proposed to me tonight."

"What? That's wonderful!" He kissed Marilyn full on the mouth.

She jerked away. "Careful. You don't want to make my fiancé jealous. He's a brute."

"I know. You lucky girl." Duncan nodded to Ben and called out, "Congrats, Ben! You sure you know what you're getting yourself into?"

"Thanks! I know!" Ben's voice came back to Duncan.

"You're gonna have your hands full."

"Tell me about it."

Marilyn shook her head. "You two. You're right, though, we need to get out of here and let the newlyweds have their wedding night. I expect to see you hanging out a bloody sheet in the morning."

"God! Marilyn."

Ben started over to claim his future wife.

Duncan hurriedly said, "Thank you. Thank you for everything you showed me."

She waved him away. "Love is love and all that." She tossed off the remark, but he could see the emotion in her face. He knew she needed to hurry away. Marilyn was not the kind of gal who favored breaking down in front of anyone.

"Go in there and make your man happy."

Ben came up beside them and pulled Marilyn away. They said nothing more and Duncan watched them until they were out of sight.

He was alone for only a moment. Peter came out wearing a pair of sweats and a hoodie, the dogs on their leashes trailing behind him. "They need a short walk before bed."

"Of course they do."

He watched as Peter headed toward the shore with the girls and it all seemed so homey, so right, so much better than some exotic honeymoon in a faraway locale. This was all he had wanted almost one year ago to the day, when he had proposed to Ben's brother in a pizza joint on Capitol Hill.

He had asked the right question then. He just had the wrong man.

Now, he had the right one...and always would. He smiled, rubbing his arms up and down.

Peter turned to him just before stepping off the pier with the dogs. "Get back inside. It's cold out here."

"Okay! Okay." Duncan headed toward the open door.

"Keep the bed warm for me," Peter called just before Duncan went inside. And Duncan leaned out, promising he would.

About the Author

Real Men. True Love.

Rick R. Reed is an award-winning and bestselling author of more than fifty works of published fiction. He is a Lambda Literary Award finalist. Entertainment Weekly has described his work as "heartrending and sensitive." Lambda Literary has called him: "A writer that doesn't disappoint..." Find him at www.rickrreedreality.blogspot.com. Rick lives in Palm Springs, CA, with his husband, Bruce, and their fierce Chihuahua/Shiba Inu mix, Kodi.

Email: rickrreedbooks@gmail.com

Facebook: www.facebook.com/rickrreedbooks

Twitter: @rickrreed

Other NineStar books by this author

Unraveling

Sky Full of Mysteries

The Perils of Intimacy

IM

Chaser

Raining Men

Blue Umbrella Sky

Third Eye

Coming Soon from Rick R. Reed

Hungry for Love

Brandon Wylde faced the form on his iMac screen with something akin to terror. Or maybe the emotion causing his mind to go blank and his heart to beat more swiftly could more rightly be called performance anxiety.

What was causing this fear of failure and quickened breath was the registration page for a gay dating website called OpenHeartOpenMind. Brandon had been all over the Internet, searching for a site that would put him in touch with other gay men looking for romance and the promise of something lasting and *not* for hookups. Now, there was no shortage of the former—the hookup sites were rampant, and as much as Brandon felt that "to each his own" was a motto worth living by, these sites were not his own. A close-up picture of an asshole (in the literal sense) or a hard dick might be titillating to some, but to Brandon it was simply a bore. How could one tell if one wanted to even "hook up" when seeing only a faceless body part? The idea gave Brandon the creeps. Did we have sex with genitals alone? No, we had sex with entire human beings, for Christ's sake. No matter how big and thick the dick was or how open and inviting the asshole (literal, again), Brandon couldn't imagine a meeting of any sort with simply a body part.

His "pickiness," as his man-whore friend Christian always said, was what kept Brandon alone and yearning at age twenty-nine. "Just go online. You can have a hot guy delivered to your door within an hour, like a pizza, a delicious, mouthwatering *pepperoni* pizza. Hold the cheese!"

Christian was no stranger to the embraces of many men, culled from sites like Manhunt, Adam4Adam, or Craigslist (or as Margaret Cho referred to it—the *Penny Saver* of dick) and, more lately, Grindr and Scruff. Christian swore by these electronic connections and, as far as Brandon could tell from their happy-hour conversations, took advantage of their charms on an almost daily basis.

Brandon shook his head and wondered if what Christian was shopping for online was more a fix than a human connection.

Brandon knew what he himself was, what he had, and the condition was incurable.

He was a romantic. As much as his hormones told him that all he really required in this world was a warm place to bury his dick, his more developed senses begged to differ.

Brandon wanted someone with whom he felt a special connection, someone with whom there was that magical spark he read about in the gay romance novels he devoured with increasing frequency, to fill the void missing in his life. Brandon wanted chocolates and flowers. He wanted love poetry. He wanted surprise weekend getaways to remote mountain cabins or quaint bed-and-breakfasts. He wanted someone to curl up next to on the couch, falling asleep together to some old black-and-white movie.

He wanted someone with whom he could share not only his body, but his life.

Christian told him, "You're never going to find the man of your dreams, unless you bring some of those wet dreams you're still having at your advanced age to life! Just get laid! No man's going to buy the merchandise without a free sample."

Really, Christian? Really? And why are you *still alone, then?* Brandon knew Christian spent almost all of his free time online. Hell, Brandon could even count on Christian to be on his phone, on Grindr or Scruff, when they were out to dinner or one of the clubs. Brandon would twiddle his thumbs with Christian nearby, oblivious and texting furiously, always on the prowl for his next hookup, who usually lurked somewhere nearby.

Why was the man never satisfied?

Brandon had a secret, one which he had never shared with anyone, especially Christian.

He was almost a virgin. He had only two pathetic sexual experiences on his résumé. First, there was an embarrassing, guilt-ridden "affair" back in high school that had lasted for all of two weeks (although Brandon wished for more). And the one time, back in college, when he had met his second paramour in the basement men's room of King Library on the Miami University (Ohio) campus. The guy wanted Brandon simply to kneel down between the stalls so he could blow him, but Brandon was far too fearful to engage in such an act and even then, he wanted more—like to see his cocksucker's face. Besides, Brandon wasn't even sure why the guy kept putting his hand under the stall, not knowing then it was a signal for him to kneel on the floor. So Brandon, romantic at heart that he was, simply grasped the signaling hand and held it.

This prompted his tearoom trick to flee the bathroom—and Brandon followed him outside.

Somehow, in the stairwell outside the men's room, Brandon convinced his bathroom suitor to take him home, to an off-campus apartment where the two young men quickly and furtively got one another off, worried about the imminent arrival of the guy's straight roommate.

That experience, sordid and unsatisfying as it was, left in Brandon a desire to chase windmills, if that's what his idealism could be called. Brandon was not going to settle. If he couldn't have the whole enchilada (the enchilada being a relationship that was satisfying not only on a physical level, but also on an emotional one), he wanted none of it.

Unfortunately for Brandon, he had come of age during a time when Internet and even smartphone connections made hooking up fast and efficient. Brandon conceded those connections might possess those benefits, but they were not for him.

He was interested in *both* of a man's heads, thank you very much. And he would not settle for less.

He believed a man who thought the same was out there. Somewhere.

Which is what brought him, right now, to the registration site for OpenHeartOpenMind. When he had finally landed upon the dating website, he was thrilled to find their mission statement on the home page, one that dovetailed with his own inclinations.

It read:

> *We here at OpenHeartOpenMind believe in old-fashioned romance. If you're looking for impersonal, easy sex and lots of it, there are*

plenty of other sites that cater to your interests. Go for them.

OpenHeartOpenMind is for the man who wants to date, who knows that sometimes delayed gratification can make the rewards all the sweeter.

OpenHeartOpenMind is for gay men who think the road to love is paved not just with physical attraction (although we'd be lying if we said that doesn't play a big part!), but with mutual respect, shared interests, and the common goal of wanting more than just merging genitals, but merging hearts and minds as well.

Good luck on your dating journey!

Below the mission statement were icons that urged the potential user to sign up and the current user to sign in.

When Brandon read those words, he quickly clicked on "sign up" because, in a way, he had already "signed up" for the very attributes the website promoted.

So now he began filling in the editable boxes on the site with his particulars: name, age, city and state: Seattle, WA, height: 6'1", weight: 198, body type: athletic. Brandon was nothing if not honest, so he quickly changed "athletic" to "beefy." He went on. Eyes: hazel, hair: dark brown, body hair: hairy, facial hair: full beard.

Brandon was relieved that OpenHeartOpenMind did not ask, as most of the other sites did, for his dick size or if he was top or bottom (although he definitely leaned more toward the former, but,as he had found, it was hard to top oneself).

Brandon came at last to the part where it asked for a headline and a short ad describing what one was looking for. And this was really the section that was giving him fits.

How do you describe your heart's desire in 200 words or less? How can you just post what you hope to find in a man on the Internet for all the world to see? Can it possibly work? Is this really the way I want to meet someone?

Thoughts like these crowded his brain, urging the more insecure part of himself to simply abandon the exercise. If he was a true, old-fashioned romantic, would he really be looking online for his true love? Wouldn't they meet casually somewhere, like a café or bookstore, where shy glances and almost covert smiles resulted in perhaps a quick conversation confirming that they might exchange email addresses, if not phone numbers? Or shouldn't they meet humorously, thumping melons down at the neighborhood Safeway? Or maybe by coincidence in, say, a fender bender at rush hour?

You are just letting your performance anxiety get to you. This is 2013, buddy, and online is how it's done these days. Although it's certainly possible you could meet a man at the grocery store, Starbucks, or jogging on the trails that surround Green Lake, this way is much more likely to get some results. And even if it doesn't, what do you have to lose? This site is not costing you anything, except for maybe some time, and by doing this, you may just be aligning the universe to give you what you've been searching for.

As your mom always told you when you went off to school, when you went off for your first job interview, or your first date back in high school, "Just be yourself."

Mom was right. He would just be his honest self, and the words would come.

DOWN-TO-EARTH HONEST MAN SEEKS SAME

I'm not looking for fireworks, just the potential.

I am a twentysomething guy, told I'm good-looking and in okay shape (kept that way not by eating right, but by logging twenty-five miles a week or so running). I have all my teeth and all my hair. My body functions normally for a twenty-nine-year-old. I don't have gas (well, not much).

I like horror movies, romantic comedies, and family dramas. I cry at the drop of a hat and laugh easily and am proud of both. I like classic jazz: Sarah Vaughn, Duke Ellington, Oscar Peterson. I love to read: gay romance, thrillers, and memoirs. I don't like sci-fi, reality TV, or selfishness. I will eat just about anything, but appreciate good food, good wine, and good restaurants.

I live in Seattle's Green Lake neighborhood, and if you can't find me at home, I am usually running around the lake—sometimes more than once.

The only thing I have that's incurable is a romantic heart. If you're afflicted with the same condition, maybe we're a match.

Want to know more? Ask me. I promise to answer...honestly.

It took a little trial and error, and while Brandon didn't think he was going to win the Nobel Prize for literature, he thought his ad made him come off okay, or at least normal. More importantly, he was pleased he had captured at least the essence of himself. There was no pretense, so he was optimistic that whatever the ad might snare, it would at least be someone who knew him for who he was.

His final task was to upload a picture of himself. He opened the file of photos on his computer called, simply, "me," and began searching for just the right one. At last he settled on one that his mom—God bless her—had taken last summer, when the two of them had taken the ferry from downtown over to Vashon Island for a picnic on the rocky, driftwood-strewn beach. In it, Brandon squinted against the sun, with Puget Sound in the background. He was tan, with a little rose along the bridge of his nose and the tops of his cheeks, and he looked happy, his dark hair sticking up against a backdrop of a blue and cloudless sky. He thought anyone could see the hope in his hazel eyes.

He clicked on it to load it to the site, waited for it to appear, and then saved his profile. He got a message telling him it would post within a few hours, after moderator review.

Well, here goes nothing, Brandon thought. *Or, maybe, just maybe, if the timing is right, the stars are aligned, and I'm very lucky—something.*

Also Available from NineStar Press

Connect with NineStar Press

www.ninestarpress.com

www.facebook.com/ninestarpress

www.facebook.com/groups/NineStarNiche

www.twitter.com/ninestarpress

www.tumblr.com/blog/ninestarpress